CRACKED
DREAMS

CRACKED DREAMS

MICHAEL BAPTISTE

A

PUBLICATION

A STREBOR BOOKS INTERNATIONAL LLC PUBLICATION
DISTRIBUTED BY SIMON & SCHUSTER, INC.

Published by

Strebor Books International LLC
P.O. Box 1370
Bowie, MD 20718
http://www.streborbooks.com

ISBN 978-1-59309-035-7
LCCN 2003116852

Distributed by Simon & Schuster, Inc.
1230 Avenue of the Americas
New York, NY 10020
1-800-223-2336

Cover Design: www.mariondesigns.com

First Printing October 2004
Manufactured and Printed in the United States

10 9 8 7 6 5 4 3 2 1

DEDICATION

*This book is dedicated to the one person without whom I would never have been able to complete my first novel. With your love, influence, and support, I have done what I would've assumed was impossible before I met you. Your guidance and advice is worth more to me than whatever proceeds I'll ever receive from the sales of this novel. Your title is girlfriend (a.k.a. Wifie), and your name is Yolanda, but to me you are "The Sh*t." I don't know where I would be in my life without you, and I'll love you to the death, mommy!*

ACKNOWLEDGMENTS

First and foremost, I'd like to thank who I owe my existence, my mother, Marie Lourdes Baptiste. I want you to know that you taught me the value of hard work and persistence. Even though I can't recall any "*Mom always said*" quotes from my youth, what I do recall is the sight of you working with every bit of energy in your body to make sure that my siblings and I always had food in our stomachs and clothes on our backs. Without words, you taught me a lifetime worth of invaluable lessons. For that, I owe you my life and every accomplishment that I make. Thank you and I love you.

To my sister, Rachel, witnessing the trials and tribulations you've experienced and how victorious you've become through it all made me realize that every cloud does have a silver lining. You *are* definitely your mother's daughter, and this fact is shown time and time again with every goal you concur—not to mention having three beautiful children, Andrew, Craig and Saintulia a.k.a. Tuli (the youngest of which shows the most character and promise [wink, wink]).

To my big brother, Junior or "*Supreme,*" thanks for the support in this project. Your assistance only lets me know that you believe in my work and you want to see me succeed. If and when I reach the goals I've set for myself, I can proudly say that you were there from the beginning and that you helped along the way as best you could...good lookin' out!

To my cousin Wise…"*peace to the Gods!*" I know you know that success for me equals success for us. I see you making moves out there on my behalf and I appreciate it like you'll never know. If I can take this thing as far as I "*vision,*" you have nothing to worry about…I got you!

Ricardine, you know we'll always have twice as much love as cousins should have one another, and that will never change. All I hope is that I can be the positive influence you need to follow your dreams. You can have anything you want in the world, just remember that first step will be the hardest. Love ya! What's up to OJ, Vanessa, Justine, Ralph, Sherlie, Valerie, Christian, Stephan, Barbara (Bobby), Jordan, Nikia, Bianca & Beatrice, Garren, Ricardo, Mimose, and my cousins that I missed, sorry but you're in my heart.

INTRODUCTION

Another "Bronx Tale." There was never one like it, and there never will be. This should just bring you mu'fuckas up-to-date; that's all. For the most part, you don't hear much of the Bronx. Anyone that doesn't grow up here would imagine that there's a constant war in the streets. In a way, they're one hundred percent correct, but it's not at all as serious as most would believe. One thing is true though; you don't want to fuck with the Bronx. Any of these other boroughs, like BK, the Q-borough, or Harlem World, they may permit mu'fuckas calling them all kinds of faggots and bitches and pussies, but not over here, dog. It can get very ugly for you in these streets. It's not the place for games, for real. As much as you don't hear about us, our streets house the most criminals. Before you get it twisted, just ask yourself one question. Who has the highest crime rate? Robbery, murder, drug traffic, prostitution, etc.…it's all here. As much as you don't hear about us, whenever you ask a nigga from the Bronx where he's from, you twist up your fuckin' face when he tells you. You know what? We don't give a fuck! You ain't got no friends over here either, pussy. Whatever you got to say about the Bronx don't mean shit. These niggas know how to get money, these niggas know how to bubble the right fuckin' way, and these niggas know how to stay the fuck out of jail. Unless, of course, you get some nigga flappin' his lips. There's always an occasional bitch-ass nigga that slips through the cracks, but that's how the game goes. When it's your turn, you gonna get it, too. You can get it from behind or dead center of your chest, eye-to-eye. You could get it from your man, or some lil' nigga, tryin to make a name for himself in these streets. There's a thousand and one different ways to get it out here, mu'fucka. So anyway you put it…a lot of niggas get killed in the Bronx!

CHAPTER 1

YEAR — 2000

It's kind of quiet tonight... Traffic's moving slowly. No movement could be recognized in the distance. Hard to believe that the first day of the new millennium had just come to a close. The streets were filled with fireworks, loud people and Y2K tension all throughout the city only a day ago. Now, there was no evidence left of the celebration that had taken place only twenty-four hours ago. No champagne bottles or horns, no confetti or balloons; just stillness. All that could be noticed through the darkness of Bronx Park up on the North Side were a few cigarette butts, empty beer cans, and the slightest scent of marijuana. Then, out of the silence, "Fuck!" said a young brother sitting on a wooden bench in the park before relighting a small blunt he'd previously put out. "Ain't shit moving out here tonight," he said, blowing smoke into the air.

Directly across from where he was sitting was a highway that had very little traffic at that time of night. On his right were stairs that led to an overpass that contained even less vehicle traffic. Ironically named Gun Hill Road, this is where only hustlers, addicts, prostitutes and pimps would dwell after a certain hour. Directly behind him was the Bronx River, also where hustlers, addicts, prostitutes and pimps could be found, but more than likely on the bottom of that shit, or floating atop.

"Damn, it's cold out here," he said, blowing into his hands before rubbing them together for warmth. This was Michael Banner, or known to the streets as "Spits," a name he'd picked from his reputation as a battle-rapper. He was what you called your neighborhood street pharmacist, pusher, hustler, or plainly put, drug dealer. He stood about six feet one and weighed about two-forty, but his baby-face could throw you off a bit. Brown skin, light facial hair and long braids described Michael to the tee.

More than anything, Michael enjoyed music; from the standpoint of a producer, writer or a vocalist. But one thing about the music business: it's not *what* you know, it's *who* you know. And then it's not even *who you know*, but *who knows you*. So Michael didn't pick music as his primary career goal. He didn't like the fact that he'd have to depend on anyone but himself to get ahead. Nope, he chose drugs. Once he'd made his first sale on the streets, it was a wrap. This is what was up. Even before then, he was always attracted to the street life. Growing up in the streets of the Bronx was considered a never-ending battle to him, and he needed to win.

"Yo, what's up, ol' timer? You i-ight?" Spits asked an older guy walking past him.

"I'm fine," he responded confusingly.

"Mu'fucka, don't you look at me funny. What you want, a dime? A twenty? How much?" Spits said angrily.

The old man, now realizing Spits was a hustler, went into game mode. "I don't even know you, young man," he said, showing a devilish grin. "How can I be sure your stuff is class A? If you give me a sample and it's good, I can make you a rich man."

Spits looked at him as if he was containing himself from exploding. "Nigga, I look new or something? I'm on grind-mode pussy, and I ain't out here to be gamed out of mines. Besides, I *been* rich, nigga," Spits said, spitting flames at the old man. "Fuckin' custees, man. They always trying to gee off!" he said walking away.

You see this was all new for Michael. He'd lost the flavor in his mouth for direct sales long ago. He'd since moved up and never once looked back. In a little over four years, Michael had turned a small-time nickel-and-dime venture into a notorious drug ring known all over the streets, up and down the East and West coasts. But now, after all of that, he was on his grind again, ready to hug the block until the early hours of the morning if necessary. That's just how the game went, according to him. Ups and downs ain't shit. Take the loss and apply some pressure of your own. But it wasn't just by chance that all four of Michael's "drugstores" got raided on the same day. It wasn't a coincidence that this happened to occur on a re-up day—of all days. Between all four spots, there was about ninety-six bricks uncut, valued at 5.7 million on the street. You goddamn right he should've been fuckin' mad. You see, all was good and money was rolling in faster, and more abundantly than was predicted, right up until his man got a murder charge.

The repercussions of these events were reminiscent of when Michael got his first taste of the street life. Even more so, he was reminded of the years prior to then, when everything was all good in the hood.

YEAR — 1996

Every morning like clockwork, Michael's three best friends, Peter, Chris and Mikey, would pick him up for school. And every morning like clockwork, Peter, Chris and Mikey would ditch while Michael went to class alone. It seemed odd, but that was the daily routine for them. They would all stop by Michael's crib because, for one, he lived the closest to the school that they attended, and two, so that they could try and convince him not to go. They did this knowing that they wouldn't all be attending class that day. While Michael was in school falling asleep in the classes that were too easy for him, the rest of the guys were running the streets trying to scrounge up paper the only way they knew how—robbing and stealing—just to support their marijuana and alcohol habits. Don't get it twisted; every so often Michael would cut with them and it would be the same ol' thing. They would go up to Yonkers to rob white kids on their way to school, just to go back down to Intervale Avenue on the 2 Train where they bought dime bags of Skunk Weed that were as fat as twenty-sacks. When they'd had enough weed to last them the day, they'd get a few St. Ides forty-ounces to sip on, and then make their way either to the park, or to whomever's home was available. This was a regular day for them. Whatever they did to get the money, they could accumulate up to thirty or forty bucks, and it would all be gone by the time it hit two o'clock when school really let out.

Michael came from a single-parent home, and all he saw growing up was his mother breaking her back to provide for him and his younger brother. He also had an older sister, but they had different fathers. She lived with her father in California, so they didn't see or speak to each other often. All Michael saw was the struggle and knew that he didn't want that for himself, so at first, he leaned toward education to rescue him from hard times to come. He figured that his mother not finishing high school, in the least, contributed to her having to work so hard for a living. So school became his out. This was how he would prevent himself from the backbreaking work he saw his mother perform to put food on the table. This went on all through Michael's life, but his views started to stray once material things became of some importance to him.

"Yo, I wonder what it's gonna be like when we get older and start getting some *real* money," Michael said to the others as they occupied a bench in Bronx Park at the bottom of 222nd Street.

"Word," agreed Peter. "I want to have a nice fat crib with a swimming pool and basketball court, yo. Word up!"

"That *would* be ill though, son," approved Chris. "We would have every bitch in the Bronx on our dicks."

"Fuck these bitches out here, nigga," Mikey said. "I'm gonna have bitches from Jamaica, Puerto Rico, and even Africa, nigga. Matter of fact, I want some Hawaiian pussy, son. That's my word!"

"On the real though, this nigga would fuck a bitch that made his dick turn green, yo," Chris said as they all shared a healthy laugh.

"Fuck you," Mikey simply countered.

The better halves of Michael's days were *usually* spent fantasizing about fancy cars, and exotic women. He wanted to travel the world twice over, and he wanted it for himself just as much as he wanted it for his friends and family. He often wondered why his father wasn't around, but never once wanted to find him or anything. Instead, he took responsibility for him. If his father wasn't man enough to provide a better life for him, his mother, and his brother, then he would make it up to them himself.

Michael and his childhood friends would endlessly talk about how they would be rich and famous. They knew for a fact they would all prosper in life. They would continuously discuss what they would do with millions and how many women they would have. It wasn't considered unhealthy for them to have a good imagination, as long as they didn't lose touch with reality too much. Growing up in their situation would make anybody try as much as possible to lose touch with reality.

Michael was always book smart by choice. It didn't come naturally to him, as did the streets. He didn't have to apply himself much to pick up street smarts because it was in fact a necessity. It was nothing for him to balance the both without one getting in the way of the other, or so it seemed. Only thing is, now he'd become more and more attracted to the streets. Although he seemed to have his schooling under control—just about finishing his sophomore year at Evander Childs High School without any complications—he thought he deserved immediate ratification for his efforts. He deserved just as much as any one of his peers, and didn't seem to be getting it. Kids his age had already experienced what he had only dreamed about. Fast cars, expensive clothes and jewelry were soon to be in his grasp, one way or another.

Now, with his second year of high school coming to an end, he had devised a plan to get some extra money over the summer. He planned that between him and his crew of friends, they could make a buy into the drug game. It had started out that the money would be for some new clothes, and some jewelry. Possibly they could even get a nice whip he and his crew could drive around, but it quickly became much more.

Spits was semi-connected to the game through his cousin, Vision. They called him Vision because he always thought he saw things differently than others. His real name was Stanley, so that could've been another reason for him wanting to change it. Anyway, Vision had made a few connections while serving time in Bear Mountain Correctional Facility. He was there for a gun possession charge but he'd aspired to be in the drug game, so he took getting locked up as an opportunity to make connections. He had just been paroled right before that summer in '96. When Spits put him on to what he had planned, he said, *"to hell with parole,"* and he was all in. He would be the connection that they needed to get their shit off the ground.

The plan Spits had devised suggested that everybody down would come up with the buy-in price of $500; just enough to get about a half-ounce of coke each. Nothing major by itself, but collectively, they could make a little noise in their little part of the Bronx. Once he introduced the idea, it was on and poppin'. It was on everybody involved to come up with their share and they all had a week to do so. Michael felt comfortable in himself, as he'd already had $500 saved for a rainy day. Others had plans of their own.

Now Chris was the hothead of the bunch. Chris adopted the call Ceelow from his given name Christopher Loew. Ceelow, or just Cee, was dark-skinned and stood six feet flat. He wore a tapered Caesar fade with 360-degree waves. He was always really serious about his appearance, and always had the whitest T's all through the summer. Ceelow planned on obtaining his share of the buy-in with the proceeds from numerous strong-arm robberies. Spits had designated him to make sure no one would try and make a move on the spot or anybody on their crew. Basically, Cee would secure the block and report anything unusual. This was perfect for Cee because anytime something went down involving the rest of the crew he got right in the middle of it anyway. So it was fitting that he handled security.

With a cat like Ceelow on your crew, you needed someone with a little more rationalism; just to even things out. That's where Pop, or Mikey, came in. Mikey got the name Pop because he would try to come off like a father figure, giving advice and looking at every situation as a possible problem that needed to be resolved. Being the only one of the crew to actually grow up with his father, plus a two-year age difference, he figured that gave him seniority. Pop's real name was Mikey Black. Ironically, Pop was the blackest motherfucker you would ever see, and he stood six-three with a nappy afro. Pop had picked up a lot from his father while he was growing up. He always worked well with his hands, and as a kid, he was often called McGuiver. That's how he intended on obtaining his share of the buy-in, from fixing bikes, cars, or doing work around someone's house. That was the easiest way he knew how to get money, plus he would be enjoying himself. Now although Pop wasn't as short-tempered as Cee, he was just as ruthless. He was designated as second to Ceelow for security measures. They would make the perfect team, and their characteristics had enough contrast to offset the other's actions.

Peter, or Trigger as they called him, would handle the finances. He would make sure that they weren't getting shorted on profit. Trigger's real name was Peter Beckford, but whoever knew him called him Trigger for one of two reasons. One would be the obvious relation to some gangsta shit. The other was because Trigger was somewhat of a playboy. So the name could also be related to how easily he "*pulled*" the ladies. Trigger could fuck your girl, her sister and best friend the next day, and hang out with all three of them the day after that with no complications. That's how he got his buy-in money. He convinced a few girls into sacrificing some sneaker money to contribute to his cause. He was slick with his shit like that. Spits also knew Trigger the longest, and they shared the same book smarts. They'd met in the first grade and had become inseparable ever since. They'd even discovered their love for music together, and would often write songs and make beats with one another. Trigger was five feet eight inches, brown-skinned and wore braids in his hair as well.

Together, they were the Time Bombs. The name came from the idea of being unstoppable. It was only a matter of time before they "*blew up*" and when they did, niggas would know they weren't to be fucked with. They'd all planned on wearing tattoos with "TB" engraved, and had also planned on getting crew rings with "TB" in diamonds once they'd gotten to where they needed to be. It was perfect.

They met at Spits' crib. For a few months, Spits—along with his mother and little brother—had occupied an apartment just off of Gun Hill Road and Onlinville Avenue. It wasn't much: two bedrooms, a bathroom, a small kitchen, a dining area and a medium-sized living room. Spits and his brother, Henry Banner, shared a room and his mother had the other. The meeting was scheduled for nine in the morning because with his mother at work, and his brother at school, they could have some privacy to discuss their plans.

The first to reach Michael's place was Trigger. Only a few minutes later, came Cee accompanied by Pop. Once together, they went to the liquor store, then to the weed spot. They would need some of these necessities if they would be deliberating for the remainder of the morning and into the afternoon.

Once back at Michael's, they all sat around the kitchen table, poured drinks for themselves, and toasted, "*Moe's, hoes and zeros,*" and officially began the meeting.

"I-ight, my niggas, let me paint this picture for ya'll," Spits began. "Now we all know the game. We've watched the older niggas do it throughout our entire lives. From Edenwald to Gun Hill, we've watched niggas get money. We've seen the real niggas get cake, and we've seen the other niggas get killed. We've grown up directly in the middle of all this shit, and now it's *our* turn. I think I've found the perfect spot for us to start." Everyone looked at Spits as if he was about to tell them the meaning of life when...he took a breath, looked around and said, "Yo, let's roll up, and go up to the roof to blaze. You can see what I mean better from there." They all began rolling up weed in Phillie Blunts and White Owls to go smoke on the roof.

As he would soon explain, Michael's whole visualization devised from Bronx Park. That's where the customers were, so that's where they would set up shop. Just on the other side of Gun Hill Road was a back block street on one side of the Bronx River, and a seating area on the other side with a little track for racing remote-controlled cars. From these two points, plus the overpass that crossed the river, they would have the street shut down. Gun Hill was already infamous for drug trading, but no one had ever thought to bring the product directly to the customer. White Plains Road was the intersecting street where hustlers from all over the Bronx could be found selling, but Gun Hill Project cats mostly ran it. They controlled the street, no doubt about it. What Spits had planned was to control the park, where the customers would actually go to smoke. The way he saw it, when you're a nervous ass crack-fiend, you don't want to walk all the way to a busy street to buy drugs where you don't know who could be watching. Nah, if the opportunity presented itself, you would buy whatever you needed right there in the park where you smoked. Made sense when you thought about it. Besides, it was only supposed to be temporary anyway. In and out, right? Whatever!

From the roof, Spits began pointing and describing the way things should be run. Trigger came up with the idea that they could make drop-offs to re-up the workers from the overpass. Cee and Pop went on to point out where the lookout points should be. They all agreed that if they controlled the traffic to the Avenue, they would have the whole shit sewn up. They all continued to pour drinks and light weed as they came up with more and more ideas for their new enterprise.

CHAPTER 2

The first week we made a little over four thousand dollars. We should've made more, but us being new and all, we had to establish clientele. With the two thousand we had for the buy, we were able to purchase a little over two ounces of coke. When we broke that down we were looking at about five grand gross, but we decided we should bag up a grand worth in samples. The only part that bothered me was that we were bagging up the same work as everyone else, so it basically only came down to convenience. The customers that came to us did because we were the closest to 'em. That was the original plan, but now it wasn't enough. So before the re-up, we decided that we needed a new connection.

I got a call on my cell phone at about three o'clock in the afternoon. As the voice on the other end started, I realized that it was my girl, Ginger. She said she had some news that I might be interested in. But whenever I heard her voice, I seemed to lose focus and drift off. I didn't even hear what she'd said at first. Ginger, or just Gin, wasn't actually her real name, but that's what I called her. I'd given her that name because when I'd first seen her, she'd reminded me of a character in a movie that had come out in '95. She stood about five-four, with an hourglass figure, caramel skin, and the prettiest eyes I'd ever seen. But you couldn't let the pretty face and the girly attitude fool you; she was still my little gangsta bitch. She didn't like the fact that I was putting the street life before school, but I'd reassured her that it would only be temporary.

"Are you listening to me?!" she asked in an annoyed tone of voice. She hated it when she didn't get enough attention.

"Yeah, I'm listening, Gin," I said, trying to make her feel appreciated.

"I have something to tell you," she said, starting from the beginning.

Ginger lived in Cornwall, New York. And the news she had was exactly what I needed to hear. She told me that she'd heard crack heads in Newburgh, a town that neighbored hers, were just dropping dead out there from some new killer shit. I was like, "I WANT THAT SHIT!" The next day, I sent Vision to scout and ask around.

After a few days, Vision reported that the coke came from some new Puerto Ricans dealing exclusively in weight. Two crazy ass mu'fuckas named Louie and Rob. When I say these motherfuckers were crazy, please believe it. They'd grown up in Carolina, Puerto Rico, just east of San Juan, with their father, Romero Ortiz. Romero, or Mr. Ortiz, was directly connected to Colombian kingpins, and controlled the drug trade in the Northeast part of Puerto Rico.

What I liked the most about Louie and Rob was that everything was fifty/fifty, and both opinions held the same amount of respect. Louie, standing at about five feet five inches, was a pretty boy type, but it didn't take from his integrity. If you let the mousse in his hair throw you off for a second, he could spit a razor out of his mouth and give you a buck-fifty (150 stitches) across your face. Rob stood about five feet eleven inches, and he was stocky. He was the complete opposite of Louie. You could see Rob's gangsta from a block away. He had an intimidating persona, and he perpetuated it.

The only problem was that they didn't want anything to do with the city. They wanted to maintain the position they'd set up for themselves in the upstate part of New York. As their father had taught them, they were trying to keep their current situation under control until they were ready to expand. Plus, they didn't trust New York City mu'fuckas one bit.

The way I looked at it, that would be perfect for us if we could convince them to deal with us, 'cause then they wouldn't deal with anyone else. That meant that we'd have the whole borough under pressure. I found that it didn't take much work to influence Louie and Rob to become our associates. When we finally met, it was like we'd known each other for years. We'd clicked right away, so Louie and Rob were considered another branch of the TB family.

I sent Vision to get an eight ball (4 grams) for starters. With the proceeds from that, plus the four grand we'd already grossed, we could get a big eighth. A "big eighth" is an eighth of a kilo of coke (125 grams), and is considered the first step to being big time. So we cut up the eight ball and put it on the block. Once that shit hit our little part of the Bronx, these custees couldn't get enough. We had the whitest shit out and everybody instantly knew it. When we went back to Louie and Rob for the big eighth, they gave us what we could pay for, plus fronted a kilo on consignment. We were ready for expansion.

The first thing we had to do was secure our relationship with those Rican cats. That way we made sure they dealt exclusively with us as far as the city sales went. Next, we got a couple of workers for the spot on Gun Hill Road while we scouted for new territory. Plus it didn't hurt to have the extra heads for protection. The newest additions to the family were these two cats El Don and Poncho, or just Don P. Those niggas were some Jamaican cats that Trigger knew from down South. Although they looked like twins, they were two years apart as El Don was eighteen while Poncho was sixteen. Both were light-skinned and short with braids. Trigger had become familiar with them when he was younger. He had family in Atlanta, Georgia and used to spend summers there. Now Don and P. were up in the Bronx for the summer, and they couldn't have come at a better time. We welcomed them to the family with open arms.

The next day was spent cooking, cutting, and bagging up 1.125 kilos of the purest coke in the Bronx. It wasn't easy at all, but we were so excited at the progress we were making in such a short period of time, that it didn't even feel like work. There was weed in the air, Hennessey in our glasses, and NAS' debut album, *Illmatic*, bumped from the stereo. When track nine came on, we all went crazy singing in harmony.

"Represent! Represent!"

Once we'd done the final total, we'd bagged 3,000 dimes, and 3,225 twenty-sacks, equaling $67,500 worth of crack cocaine. When Trigger said how much we'd bagged up for the first time out loud, silence fell over the room. No one could say anything to fill in the blanks, so we just stared at one another. Finally, Cee put his glass up for a toast. "Moe's, hoes, and zeros."

We hit the block that night. Don P. and Ceelow manned the spot on Gun Hill Road., while Trigger, Pop and I went to the new spot. It was located on 224th Street and Bronx Boulevard. Pop thought that it would be a nice place to set up shop. That's where we'd all grown up, but he was the only one that realized the traffic controllability from that point so he'd presented the idea to the rest of us. Each spot was in possession of two G-packs each. A G-pack was a thousand dollars' worth of work. Re-up bundles were left in the parking lot behind my building in case either of us ran out. We kept contact through payphones and beepers.

Between eight-thirty and midnight, we'd finished both our packs. It had started out slow, but once the first few sales were made, they kept coming. It started moving like hotcakes, a five-sale here, and a twelve-sale there. We needed to re-up fast. I immediately got in a cab to Gun Hill to get the stash. I had the cab drop me off on the overpass so that I could check on the others.

"What the fuck?" From the overpass, I could see two guys with guns pointed at Ceelow, Don and P., plus one more waiting in a beat-up, charcoal-gray Honda Accord.

"Where the paper at, dog?" said one guy to Cee with a chrome .9mm pointed directly between his eyes. "Give that up, little nigga. Don't worry, you'll live," said the other to Don.

My first instinct was to run down there and beat the shit out of those bitch-ass niggas, but that wouldn't have been the smartest thing to do. So, I did the sharpest thing I could think of. I stood at the top of the stairs leading down from the overpass, pointed like I had a gun, and screamed, "You bitch-ass niggas want it with the Time Bombs?" When they saw me, they automatically anticipated me firing, and fired first in my direction. When the first shot went off, I hit the pavement. Then two more went off.

Ceelow took advantage of the situation like I had hoped he would. Realizing what I was doing, he acted on it without missing one beat. When he saw that I had all of their attention, he hit the guy closest to him with a left hook, dazing him. Don immediately spit out a razor he had hidden inside of his mouth, and split the right side of the other guy's face open, sending blood flying through the air. By now, Poncho had gotten hold of the black .38 Special that was just pointed at his face and began striking him with it until he hit the ground. Cee did the same with the .9 mm.

All I heard were the car's tires screeching as the driver fled, leaving his boys behind on the floor bleeding. I rushed to the bottom of the stairs, where we continued to beat on the remaining two so-called stick-up kids. Assuming enough stress was relieved, and that the culprits had taken enough of a beating, I attempted to calm everyone down. Cee, on the other hand, didn't agree and continued violently beating the guy with the butt of the gun. When I tried to grab him, he pushed me off and pointed the gun at the back of his head as he lay face down on the floor. I looked in Ceelow's eyes, as they opened wider and wider, and saw an expression I'd never seen before. He looked as if excitement filled his entire body, from his fully extended eyebrows all the way into his fingers, which were twitching on the tip of the trigger.

"My nigga, relax yourself and think, dog," I said in the calmest voice I could. "This nigga ain't worth it, son. Not here...not now."

He made eye contact with me and slowly took the gun from the back of his head. I put my arm around him and attempted to walk away when, suddenly, he broke free of my grasp, running back to where they still lay on the ground and put the gun right back to his head. *BOOM...BOOM!* He shot him in the back of his head twice. He then turned the gun on his unfortunate partner in crime. *BOOM! BOOM...BOOM! BOOM! BOOM!* He put five shots in his back and dropped the gun as he walked away.

"Ya'll ready?" Ceelow asked, trying to conceal the fact that he was still shaken up.

I couldn't believe it. I just stared at him in amazement, unable to move. Police sirens gave me back focus as they could be heard from above us on the overpass getting closer and closer. We automatically took off running. It was almost impossible to see much down there, in the darkness of Bronx Park, so the police didn't get a glimpse at us fleeing. When we got back to 224th Street, I told Trigger and Pop that we should pack it in for the night. They asked no questions. They just nodded in agreement, as they had seen a few police cars pass them with sirens blaring. We spent the rest of the night drinking and smoking in the lobby of the building that we'd all grown up in. We spoke nothing about it the entire night. It took me until the next morning to actually realize what had happened. We'd reached another level of the game that night. We could never go back now, and that's just what I was afraid of.

CHAPTER 3

Two months had passed since Spits and the rest of the Time Bombs had started their drug enterprise, and it seemed as though they had seen the worst of times. They had really come a long way since that early morning on the roof. In only two months their growth and maturity could've taken the average sixteen-year-old the rest of his life. Soon after the robbery attempt on the crew, they'd all gotten arms of their own, and rarely were they without them. All that happened that night would never happen again if they could help it. They also stopped using the spot on Gun Hill Road because the two dead bodies put the area under close observation by the NYPD. So along with the spot on 224th Street, they had Vision rent a room on 219th and White Plains Road on the top of a candy store. The rent was cheap, and the door was reinforced with steel. They cut down the access anyone had to them so they wouldn't find themselves in the same predicament as in the park. Besides, they had the fiends on lockdown. Wherever they moved, the customers were sure to follow.

Now with the new school year right around the corner, Spits found himself in a dilemma. He'd originally planned on putting school before the drug game, but he also couldn't have imagined in a million years that he would profit as much he did. In two months TB moved about seven kilos collectively. That's about four hundred and twenty grand. Personally, Spits had over twenty thousand saved, but only a portion of the family's proceeds went to individual members. Besides a car they'd bought for business purposes, the lump of the profit got reinvested. It was imperative that they had enough product to supply the many customers they'd obtained in the past couple of months. On top of the two spots they had under control for hand-to-hands, they also started making weight sales. The best thing about buying weight from them, besides the fact that nobody had better work, was that they delivered. If you called Spits for a small eighth, you would have it within thirty minutes. That saved you the time it would take to go to the weight man. That way, you could anticipate when you'd be finished and give them a call. By the time they came, all you'd have to do was buss it down, and get right back on your grind.

Things were looking so promising for them with all of the advancements they'd made. *Maybe I can just postpone for a year, or maybe two,* Michael thought to himself time after time. *I'm still young. I have enough time to go back.* He tried over and over to justify to himself that he was doing the right thing, until finally he just said, "Fuck it."

As Spits slid in and out of highway traffic on the Bronx River Parkway in what they all called "The Family Car"—a 1992 white Nissan Maxima—he found himself zoning. The sky was a light shade of gray, and the air had a hint of moisture as if rain were near. Spits was on his way down to 169th and Simpson Street to make a drop, and had been studying his options. He still had some regrets as far as his decisions regarding school, and it was on his mind twenty-four hours out of the day. He'd decided that he needed a vacation. Some time away from New York would be just what he needed to get his mind right.

He'd decided to visit some family in Florida. His cousin Anthony, or Tone, was attending a college in Daytona called Embry Riddle, a college specializing in aeronautics. As far as Spits was concerned, Tone somewhat had his shit together. He knew what he wanted to do, and he was going for it. Maybe Tone would be the positive role model he needed to get his priorities in the proper perspective.

"Hello?"

"Yo, what's good, my nigga? It's Spits."

"Oh, what's up, my nigga?" Tone asked, excited to hear a voice from back home. "What's crackin' up in New York?"

"Everything is cool out here, na'mean. How's the school situation?"

"Things is i-ight down here, but these school loans are killing me. What ya'll niggas been up to?"

"Oh, we killin' 'em out here, kid. If you was up here, you wouldn't have to stress no school loans and shit, but we'll talk about that another time. Yo, ain't ya birthday coming up soon?"

"Yeah, in a few days, on the 26th. Why?"

"I think I'm gonna come down there and check you, son. I need to get away from New York for a bit to get my head on right. That's cool?"

"Hell yeah, I'll see you then."

"I'll call when I touch down, my nigga. Peace."

Once they'd hung up he couldn't even conceal his excitement. Michael called Ginger first to let her know that he'd be out of town for a few days. He knew she'd be mad at first, but she'd have to understand his situation. If anybody could appreciate his intentions, Ginger could. She knew him better than anybody. Ginger, like Michael, had grown up in a single-parent home. Her father had fallen victim to the street life and was sent away while her mother was still pregnant with her. Her mother struggled to provide for her family just like Michael's mom. Seeing what her father and the street had put their daughter through made Ginger's mother pursue a career as a police officer. Once she'd become a part of the NYPD, she'd moved Ginger into a good neighborhood upstate to shield her from the street. It worked. Even though Ginger rebelled a bit, she'd still grown up with more opportunities than the average kid from the old neighborhood.

When he hung up with Ginger, he called Trigger, and told him to let the fellas know what was up. He strongly emphasized that it would be on the rest of the family to hold the fort in his absence. He told him that he was going to drop the car off at Pop's house, if he needed it for anything, and then they hung up. When he went to Pop's crib, they had a lengthy discussion about life, he wished Spits a safe trip, and he was off. Pop looked extremely pleased with the way things were going. As Spits left, he realized that he'd never seen Pop so happy and content with his life. Everything was moving smoothly, and Spits couldn't wait to get down to Daytona.

The next morning was chilly out, and the clouds had turned a darker shade of gray than the day before. As Spits looked out of his bedroom window, raindrops started to tap on the sill, and he thought to himself, What a good day to leave New York. He rolled over and started getting ready. He grabbed a small bag that he'd packed, and made his way for the door. He thought to give his mother a call at work before he left, but he knew that she wouldn't approve. He wouldn't tell her until he'd already reached Daytona, when the damage was already done. He'd have to suffer the consequences when he got home.

Spits reached Daytona Beach International Airport at about 2 p.m. With no bags to claim, he headed straight outside to catch a cab to the hotel. Once in the cab, he couldn't help but stare outside the window at the sights in amazement. This was Michael's first time in Florida since he was a kid. An aunt of his had a house there, in Port Charlotte, where his mother would take him and his brother on vacation from time to time, but he didn't remember Florida like this. With the palm trees swaying from the slight breeze, and the clear blue sky, Spits could finally take a deep breath of the fresh clean air and relax.

He'd originally planned on booking a room at a Best Inn Hotel located on Bostwick Avenue—a couple of blocks from the beach—but given the exceptional mood he was in, he had the cabdriver suggest other arrangements. So they proceeded to the Hilton Daytona Beach Resort located on South Atlantic Avenue on the beach strip. While his first attempt to check-in was unsuccessful due to his age, he figured that a little cash would be more effective than a state ID, and it most certainly was. He then checked in and anxiously went upstairs where his suite was located. Once he found the door, he stuck the keycard in the slot until the green light lit up. He opened the door, and stood there in the doorway with his jaw dropped. He couldn't believe his eyes. It seemed as if he were in a dream.

The entrance was met on the left with a full-sized bar stocked with all kinds of brandy, cognac, vodka, whiskey, scotch and anything else you could think of. To left of the bar was the living area, and it was complete with two plush leather sofas, big wall-sized mirrors, a fireplace, and a television set inside a rotating pillar so that it could be directed toward the sleeping area.

On the right side of the living area were two doors that opened outward to the terrace. Next to that was the sleeping area that was laced with a nice big king-size bed, nightstands and dimming lamps. Then, there was the bathroom. The bathroom split into two separate toilet areas closed off by mirrored doors, with a huge vanity mirror in the middle, and double sinks. Behind one side was a toilet with a stand-up shower, and behind the other, a toilet and a Jacuzzi. Jet-black carpet flowed through the entire space with the Hilton logo placed in key areas of the floor. From the terrace you could see the entire beach strip and all of the other smaller hotels that sat to the right and left. Just looking at the sky from this point could calm a wild animal. As the sun set into that powder blue sky, it started turning orange and then red. Captivated in its beauty, Spits couldn't help but to just stand there, staring for a while until the sun was gone. He then got into the Jacuzzi to relax for a while and think. When he was done, he got into the huge bed and dozed off watching *Thundercats*, his favorite childhood cartoon, on the Cartoon Network.

Spits woke up early the next morning, and that day was even more beautiful than the last. He called room service to order breakfast, got a quick shower and, by the time he was done, his breakfast had arrived. He quickly ate and headed out. The first thing he wanted to do was hit the mall for some new gear, so he caught a cab to the Volusia Mall. He hit all the urban spots and designer clothing stores for the newest designs. When he finally felt like he had done enough shopping, he had seven or eight bags filled with Coogi, Iceberg, Armani Exchange, Timberland boots, and Nike Air Force Ones. Before he could leave, he stopped in a jewelry store called Atlantis, where he saw a gold Cuban link chain he liked. He put it together with a gold pendant in the shape of a dragon flooded with diamonds, and paid for it in cash with no hesitation whatsoever. He also bought a charm bracelet he thought that Ginger would like, and then he was on his way. The gift he'd bought for Ginger reminded him of how much he missed her. He called her as soon as he got back to the hotel to let her know he was safe, and that he was already having a great time. When he got off the phone with Ginger, he called Tone, and they made plans to link up later on in the evening, giving him the opportunity to take a nap before they came to pick him up.

The time was ten o'clock when Tone called Spits in his hotel room to wake him up from his nap and let him know they'd be there in forty-five minutes. After a quick shower, Spits selected an outfit from his shopping spree earlier in the day. Spits looked at himself in the wall mirror and fell in love with what he saw. He picked out an Armani Exchange linen short set to wear along with a pair of Gucci sneaker/shoes. As he was tying his shoe the phone rang. It was Tone.

"What up, son?" asked Tone. "You ready, or what?"

"Yeah, I'll be down in one second," Spits said, rushing him off the phone.

He hung up and took one more look at himself in the mirror. He polished off the face of his watch to make sure it carried the proper gleam, adjusted his new chain so that it fell correctly on his shirt, and gave his reflection a grin and a wink before leaving.

Tone, along with one of his boys from school named Will, took Spits to a new club he had heard about out in Orlando named The Palladium. At the door Spits paid for all three of them to get in with VIP passes and after they did a couple of rounds around the dance floor, they headed upstairs to get a booth in the VIP lounge.

"What can I get you guys?" the waitress asked.

"Yeah, give me a crown and Coke," requested Tone.

"Yeah, I'll have some Henny straight up," said Spits.

Will would order the same but the waitress cut him off before he could finish.

"Y'all got to buy bottles to sit here. If not, you'll have to go downstairs to have your little mixed drinks," she said in a tone that suggested they wouldn't be able to afford it.

"Okay then, let us get three bottles of Moet then, i-ight, shorty," Spits said, pulling a knot of hundred dollar bills out of his pocket. "That will be all, for now!" he said, waving her off.

"Damn, son," Tone said, showing his amazement at the stack of money Michael had revealed. "You holding like that?"

"Yeah, I got this. We gonna make this bitch feel like a real dumb-ass tonight.

Who the fuck she think she is?" said Spits, still showing a little bit of anger at the waitress' comment.

"Oh, fuck that bitch, son! Where did you get all that paper?"

"My nigga, I told you we killin' 'em up top," he responded, referring to his recent narcotic escapades in the Bronx.

"I heard you when you said it, but I didn't know it was like that though, son," said Tone in disbelief.

"Yeah, it's a serious situation now. We got a tight little crew, too, son. We gonna make some real noise in a minute, kid," said Spits, referencing the plans they had for the future.

Tone showed much interest. "Word? You gonna have to put me on, my nigga. This school shit is fucking my pockets up."

"I don't know about that," Spits responded, disinterested in corrupting a family member. "That might not be a good idea."

As they discussed things further, Tone went on to mention that he'd already obtained his private pilot's license with the hours of experience he had. That would be perfect if Tone was going to set up shop down in Daytona. He could charter planes without a problem, and security was minimal. He also pointed out that his school was predominantly filled with, "white boys who only did drugs," to quote his words exactly. He wouldn't even have to cook or cut the coke. He could sell it to them raw, and for the prices they were already paying, he'd make a killing. Although Spits took it all in, he didn't let on how fascinated he really was. He'd already planned out what they could accomplish in his head, but he needed more time to think about it before he told Tone anything.

"Calm down, cousin. We'll have all the time in the world to talk about this shit," Spits said. "I came down here to get away from all that temporarily. Feel me?"

Tone agreed and they continued to drink.

It had passed midnight while they were talking and it was now officially Tone's birthday. They lifted their bottles for toast to "Moe's, hoes and zeros" and just as Spits was about to take a sip from his glass, he got a page with the code for emergency: 9-1-1.

CHAPTER 4

The day I got that page was one of the worse days of my life. I couldn't believe that while I was having the time of my life in Florida, something that fucked up could be happening back home. When I finally got to a payphone to call the number that was left on my pager, I found out that the room we were renting on 219th Street had been raided by the police. As soon as I heard the voice on the other line, I knew something was wrong.

"Yo, what up? Somebody paged Spits?"

"Hello, is this Michael?" asked the man on the other line with a very shaken and cracked voice.

"Yeah, who's this?" I said, confused.

"This is Peter Sr.," he said. "I'm Peter Jr.'s father. He said that you'd be able to help us get him out of jail."

"Jail?" I asked with a puzzled look on my face. "What the fuck is he doing in jail? Um, excuse my language, Mr. Beckford, but you can understand my confusion," I said to give a responsible impression.

"Don't worry about it, son," he said, trying to make me comfortable. "He told me that you were out of town, and that he needed to speak to you directly. He's currently being held on one hundred thousand dollars bail. He was charged with possession of an illegal substance, intent to distribute and resisting arrest. Look, there are a lot more details that I'd rather not tell you over the telephone. How long will you be out of town?"

"I'll be there in the morning," I responded. "When you speak to Trigger, I mean Peter, tell him to call me at my girl's house, anytime in the afternoon. I'll be waiting for his call." I figured no one knew where Ginger lived, so I could avoid being greeted by the authorities upon my arrival.

"All right, Michael," he said, sounding pleased. "I'll let him know. Peace."

"Peace."

I immediately got Tone to take me back to the hotel so that I could get my things. When I got there, I called Ginger and told her that I'd be at her house in the morning. I told her that it might not be safe for me to go straight home, so it was important that someone be there when I arrived. When we hung up, I checked out of the hotel and went straight to the airport from there. I got a ticket for the next flight out but it wouldn't be departing until seven-thirty. I'd reach New York with only a little bit of time left to get upstate to Ginger's house by noon.

The flight was on time and it landed at LaGuardia Airport at 11:30 a.m. A cab from the airport got me to Ginger's by 12:10 p.m. If I'd gotten there a minute later, I would've missed his call since the phone rang as soon as I walked in.

"Hello?" I said with anticipation. An operator came on the line and informed me that there was a collect call from Peter and I quickly accepted.

"Hello?" said Trigger, sounding very distant and emotionless.

"Yeah, son. How you holdin' up in there, kid? Ain't nobody fucking with you, right?" I inquired, trying to come across relaxed and in control of the situation. "I'm gonna get you outta there, son. Don't even worry about it."

After a few seconds of complete silence, he spat, "Yo, he just kept shooting, son."

I was without a clue. I waited for him to finish, but he didn't. Then he said, "He just kept shooting, and shooting, and shooting. I tried to tell him, 'Yo, son! Don't! We already caught! They got us!' But he didn't listen. He just kept shooting, and shooting, and shooting."

"Who are you talking about, dog?" I asked, trying to understand.

"You don't know?" he asked confusingly. "They didn't tell you. I'm talking about Pop. He's gone. They sent him back to his essence, kid."

My heart stopped. I couldn't even breathe. It didn't hit me until I looked up at Ginger, and she had tears in her eyes. She thought I knew. I couldn't contain myself any longer. Once Ginger looked at me, I saw the pain that she felt for me and for Pop and for Trigger. As the tears that began forming in my eyes, I quickly buried the emotions deep inside me as Trigger continued telling me the story.

"He came to pick me up early yesterday morning. The night before had been real good for our spot on 219th. Shit was moving like water. We thought it would be best to keep it fully stocked. So that morning we cut up half a brick to re-up the spot with. On our way out, we weren't even halfway out the door before the police rushed us. When I saw them approaching, I went to shut the door, but they beat me to the drop. Pop had already run back upstairs for the Mac-10. Like eight of those pigs went upstairs after Pop, and as soon as the first one hit the top step, the shots started. They had me pinned down at the bottom of the stairs when I screamed to him that we were caught. All I could hear was the rattle of the shots being let off from the Mac, one after the other, while Pop screamed like a maniac."

"What happened next?" I asked in suspense.

"He took out like six of those mu'fuckas before they got him. He gave it to five of them upstairs, and then he got away from them to come back toward the stairs where they had me pinned down. He hit one of the dudes holdin' me down in the head twice before another cop caught up to him from behind. Yo, I saw his brains hit the fuckin' wall, my nigga. He went out like a straight-up gangsta, dog. After I saw that shit, it took five more of them to hold me down. When they finally got me to the precinct, those punk mu'fuckas beat the shit out of me for what seemed like forever. I guess for their partners and shit."

"Yo, I'm gonna get you out of there, son. I got you; don't even worry about it. I got you," I said with redness in my eyes. I wasn't playing one bit either. Whatever it took, I was going to get my man out of there.

I reassured Trigger that I'd hold him down like steel. In turn, he reassured me that the police wouldn't be waiting for me when I got back to the Bronx.

I should've known that he wasn't a rat; especially as long as we'd known each other, but sometimes you have to put your brain before your heart. Besides, I didn't even know who'd snitched to begin with. How the fuck did they know about our little organization anyway?

Seeing the stress in my face as I sat there with my head in my lap, Ginger came over to me in an attempt to comfort me. She stood up in front of me and began rubbing my shoulders. When I looked up at her, she wiped the tears from her eyes, kissed my forehead, and got on her knees in front of me, resting my head on her shoulders. Just the feeling of her soft, warm body up against mine as we hugged immediately made me feel much better. She began kissing my neck passionately, and then unbuttoned my shirt, kissing my chest with more intensity. In seconds, my shirt was off, and she slowly started to undo my pants while she gently kissed down to stomach. Before my pants were all the way off, I'd already grown to the extent of my erection as the anticipation grew. Once I was completely naked, she glanced at me and smiled as she stroked my fully enlarged penis with both hands. Without her even breaking eye contact with me, I watched myself disappear into her mouth. It felt like I was in heaven as she motioned up and down, but unfortunately I couldn't stay in this heavenly place for much longer before I would explode. I soon felt myself ready to ejaculate, so I lifted her head back up and began kissing her deeply. I took her in my arms and carried her upstairs to her bedroom where we would continue what she'd started. As I laid her down on the bed, I removed all of her clothes slowly. When she was completely nude, I began caressing her breasts and kissing them softly. Soon, she was pushing my head further down her torso until I was between her legs. I began tenderly kissing her inner thighs, and slowly moving inward. When I reached her clitoris, I teased it with the tip of my tongue, making her jerk and moan until she begged me to stop so she wouldn't cum prematurely. Laying me flat on my back, she mounted my throbbing penis, and inserted me inside of her, moaning more and more as I sunk deeper and deeper.

"Cum for me, Daddy," she said with the sexiest, most sensual voice I could imagine. That's all it took. Within seconds I was ready to explode.

The intensity grew with every movement. I felt a rippling wave flow through my body as I began to erupt. With her hands clenched into my chest, her grip grew tighter and tighter as she came right along with me. When we were both through, she laid her head on my chest, and fell asleep to the sound of my heartbeat.

All over again, my mind started to race as I lay in Ginger's bed smoking a cigarette, while she slept beside me. All of the stress from when I'd first hung up the phone with Trigger came rushing back. I'd need to get a lot of money together for this shit. Bail money was the least of my worries. We were going to need a good lawyer for Trigger, and for any one of us that caught a case. It was time for grind mode.

I called Tone first. I had to see if he was really serious about all that shit he was talking in Daytona. If I was sure of his dedication, I'd call Louie and Rob next. I had to set up a meeting with them to propose that they transport in and out of the States through me for a reasonable price, while I purchased directly from Mr. Ortiz. That shit would be perfect.

CHAPTER 5

YEAR — 2000

"Here this mu'fucka go again," Spits said to himself as he spotted the ol' timer from earlier approaching. He looked to the left, and all he saw was the blackness that consumed the Bronx Park at 4:15 a.m. He looked to the right, and there was nothing but a blinking streetlight on the other side of the overpass. That was it. It was just him, the darkness and the damn blinking streetlight. Considering the limited resources, Spits started to look at this ol' timer as his only option. He got his attention and signaled for him to come over to where he was sitting. Once he got there, he began to run a little game of his own.

"What's up, Money?" said Spits.

"Money?" he said with uncertainty.

"Uh-huh, that must be ya name, nigga. You said you gonna make me rich, right?"

"Yeah, that's what I said. But you young bastards nowadays think you know every fuckin' thing."

"Listen, mu'fucka," Spits said as he brandished a chrome .45mm pistol. "Don't think for a second that you can't get it. My kindness is not to be mistaken for weakness, pussy. Just cuz you don't know me, don't mean I ain't known. Now, I got a proposal for you," he said, now raising the pretty pearl-handled cannon to the side of the guy's head. "Either I could let you have it, or I could let you hold sumthin'. Make a choice."

"Sorry, sir. I didn't mean any disrespect. What do you want me to do?" the man asked with obvious fear in his voice.

"Yeah," Spits said, lowering the gun. "You gonna do some legwork for me. For every ten sales you bring me, I'll let you hold sumthin'. Feel me?"

"Sounds good to me, sir. Sorry for the disrespect, young m-man—I mean, sir. Umm, what should I call you?"

"Call me Spits, Money."

"Spits? You're Mike Spits?" he asked, realizing whom he had been bad-mannered toward. Realizing that his shit-talking could've just gotten him killed, a little ass-kissing couldn't possibly hurt.

"Yeah, now go ahead and make me some paper."

At first, Spits felt better when the ol' timer realized who he was, but that quickly faded. It actually made him aware of whom he had become in such a short time period. Four or five years ago, he wouldn't have cared whether or not some nobody crack-fiend knew his name. His priorities had changed completely, and he regretted every decision he'd made since that summer of '96. For the first time in years, Spits was actually genuinely considering retiring from the game. The day had to come sooner or later. Better sooner, than later.

"Damn, it's already four-fucking-thirty, and I ain't moved shit out here yet," said Spits, beginning to show his frustration. As he sat there on that park bench for all of those hours, he started to realize that the park hadn't changed much at all since they'd first started. Still, it sure wasn't like it used to be.

YEAR — 1997

"Yo son, turn that shit up," said El Don from the back seat of Michael's brand-new Lexus LX450, as they breezed past their old spot on Gun Hill Road without even giving it a second thought.

"That's that shit," Poncho said in agreement. As Spits reached for the knob, realizing what song was coming on, he bumped the stereo to its maximum volume. As the beat started to settle, and the hook came in, they all began singing along.

"You belong to the city...You belong to the night...In the river of darkness...He's the man of the nigh...t"

Jay-Z's new album, *In My Lifetime Vol. 1*, was crucial to have bumping in your ride; especially a ride like Michael's new Lex truck. It was a silver '97 LX450 with a tan leather interior, a six-CD changer, set in a cherrywood grain dash. It had a power sunroof, tinted windows and it was sitting on some 20-inch Pirellis. It was his new toy, and he loved it. Needless to say, his new ventures into the drug game had been most profitable.

His idea to transport for Louie and Rob Ortiz had gone over well with the brothers; they'd been extremely excited to get started as well as Spits. Between September of last year and now, Louie and Rob had brought over 50 kilos of cocaine to the States from Puerto Rico through Tone and Spits. That's not even counting the bricks Spits flew in for TB distribution. They'd become an enterprise worth millions of dollars collectively.

Now that the TB Family was worth a little paper, they'd started to act like it. Just as planned, they'd all gotten tattoos on their right forearms that illustrated the love and dedication they had for each other. They had an insignia designed that fit them perfectly so that no one else could have it that read: "T.B.T.B.T. – Time Bombs the Bronx Terrorists." They'd also followed through with their original plans to get TB rings flooded with diamonds. They'd also gotten their own apartments respectively. It was definitely their time to shine.

With all of the success, the Time Bomb Family had become a crack-household name all over the Bronx, including the police departments. They often had to grease off numerous police officers from two or three different precincts just so that they'd turn their heads a bit while everything transpired. They didn't have any particular officers on the payroll, but whenever they were faced with that type of situation, they gave no hesitation. Everyone on the streets of the Bronx knew who the Time Bombs were. Their reputation spoke for itself, and it was so thick you could feel it whenever any one of them walked into a room.

It took only a few days after Spits had gotten back from Daytona for them to get the money together to post the $100,000 bail for Trigger, and he'd been awaiting trial ever since. The lawyer Spits had retained for Trigger,

William D. Oberman, had gotten his trial pushed back so that they'd have sufficient time to get his defense ready, or if worse came to worst, construct a contingency plan if he had to go on the run. But the courts wouldn't wait much longer, no matter how good his lawyer was, and he was good.

William, or "The Doberman" as they called him, was the lawyer for all of Mr. Ortiz's associates in the States. TB had become of some importance to his organization, so he plugged them in. It was in both of their best interests. The Doberman had over fifteen years of experience under his belt. He'd spent a substantial amount of his career as a district attorney in Columbus, Ohio, but soon discovered his love for money was greater than his passion for justice.

Anyway, until that date came for Trigger to come before the judge, he was free to roam the streets. In fact, they were on their way to pick him up at that very moment. With Spits driving, Don and P. riding in the back, and Ceelow up front, they were going to scoop up Trigger at his crib so they could go meet some prospective buyers in Washington Heights, on the Upper West Side of Manhattan.

"Where this mu'fucka at, dog?" asked Spits, worrying that they might be late for their meeting. "Yo, Cee, you called this nigga before we left the crib, right?"

"Yeah, nigga. You was standing right there when I called him!" responded Ceelow as Spits tried to shift the blame to him. "He probably up there with some bitch."

"Word up," agreed El Don as he passed a newly lit blunt to Poncho. "My nigga always got a broad buffing his tip."

Don's comment made them all laugh; except for Spits. He got angry and didn't think it was a joking matter.

"Yeah, well that's gonna be his downfall," said Spits with no humor in his voice whatsoever. "The day you let a piece of ass get in the way of business, is the day you might as well hang it up," he said, now directing his words toward the rest of them.

"Here this nigga come," said Poncho, pointing toward Trigger's front door. "Yup, and there's the hoe that he must've been smashin'."

Trigger walked toward the car, after dismissing the female he'd come out of the building with, and then jumped in the car. As they drove off, Spits shot him a disappointing look as he described the perverted activities that had kept him too busy to realize how late it had gotten. He went on to express to the crew his deepest apologies and they all, including Spits, brushed off the incident entirely.

When they finally arrived they were twenty minutes late, and if these Dominicans were anything like Spits, they wouldn't tolerate tardiness. They met at a place called Fernando's Coffee Shop on 153rd and Amsterdam Avenue. They were there to meet up with Pitto and Willie Hernandez, two Dominican coke-pushers looking to take over the Washington Heights drug trade via the TB organization. When they pulled up, they were greeted by four large gentlemen standing in the front of the establishment. It may have been an attempt on the part of Pitto and Willie to look intimidating, but that shit didn't work a bit on Spits and the rest of the crew.

"Look at these mu'fuckin' *oye's* tryin' to look hard over here," said Spits. "Fuckin' amateur night and shit…who they supposed to be scaring?"

"I don't know," Cee answered. "But I know if one of them try and pop off, I'm gonna knock somebody ass the fuck out."

"Anyway," Spits said. "Let's see what these mu'fuckas is talking about. Yo, just in case, make sure all of ya'll got a slug chambered, and if I say 'let's get down to business,' start blazing, i-ight?"

They all nodded in agreement, and then Spits, Trigger and Cee got out while Don P. waited in the truck.

As they walked toward the door, without any words being spoken, the four guys parted for their entry. They were then directed to the rear of the coffee shop where there was a table set up for their meeting. When they arrived at the table, Pitto and Willie sat there staring up at them as if disgusted at the sight of them.

"Pitto," Willie said. "Tome este como una lección aprendió a no tratar con Negro," he said as he looked Spits up and down.

"Oye mu'fucka," said Spits, showing a little rage. "No me subestime apenas porque soy Negro. We here, ain't we?"

"What did he say?" whispered Ceelow to Trigger.

"He said 'that's why you should never deal with Blacks,'" answered Trigger. "And Spits told him not to underestimate us. These mu'fuckas is basically trying to play us."

"Now," Spits said. "If we're through playing childish games, don't we have some things to take care of, so we can get the fuck outta here?"

Aside from the way the meeting began, it turned out successful. They came to an agreement to take fifteen kilos of pure Colombian coke that they'd purchase quarterly throughout the year (every three months). Now, this deal was just for openers, but it would still bring the Family approximately $1.8 million over the course of a year, and every year that followed. The first payment was due in one week at a location that would be later determined. This relationship looked promising for the Family, as all they would be were middlemen for an extremely generous fee. While they paid $10,000 per kilo, they were charging $30,000. The price was high, but the quality of the product suggested that price to be a suitable one. Besides, once they had a sample, they couldn't even pronounce "too much money." Plus, Spits reassured them that they'd handle all of the transportation involved. They couldn't be more satisfied.

By now, the TB Family was moving two kilos monthly through Tone down in Daytona Beach. They transported approximately twenty-five kilos for the Ortiz Brothers every month. Along with some street corners they had under control along Bronxwood Avenue that they called "The Woods" they had an apartment set up for hand-to-hand sales and a phone number that you could call for weight volumes. And now with this deal set in motion, it put their average gross at about $2.96 million every three months (give or take a few hundred grand). Whoa!

When they left Fernando's, they parted ways once back in the Bronx. They all had to get back to the crib to get ready for that night. A celebration was in order and if they knew how to do anything, it was party. When Spits reached his apartment, he went fumbling through his closet for the perfect outfit. When he was finally satisfied, he had a jet-black Iceberg leather pair of pants laid out with a jacket to match jean-suit style. Under that he would put a charcoal gray and black Iceberg sweater and the skull hat to go with it. On his feet would be a crispy pair of Wallabee Clarks, black with the sides dyed charcoal gray. He posed for himself in the mirror while adjusting his sleeve on his new Cartier watch so that the diamonds in the bezel could be shown. He polished off the ice on his right-hand ring finger where he wore his Time Bomb crew ring, and he was ready to do it up until sunrise.

They'd all meet on the Block for a little fashion show before they were off. Spits insisted on reaching there after everyone had already showcased their gear so that he could blow up the spot. He pulled up in his newly waxed Lexus LX450, with the streetlights gleaming off the hood. As the driver's side window came down Spits let his hand hang out, and the ice sparkling from his watch was even more blinding. When he smiled out of the window, they all began to holler in awe at the show he was trying to put on.

Capone -N- Noreaga were supposed to be performing at Jimmy's Café in the Bronx that night, and Spits intentionally had their debut album *War Report* bumping from his system. When the door opened, the song playing was suited perfectly for the situation. After they'd all given each other pounds and hugs, they began singing along with the music.

"T-O-N-Y…Invade NY…Multiply…Kill a cop…Me and you…You got beef…I got beef."

It had become the new street anthem in the Bronx and every other hood you could imagine and for good reason, too; especially for the Time Bombs. The streets had been eagerly awaiting this type of bomb since the *Infamous* album in '95. As laid-back as the vocals were released, it still brought the animal thug out of you. As the crew went on chanting, Spits took a long hard look at their circle. He looked at them all closer than he'd ever looked at them before and said to himself, "This is my family."

They had more fun that night than they'd ever had. It was like a new life party, or like a huge weight had been lifted off their shoulders. They finally could relax in knowing that they'd be financially set for the rest of their lives. It was the most comforting feeling to have.

The night was temporarily saddened at the news that Capone wouldn't be performing, as he was picked up by the police on a robbery charge, POSSIBLE LEGAL ISSUE but Noreaga still came out and did his thing. When the crew was tired and sweaty from going crazy on the dance floor, they all met back at a booth in the VIP area. As the best night of their lives together came to a close they gathered around the table, each with a bottle of Cristal in hand, and still toasted to "Moe's, hoes and zeros" for old times' sake. They also vowed that the next toast, and from then on, would be to "Dom P's and palm trees" respectively.

CHAPTER 6

Monday, March 17, 1997 was the day Trigger's trial was set to begin. It was a cold and rainy day in New York but you couldn't have asked me, because I was in sunny California. My intentions weren't completely political; I mean, I had no desire to be anywhere near the courtroom, but for a while I'd wanted to visit my sister, Rachel. Rachel and I hadn't seen much of each other during our childhood, but we'd gotten closer to one another as we grew.

While I was there, I stayed with her at her apartment complex in Sunnyvale, California called Oak Pointe Apartments. It was a real shitty neighborhood and the complex security was some real bullshit, but she had a duplex three-bedroom apartment to decorate, and it was decked out top to bottom. Her living room consisted of two cream-colored leather sofas with a light-gray trim and pillows that matched. A glass coffee table was set in the middle of the room in front of a big-screen television with a satellite connection and DVD. Wall-to-wall carpeting flowed through the entire apartment, also cream-colored with a light-gray border, and vertical blinds shielded the apartment from the sun. She had a master bedroom, a guest bedroom and turned the last room into an office that she mostly used for her schoolwork. She attended California State University pursuing a degree in nursing, and also maintained a job at the San Jose Hospital as a nurse's aide. Her father mostly paid for her education expenses, while her bills were up to her to handle. She had a nice little setup out in Cali, and she made her little brother proud.

I'd arrived the Friday before and had only intended on staying a couple of days, but it quickly turned into a week. Since it had been so long since we'd seen each other, we took advantage of the time. It was a relaxing experience to just hang out without having to deal with the day-to-day bullshit that consumed most of my time in New York. Trigger and the Doberman were working hard on his defense, so it was left up to Ceelow to handle most of the responsibilities regarding business. I made sure to call back home at least twice a day to find out how the trial was going, and if there were any emergencies related to the Family. I would be back in New York in time for any support Trigger needed when it started getting down to the nitty-gritty in court. As for now, I felt like a seventeen-year-old again, and I didn't mind at all. We went to theme parks in the day and to restaurants and nightclubs in the evening. We even blew some California chronic together. Rachel was like my best friend, and it didn't at all feel like we'd spent so much time apart. But honestly, after a week had passed by it was time for me to return to the grime where I belonged. I started to feel homesick, so we had to part ways. I promised her that it wouldn't be long before I came back to visit, and we said our good-byes.

The night before I left, I called Ceelow to inform him that I'd be there in the morning, and that we needed to have a meeting so we all could be brought up on current events. My flight landed a little after nine o'clock, and Trigger and Cee were waiting for me in Trigger's Range Rover.

"What's up, son?" Ceelow asked as I exited the airport. "How was the flight?"

"It was cool, you know," I answered. "Different toilet, same shit. How ya'll holdin' everything down in our borough?"

"Shit, everything is still under control over here, dog," Trigger answered. "We got the city under lock and key, my nigga."

"Cool, ya'll niggas ain't eat yet, right?" I asked.

"Nah, Don P. gonna meet us at M&G's over there on 125th Street," answered Trigger.

"Oh, i-ight. Let's get over there then," I said. "I'm hungrier than a mu'fucka."

As the truck pulled off, it didn't take long before they started making inquiries about California.

"So, what's good?" asked Cee. "Tell us how it is out there in Cali."

"Oh, it ain't nothing like over here, dog. Everything is the opposite. The way we like to relax and hang out is not how they do it out there. Besides that, the niggas are all arrogant and conceited. Because of the men-to-women ratio out there, the broads have to push up on the dudes. Rachel introduced me to some of them niggas though. I mean they mad cool and all, but they too wild and shit. I even got into it a bit wit some niggas out there, and the cats that I was with held me down. They even let me hold a pistol so I could be ready for anything. I got some real niggas out there, for real."

"Oh, word," Trigger said. "Maybe we could set something up out there, too."

"You never know, dog. We just might," I said, already thinking way ahead of him.

When we arrived at M&G's, El Don and Poncho hadn't reached there yet, so we waited for about twenty minutes before we just said, "Fuck it," and got a table without them. I ordered some home fries, beef sausage and a tall stack of pancakes. Trigger got cheese eggs, grits and salmon, and Cee had an order of waffles with bacon on the side. Once we'd all placed our orders, we started discussing issues of business.

"How's the trial going?" I asked.

"Oh, we ain't really get down to it yet," Trigger replied. "Everything is moving in slow motion and shit. They picked the jury though; a bunch of crackerzoids. The Doberman said that our best defense is that we didn't know that it was police runnin' up on us, being that they never identified themselves. On that alone, he said that all of the evidence would be inadmissible. Besides that, we gonna see if we can turn a couple of those jurors to force our hand, or get a hung jury. These are all the Doberman's ideas. If you ask me, I should just fucking disappear right now, you know?"

"Yeah, I feel you, dog," I said in agreement. "But let's just put some faith in our Doberman, and see what he can do with it. If it comes down to that, I know exactly what to do. Don't even worry about it, my nigga."

"I-ight, son," said Trigger, showing no worries. "I know if you say you got me, you ain't bullshitting."

"What's up with you though, son?" asked Cee. "You just want to be flying off everywhere and shit. You i-ight, dog?"

"Yeah, I'm cool, now. You just have to get out of New York every once in while, so that you can come back and appreciate all of this dirt and grime, you feel me? Besides, I ain't even really go nowhere yet. You'll know it when I'm really doing it up."

"Oh, i-ight," he responded. "I got you in my radar now. You ain't trying to leave a stone unturned, huh?"

"See, now you feel me," I said with a grin as I winked at him.

As the food arrived, the conversation came to a halt. We all began devouring our meal, and then Don P. pulled up in a black Ford Expedition.

"Here these niggas go right here," said Trigger as he pointed out of the window. "I wonder what the fuck took them so long."

As they entered the restaurant, car tires screeching directed our attention to the street. All that could be seen from the restaurant window was a gray car turning the corner in a hurry. No one gave it a second thought except for Poncho, who thought the car looked familiar, but then brushed it off. Once it was out of sight we all paid the shit no mind and directed our attention as to why Don and P. were late.

"What's up, son?" I asked. "Where were ya'll mu'fuckas at?"

"We had to go to Central Bookings real quick to get this nigga Little Jay out," answered El Don. "He got picked up last night outside his crib. He wasn't even dirty, or nothin'."

"If he didn't have no work on him, why'd they take him in?" asked Trigger.

"The nigga had like eight grand in cash on him," answered Poncho. "He was coming home for the night from The Woods."

"That nigga's a dick," blurted Cee. "What he doin' with all that money in his pocket? Why he ain't sending somebody to drop off after every two grand like he supposed to?"

"I don't really know," responded Poncho. "But the kid is smart though. If he didn't drop off, he must've had a good reason. He did say some shit about not being able to trust the new nigga we put with him up on 227th."

"Who's he talking about?" I asked. "That nigga Roscoe?"

"I ain't too sure. Let me look into it," said Poncho. "I didn't get all the details because we were in a hurry, but I'll holla at you."

When we were all done with breakfast, I had Trigger take me to my crib so that I could drop off my bags and get my truck to run some errands. After everything, I'd end up over at Ginger's place all the way upstate. I often tried influencing her to move in with me, now that I had my own place, but she'd just reiterate the fact that she didn't want to leave her mother all alone. I didn't want to come between her and her mother, so I backed off. It also benefited my situation if I ever needed to disappear really quickly, so it worked out. Her mother was hardly ever home anyway, ever since she'd made detective. It was kind of ironic though…a detective's daughter in love with a notorious drug dealer. If only she knew.

"Hi, baby!" she said with excitement as she fumbled to unlock the door. "When did you get back? Why didn't you tell me you were coming over? I could've cooked something for you. I missed you so much, baby. How was California?"

She opened the door and gave me a big hug and kiss before I could answer any of her questions. The love she showed me was indescribable. It was so genuine that I could never doubt her sincerity for a second, or think that she was putting on a show, or saying things just to make me feel good. She really loved me a lot and I loved her just as much. She was my baby, my precious little Gin.

"Relax, Gin," I said, trying to calm her down. "One question at a time, Mommy."

"All right then, Daddy. Just go upstairs and wait for me. I'll be up in one minute, okay?"

"Cool, don't keep me waiting too long."

She was upstairs in no more than two minutes with a Corona in each hand and wearing nothing but a smile. I looked up at her and thought to myself, *That's why I love her.*

✪✪✪

That night, while Spits lay beside Ginger asleep at her place upstate, it was nowhere near bedtime on the streets of the Bronx. What El Don and Poncho had planned, the streets wouldn't even be ready for. As they sat in Poncho's black Expedition on 227th Street between Barnes Avenue and Bronxwood Avenue, they were patiently awaiting the arrival of one of their workers, Roscoe. They'd been waiting almost two hours for him to show up, and there was still no sign of him. It had gotten as late as 2:45 a.m., and his ass was nowhere to be found. Then after a quick glance at the side-view mirror, without saying a word, El Don opened his door on the passenger side of the truck and exited the vehicle. He walked down toward Barnes Avenue and made a right at the corner. Ten seconds after that, Roscoe came walking past the truck. Poncho saw him pass, but waited for him to get three-quarters of the way down the block before making a move. He then opened the door, got out of the car and called to him, "Yo, Roscoe! What's up, nigga!" Roscoe, a little tentative, turned around and tried squinting to clearly see whom it was that called his name. As he stood there uncertain, the figure that he saw from up the block uttered the words, "Let me holla at you right quick, nigga!" Still confused, he reached for his waist where he had a Glock .9mm tucked under his belt. Suddenly, all he saw was black. El Don came from behind him and covered his face with a black laundry bag. When Poncho saw his brother make his move, he made his way to where they were, and proceeded to assist in getting Roscoe in the back of the truck. Once they got him in the truck, they took the gun he had hidden underneath his shirt and struck him on the back of his head with a crowbar. Roscoe lost consciousness once he was hit with the blow and could give no more resistance as they tied his hands and feet, and gagged him. When they were done, they closed the back door and drove off.

✪✪✪

"Mommy," I said, trying to get Ginger's attention, as she lay next to me peacefully asleep. "Gin, are you awake?"

"What's wrong, Daddy?" she asked as she yawned and turned over to face me.

"Nothing, I was just thinking; that's all," I responded.

"Thinking about what?"

"I was thinking we should go away somewhere, just me and you. Like Bermuda, or Jamaica, or to the Bahamas. Just somewhere far, you know."

"But, Daddy, you know how terrified I am of airplanes. Why can't we just go to Miami or something like that?"

"Come on, fuck Miami," I said, a little annoyed at the familiarity of the conversation. "I want to see other kind of things, Mommy. I want to go somewhere exotic for a real vacation. I want to go somewhere that can make me completely forget about all this shit that happens every day in the streets of the Bronx. That's how it was in Cali, but I still missed you. I want you right there with me."

"So, Daddy, you can go to all of those places. Don't let me stop you," she said, trying to conceal the fact that she wouldn't rather be without me.

"Listen, I ain't goin' nowhere like that without you, Mommy. That's for real. If and when I experience that type of shit, I want you to be right there beside me. What's wrong with that?"

"Nothing, I guess. But what about the flying part?"

"Mommy, don't worry about that. You think I'd ever let anything happen to you?" I asked, looking directly in her eyes waiting for a response.

"I know, Daddy. I know you'd never do anything that could hurt me. Well, just let me think about it, okay?"

"That's good enough, Mommy. Just think about it and holla at me."

"I love you," she said with an innocent little smile on her face.

"I love you, too."

✪✪✪

"Yeah, mu'fucka. You thought that you could just rob us blind and never face the consequences, huh?" asked Poncho with a black Tec-9 at the side of Roscoe's head.

"No, please," pleaded Roscoe with his shirt drenched in sweat and his face covered with blood. "I never once stole anything from you. I swear it."

"Uh-huh, you a lyin' mu'fucka, ain't you?" asked Poncho. "You tried to be slick, but we got ya fuckin' pussy ass now though."

"No, I didn't. Please, you have to believe me. Don, please tell him I'd never do something like that," he said to El Don, as if he could get sympathy from him.

"Oh, you wouldn't, huh?" Don asked. He walked over to them and took the Tec-9 from Poncho, lowered it away from Roscoe's head, and then he lifted it back up quickly, swinging it across Roscoe's face in a downward motion. "Why the fuck should we believe you?"

"It wasn't me. I swear it wasn't me," he went on with his mouth now full of blood and running down his jaw.

As Roscoe continued to profess his respect for the Time Bomb Family, and how he could never have done what they were accusing him of, Poncho pulled Don to the side as if trying to conceal the topic of conversation. When he felt they'd put enough space between them and Roscoe he questioned him in a voice that didn't suggest he was trying to keep him from hearing anything at all. "What you want to do with him?" asked Poncho to El Don.

Roscoe stopped pleading while El considered a suitable punishment. As he looked around the room, he could see no exit available for the situation they had him in. He was on his knees tied to a heater in the corner of a room in what seemed to be an abandoned building. He was also left clueless as to his location due to the boards on the window. It would've been completely pitch black if not for the flashlights they had. His strength was fading; he wouldn't be able to take much more beating. His mind was racing and he didn't know what to do, until he came to the conclusion that there was nothing he could do...but listen, and wait for his fate.

"I don't know," El answered, pausing, and then taking a glance at Roscoe until his attention was at its peak. "We could cut off the nigga balls and feed those shits to him. Or we could pull out the nigga's fingernails with a pair of pliers and shit. Or we could take his ass down in the basement and feed him to the mu'fuckin' rats."

As Don went on and on about the different things they could do to Roscoe before putting him out of his misery, he began to grow more and more terrified. He couldn't take it anymore. He was ready to tell them everything he knew with the small chance that they might let him go, or probably just kill him quickly. Even as he was ready to talk, his hesitation left El enough time to figure out the perfect way to make him talk. He left the room and when he returned, he had a grin on his face that would've done the job all by itself and in his hands a canister of gasoline. After lighting a cigarette he walked over to Roscoe and began pouring the gasoline all over him and on the walls next to him. His attempts to halt El's actions went unanswered until the canister was completely empty. When he felt Roscoe was ready to tell all, he got down on a knee and let him sing the song in his ear. As the information began to flow, Roscoe asked that if he told, that they'd just kill him quickly and El agreed. When the questioning came to an end, El walked away from Roscoe while he was still dripping gasoline, and went over to Poncho. They conversed for a moment amongst themselves as Roscoe sat silently, watching, waiting for his death.

"What are these fuckin' bastards talking about?" he asked himself as he began to get impatient. He knew his fate was leading toward his demise, and it was just killing him to wait any longer. It was torture for him to just sit there not knowing what they were going to do to him, and to know that he would have to bear with whatever they had planned. As his thoughts started getting more and more rapid in his mind, his entire body grew tense and he began to cry uncontrollably. When he looked up at Don P., ashamed of his appearance, they'd begun making their way to the exit. He suddenly became calm, let out a sigh of relief, and then thought to himself, Thank you, God. They're going to let me live.

Just as Roscoe's hysterical cries came to an end Don P. stopped at the doorway. They stood there for a second before El turned around and looked into Roscoe's eyes with a grin on his face.

"Oops," he said, snapping his finger as if he'd forgotten something. "It almost slipped my mind. Catch this, you rat mu'fucka."

He flicked the cigarette at him as they both laughed wildly. They watched closely as Roscoe yelled and fought to get free, just to make an attempt at putting out his flaming carcass. He pulled at the pipe he'd been tied to as pieces of his skin burned to the wall and peeled off his body. The smell of burning flesh and the screams he let out didn't break Don's and P.'s concentration once, as they left conversing of their findings. They left him on the floor ablaze with no regard, and with only one thing in mind: contacting Spits as soon as possible.

✪✪✪

My cell phone rang around 4:40 a.m. as Ginger and I were about to roll over to go back to sleep. It was Poncho. He sounded a bit distracted and confused as he spoke, but I knew it had to be serious. He said that he had something important to tell me, and that it couldn't even wait until later in the morning. Disregarding the numerous requests by Ginger for me to stay in bed, I got dressed and ready to leave. I had business to handle. I reassured her that I wouldn't have kept it from her if something were wrong and that there was no reason to worry. I told her to go back to sleep, and then yelled a promise to speak to her later as I shut the front door.

Roscoe had made some serious accusations after the beating he'd taken that night. He'd said a lot of shit that Don P. didn't want to sit on—not even for the rest of the night. When I finally met up with them, it was 6:00 a.m. We met at Baychester Diner on Baychester Avenue and Boston Road.

"What's good, son?" I asked as I walked toward the entrance from the parking lot.

"Good?" asked Poncho. "Ain't nothin' good, dog. Your boy Roscoe made sure of that shit."

"Where that nigga Roscoe at, anyway?"

"Oh, you don't have to worry about him, dog," answered El. "You won't ever hear any more negativity from that hot boy, feel me?"

Don P. chuckled a bit, and then we all went inside the diner for breakfast. After we'd been seated and placed our orders, Don P. began to run down the specifics of the get-together from earlier in the morning.

It seemed as though Little Jay had noticed that the profit from the spot he worked on 227th Street had been coming up short the last couple of weeks. What stood out was that the amount was always the same, five percent. If they estimated thirty grand, at the end of the night they would only have $28,500. The rest of the Family never noticed this because Little Jay would always make up the difference out of his own pocket. He wanted to find out who was the thief before he raised any eyebrows, and then he'd report them. He figured out that whenever he sent Roscoe to drop off, that's when their profits took a loss. The night he was arrested was the first night he'd decided not to send Roscoe on the drop-off, but he never got a chance to report because he was taken through the system that night. When Don P. were done explaining the story up until this point, I was surprised but didn't feel that it deserved as much importance as they were placing on it.

"All right," I said, uninterested. "That's what ya'll mu'fuckas thought I needed to come out here from in the bed with my broad to hear?"

"Nah, son," answered El. "We saved the best part for last."

"Okay, spit it out."

"After a few hours of getting his ass beat, Roscoe finally admitted that he'd been stealing from us. That's not the only thing though, son. He said that it wasn't his idea and that Ceelow put him up to it."

When El was through I had a furious, but confused look on my face. It was so hard to believe that someone from the crew I considered family would steal from us. Since we'd both been little, it was us that had spoken about getting money together the most. We'd had the longest conversations with one another about the numerous things we could buy with the money we made. With all of these things running through my head, I wanted to find him, and lay him down wherever he was, but I had to calm down. I had to figure the right course of action to take.

"Yo, let me sit on this for a while," I said after minutes of silence. "I'm gonna handle this shit personally, ya heard? We ain't about to start a war within the Family because of what some bitch-ass rat mu'fucka said to save his ass."

"Yeah, I got you," said Poncho. "For whatever, my nigga. All you got to do is holla."

"Word up, son," agreed El.

After my conversation with Don P., I realized that it didn't matter how long you knew someone. You just can't trust them unless they just that type of nigga. I saw their honesty and dedication when Don P. said that they'd hold me down, and I hadn't known these niggas ten years like I'd known Cee. "Whatever," I said to myself. If this information would prove true, then it was just a situation that needed to be dealt with. Two and two is always going to equal four, you know?

CHAPTER 7

Today was a busy day for Spits. He had some business to take care of. When Spits would get in these moods, the only thing that could relax him was listening to a little Sade. He got in the truck late that morning, pressed play on the CD player, and immediately became tranquil as the soothing sounds of his favorite song "Kiss of Life" came through the speakers. He sat back in his truck with the windows rolled up and zoned out for a minute before he pulled off. He then began his morning grind with a delivery run to Burke and Arnow Avenue. There were some new young Puerto Rican cats out there starting to make a name for their crew. They called themselves "The Chosen" and the only problem was that whenever they made a request, it would always be for a little at a time. That must've been the only flaw in the whole delivery process; niggas would take advantage of the no-risk factor. But Spits had a plan devised for such occasions. One of Spits' run-men, Vic, informed him of the situation. He told him that their money was never short but the requests were always mediocre. He'd make the drop personally to have a talk with them.

✪✪✪

"Yo, what up, my nigga?" yelled Bobby as a he saw a friend of his drive past. The car stopped halfway into the block and reversed to where Bobby had been standing waving his arms. When the car stopped, out came D. He tried concealing his happiness but soon gave in to a huge smile. He hadn't seen his man Bobby in a while.

Bobby and D. had been friends for over ten years. They'd grown up in Edenwald Projects together and hadn't seen each other since Bobby had been sent away for an assault charge. He did four years out of a three-to-six sentence and had been home for a few months. Bobby and D. used to be a stick-up team back in the days before Bobby got sent away. They'd lost touch since then, but the love they had for one another was still strong.

"What's good, son?" asked D. as he gave Bobby a hug. "How long you been home?"

"Oh, about like three or four months now," responded Bobby.

"Damn, Bobby. It feels like it's been forever. What you been up to nowadays, son?"

"Same shit, same shit, you know?" responded Bobby. "Ain't nobody called me Bobby in a while, but other than that, the God ain't change a bit, feel me? I see you ain't changed either. You still driving that bullshit Accord, huh?"

"Yeah, you know," said D., shrugging off Bobby's insult. "Shit ain't been the same since you got knocked, my nigga. We used to do it big, but ain't nobody left out here that's still thorough. I was doing sticks with Drew and that nigga Pone for a minute, but that shit ain't last too long, so I just been doin' me."

"Why?" asked Bobby. "What's up with them niggas?"

"They both dead, son," answered D. with a low drop in his tone. "They got bodied and shit. But fuck all of that, son; I heard you was home, but I didn't know where you was laying."

"No doubt," responded Bobby as he pointed to the house behind him. "This is me right here. I'm renting a little room up there on the second floor. It ain't much now, but I'll be back up to par in a few, na'mean? I'm home now."

"That's cool, playboy. Now we can do it up like back in the days, for real."

"Word! Yo, umm…where did you, umm…" said Bobby as he couldn't quite get the words out.

"Huh?" asked D., expressing his confusion.

"Umm, where did you hear that I was back home?"

"Oh...that nigga Bernard and all them niggas from the 8th. They told me that you was back making mad noise, making it hot again. I don't know why, but it sounded like they wasn't too happy to see you home. What's that about?"

"Fuck them niggas, dog," responded Bobby as his voice started to rise. "Them niggas is just haters; that's all. I could leave them niggas with rabbit ears whenever I feel like it, and they know that shit. They can't fuck with me. They scared now that I'm home because they know I got that knockout blow and I buss my gun. They gonna know in a minute though, you heard?"

"Yeah, I ain't feeling them niggas like that anyway. They think they own the whole White Plains Road now."

"Oh, word?" asked Bobby, already plotting. "I'll see what they working with. Yo, you want to come up for a while? I got to make a phone call."

"Oh, all right."

✪✪✪

"Which one of ya'll mu'fuckas is Johnny?" Spits asked as he pulled up to the corner, which was too crowded to tell anyone apart.

"What you say, pa?" one of them asked as the others looked on.

"You heard what the fuck I said," Spits shot back. "Are you Johnny?"

"Yeah, that's me," he said, approaching the truck still perplexed.

Spits waited for Johnny to get close enough to the truck before responding as to not let anyone else hear what he said. "Well, I'm Spits, nigga! You know me now?"

"Oh, my bad, pa. You never know out here, feel me?"

"Whatever, mu'fucka. Listen, hop in so I can holla at you. We gonna take a ride right quick, dog."

"Give me a minute," he said as he turned around to talk to the rest of his crew. "Ayo, that's that nigga Spits in the Lex over there, kid. He wonna holla, so I'm gonna take a ride with him. I'll be right back, i-ight, ya'll?"

They all agreed and gave their personal handshake before he turned back toward Spits. He jumped in the passenger side of the truck and they were off. Spits went East on Burke Avenue and made a left turn onto Bronxwood Avenue. Once they got to the area they considered "The Woods" he slowed down a bit so that the conversation could have visuals.

"You see all of this up here?" Spits asked Johnny. "All of this shit is for the Time Bombs. All these niggas out here work for the Family. Now, my man Vic told me about you and your crew. The Chosen, right?"

"Yeah, pa," he responded, as he was excited that someone knew their name. "I hope he didn't have nothin' bad to say about my crew."

"Nah, he told me that ya'll always got your paper straight, and that ya'll not the type to feed off the re-up money with petty bullshit," said Spits. "The only thing I had a problem with, was the fact that you dudes would call five or six times a day to re-up with eight-balls. Now, I know ya'll get it poppin' over here. Why don't ya'll ever take a bigger bite of the weight?"

"The problem isn't moving the product, bro. With all due respect to you and all your peoples, we'd rather hold out and let ya'll take all of the possession risks. We know how much shit we can move in a given amount of time, so why have more than we need. Feel me, bro?"

"Yeah, I feel you, dog, but peep game, Johnny. If we're going to pretend like ya'll mu'fuckas are workers for us, then ya'll mu'fuckas might as well be workers for us," Spits said before pausing to shoot a grin and wink an eye. "Now, whatever you make gets reinvested anyway leaving ya'll no spending money, so I think that it would be in your best interest to formally involve yourselves with our organization. That means that we'd put up all the white, already cooked and bagged, and you and your crew get a percentage. Does that make sense?"

"I don't know," Johnny answered, showing a little doubt. "That just sounds like ya'll get all the control."

"You a smart mu'fucka, Johnny," Spits said with a chuckle. "But do the math. It's the difference between you guys taking home $1,000 a week, and $10,000 a week. You don't have to answer now, but I'll send someone for a response tomorrow morning."

✪✪✪

As Bobby hung up the phone, he turned to D. and said, "Yo, peep this," as he handed D. a black Desert Eagle. "You like that?"

"No doubt. This shit is pretty, for real," answered D. "This is what I need."

"I could get you one if you want, son."

"Oh, word?" Bobby asked with excitement.

"Yeah, you remember my uncle that lives down South, right?"

"Yeah, you talking about Richie, right? He still in the army?"

"Yup, he get all kinds of gats easy. For good prices, too. He be hooking me up so I can sell them shits up here."

"Oh, that's flavor, son. For real."

"Yeah, I had that one for a while now. That joint got..." said Bobby, pausing like he heard something. "Did you hear that shit, son?"

"I ain't hear shit, dog," responded D. "You all right, man?"

"Yeah...I'm cool. Anyway, what was I saying?"

"You was telling me about the gat," said D., still playing with it.

"Oh, yeah. That shit got mad bodies on it, kid," Bobby said as he went looking through the closet.

"Oh, shit! I forgot I was supposed to go check my baby mom's, right quick," D. said as he jumped up to leave. "Yo, don't go nowhere. I'll be right back."

"All right, dog," Bobby said, still fumbling through his closet. "Where the fuck did I put that shottie?" he asked himself.

"One," yelled D. as he exited the room, dropping the gun on the floor before he left.

"Yeah-yeah, dog. One."

✪✪✪

Before Johnny could even respond to the offer that Spits had laid out, he got a phone call and dropped him back on Burke Avenue before speeding off. He still had other matters to attend to that superseded the importance of these "Chosen" dickheads. Before anything, he went to go check this nigga he knew from his high school days. Some dirty nigga named Tec.

Now, Tec got his name from…well, it's obvious how you get a name like Tec, but it's one thing to just say "yeah, call me Tec," and it's some completely different shit to never even have to ask anyone. If you'd ever heard about him or met him, you'd know why that was his name and you'd call him nothing else. Tec was the gun man. Any kind of toaster you could think of, he bussed it before and would have it for sale if you requested. He could explain in detail everything about any gun, but the only thing was he wasn't exactly "all there" upstairs. Tec had supplied the basic needs of the TB Family in the past, but Spits had put in a special order and was just notified of its availability.

When he reached Tec's block, he made a right turn onto Laconia Avenue, between 229th Street and Grenada Place, and double-parked in the front of the house that he lived in. As he turned the engine off, he saw Tec walk past his truck on the right side. He tried calling to get his attention, but his shouts fell short of Tec's ears. In a hurry, he jumped out of the truck and went after him. Finally catching up to him halfway into the block, he realized he had a shiny black shotgun under his coat. When he attempted to give him a handshake and ask him what was going on, Tec raised the polished cannon and pointed it directly in between Spits' eyes and cocked it. Ultimately realizing who it was that he'd just pulled a shottie on, he quickly lowered the shotgun and apologized.

"Oh, shit," said Tec with a chuckle. "My bad. I didn't even see you there. Where the fuck did you come from?"

"You didn't see me?" Spits asked sarcastically. "Where did I come from? Nigga, I was calling your fuckin' name from down the block."

"My bad, son. I was just on my way to…uh, I was on my way down the block to…" he said with a blank look on his face. Then, when he finally looked down at the huge gleaming shotgun he had tucked under his trench coat, he said, "Oh, that's right! I was on my way to 228th right quick. Yo, just wait for me in my crib. I left the door open. I'll be right back."

Before Spits could even reply or attempt to probe as to why he was walking down the street in broad daylight with a fucking monstrous shotgun underneath a trench coat, in the middle of April at that, he was gone.

So Spits, being the curious mu'fucka that he was, went up to Tec's house to wait for him. He walked up one flight of stairs and straight to the door of the room Tec rented. As he entered the unlocked room, he almost tripped over a .44-caliber black Desert Eagle that Tec had just laying on the floor in the front of the door.

This dude is crazy, thought Spits to himself before picking the pistol up off the ground. He shifted the shaft back enough to see a slug in the chamber, then removed the clip. As he examined the fully loaded clip, he heard gunshots go off that didn't seem too far from him. First, a clutter of small shots fired, and then three loud booms could be heard. After that, silence. He inserted the clip back into the pistol and put it back down on the floor, but realizing his fingerprints were still on it, he quickly picked it back up and rubbed it off on his shirt. When he was done he got up to take a little peek out the window, and he caught a glimpse of Tec running around the corner. He had a look on his face that considered to anyone watching him that he didn't even know why he was running, but that he just had to be. He made a sharp turn into the gate in the front of the house, and in seconds he was in the room standing in front of Spits, breathing hard and coughing with sweat running from his forehead. He shut the door behind him and dropped the shotgun on the floor next to the bed.

"What the fuck did you just do?" Spits yelled with a shaken voice. "That was you bussin' off just now?"

"Yo, calm down, son," said Tec, wiping the sweat from his brow. "That wasn't nothing, kid. Those niggas had it coming. Look how much paper them niggas was holding, son."

"Son, you buggin' the fuck out, or what?" asked Spits. "There's ways you do things, nigga. You can't just be running up on niggas in broad daylight. There's only a matter of time before you gonna get it, too. You can't be so reckless, dog."

Tec paused for a bit, looking as if what Spits said had started to sink in, and then said, "Whatever, nigga. You want the thing, or not?"

"Yeah, nigga," said Spits, giving up hope. "Let me get that so I can bounce before the police run in here shooting shit up."

Tec reached under the bed and pulled out a silver briefcase. He laid the briefcase down on the bed and opened it, facing Spits. When it was opened all the way, two chrome pearl-handled .45 Magnum pistols stared up at Spits. He was hypnotized at the sight of them. Engraved in the pearl handles was the exact logo each member of the Time Bombs had tattooed on their forearms. Immediately satisfied with what was presented to him, he instantly paid Tec the suggested price and left in a hurry with the briefcase under his arm.

✪✪✪

As D. pulled back up to Bobby's place, he saw someone exiting the house holding on to a silver briefcase for dear life. It took him a minute but he finally realized who it was, and when he did, all of the hate he had in his heart for him came rushing back. "That's that bitch-ass nigga, Mike Spits," he said to himself. "What the fuck he doing coming out of Bobby's crib?" All the pain and frustration from their first encounter came and hit him like a ton of bricks. "I knew I should've bodied all them niggas when I had the chance." Before D. got the proper opportunity to make his move, Spits had already jumped into his truck and sped off. His first instinct was to follow him, but reluctantly changed his mind. He decided that it would just be smarter to tell Bobby in detail what had happened, so that they could plan something out together.

D. got out of the car and before he could cross the street toward Bobby's crib, he suddenly saw police cars approaching from both sides. His immediate thought was to flee as he assumed they were after him for one of the many crimes he'd committed in the past, but they weren't headed in his direction. He made a sharp left away from Bobby's gate as the officers blew past him and into the house. Seconds after they were in the house, wild gunshots started going off. The shots would last for no longer than five seconds, before they came to a complete halt. That was it. It was all over now, and neither D. nor Bobby could've ever seen it coming. He knew then that his man Bobby was gone, and his entire body started to feel numb. He couldn't even focus on anything that mattered. All he thought about was the times they'd had, and the fortune they'd seen together. They'd never get a chance to catch up and reminisce about those old times, and it would never again be how it used to be. The sky seemed to get dark directly over his head, and a cool breeze came through the block. D. felt a slight chill run up his back that made his shoulders shiver. He zipped up the velour jacket that he had on and put his hands in his pants pockets. As he walked back in the direction of his car, his immediate feeling was to take it all out on Spits. He blamed what had happened to Bobby on him, as he hadn't known what Bobby, a.k.a. Tec, had done just a few minutes ago down the block on the 8th. It was no one's fault but his own that he was gone now, but that was the furthest thing from D.'s mind.

"When I catch up to that nigga Spits again, it's on," he said, pulling away from the curb. "It's on."

CHAPTER 8

"Please stand. Court is now in session. The honorable Judge Marilda Rosenberg presiding."

"What?" asked Trigger in disbelief. "Who the fuck is she?" he asked as he stared at his attorney to wait for a response.

"I'm not sure, Mr. Beckford," said William. "This is very unorthodox."

"Well, you better do something quick, Doberman. That's, of course, if you like your fucking job."

"I'll get to the bottom of this, sir," said William as he stood to request the attention of the judge. "Please, Your Honor, may I approach the bench?"

"There will be no need for that," said the judge. "I'll answer any and all of the questions you may have once I am through."

"Thank you, Your Honor," responded William as he sat back down.

"Now, I know that this may come as a surprise to many of you. And I know that this may not be considered conventional practice, but I will be acting as judge for the remainder of this trial. There are details regarding this situation that will not be revealed at this time, due to an ongoing criminal investigation surrounding interactions between the defendant, Peter Beckford, and the previous judge, Edward R. McHullan."

"This is an outrage," said William, as the rest of the courtroom came to an uproar.

"Order, order in the court!" yelled Judge Rosenberg. "I will have order in my court or you will all be escorted out of the building."

"Your Honor, I would like to go on the record as objecting to...," said William before the judge cut him off.

"Your objection is duly noted, counselor, but I was not yet through. This case will be under strict observation, as well as any connections to criminal involvement on the part of the defendant. Now, I will need until tomorrow to get up to speed as far as deliberations before my arrival. Court is now in recess until eight o'clock a.m. tomorrow morning, May 11th." When she was done, she got up and walked back into her chambers, where she could get ready for the morning. All Trigger and the Doberman could do was stare at one another in awe.

I got the call that morning from Trigger, and he told me what had just happened as he exited the courtroom. Things were all messed up now, and we needed to have a roundtable meeting as soon as fucking possible. I told him to call everybody, and have them all meet me at my crib at noon. When I hung up the phone with Trigger, I sat out on the terrace, and thought for a while. Things had to go down with complete precision or it would not work at all.

They all arrived together promptly at twelve o'clock noon. We sat around my dining room table and officially began our meeting.

"Everything is all fucked up, Spits," said Trigger, opening the meeting. "What the fuck we gonna do now, son? Damn!"

"All right, calm down, my nigga," I said, trying to slow down the pace of the conversation. "Just fill in all of the blanks for us, Trig."

"Listen," he said in a calmer voice. "This new judge they got on my case just put our progress in reverse. Son, they launched a criminal investigation on the judge that me and the Doberman paid off. Now you know that nigga's gonna rat. Before anything, we need to find his ass, and put him to sleep before he start flapping his lips."

"Nah, listen," said Spits, disagreeing. "The way that all went down left no paper trail back to us. We sent a nobody to make the proposal on the Family's behalf. There's no way he can tie us to the money he took. Now if he turns up dead or missing all of a sudden, then they'll really be in our asses. We'd just be making ourselves hot."

"Yeah," agreed Trigger. "That's true, but what about this new judge? You think we can turn her, too?"

"I doubt that, son."

"The thing is, with the judge in our pocket, we controlled the whole trial. Without that, they're just going to readmit all of the evidence that our judge deemed inadmissible. All of his rulings are going to be fucking overturned and shit. I'm fucked, dog!"

"Relax, Trig," I said in a calm and collected voice. "We gonna figure this shit out, son."

"Yo, you a little bit too much on the nonchalant side of this shit, son," said Trigger, implying that I wasn't as worried as everyone else. He was absolutely right. I wasn't as worried as everyone else was because I'd already anticipated this situation. I knew exactly what we were going to do.

"All right, fuck it," I said, finally letting my thoughts out. "I know what we can do."

"What?" asked Trigger while everyone else waited for my response.

"You," I said, pointing at Trigger. "You gonna be the new boss of our West Coast operations."

"What the fuck you talking about?" asked Ceelow.

"That's the only way this problem can be solved. Now, we all know that if this trial gets a brand-new judge to start poking around and looking for an example to set, that even the jury won't rule in our favor. Fuck the money we paid those cocksuckers; they'll shit on us real quick when faced with the possibility that they could do time. The only way to beat this shit is to outrun it. I don't give a fuck how much money we throw at this courtroom, this new bitch ain't letting it stick to her pockets for one second."

"Well, what the fuck's on the West Coast for us?" asked Poncho.

"Opportunity, dog. The time I spent out there ain't go to waste. I met a few real niggas out there, and on some real shit, all it would take is a phone call and they'll be ready for whatever. It's that real, son. You know gangsta recognize gangsta, and they respected my flow. They want to get it just the same, son. They even hungrier than we were when we first started."

"Word?" asked El. "You sure about this, dog?"

"One hundred percent, my nigga. As a matter of fact, I spoke to my sister before ya'll got here and she said you can even stay there for a while until shit starts really jumping."

"Oh, that's love for real, son," said Ceelow. "She a real gangsta bitch, huh?"

"Listen," I said with a stern voice. "Just so that ya'll niggas know, there ain't gonna be no disrespect in anybody's mouth regarding my sister, Rachel. That's still my sister, ya na'mean. Don't get it twisted."

"My bad, son," said Cee. "You know what I mean, right?"

"It ain't nothing, dog," I said, relaxing my tone. "I'm just bugging. I know what you meant."

"Anyway," Trigger said, interjecting. "When and how is all of this going down?"

"All right, peep this. If this is going to work properly, you can never get out of control out there. As soon as some overworked dickhead pig takes a peek into your history, he gonna see a fucking big ass warrant for your arrest staring back at him. All they need is a reason to take you down, and you'll be extradited back to NY facing trial again. You'll have to come in contact with no work whatsoever, so that they can't tie you to shit. Them mu'fuckas out there need not even know your real fucking name, na'mean? You'll be a completely different dude out there at all times; no matter what. If you call your mom's, that's your ass. We have to assume that everything that's connected to you, is connected to the mu'fuckin' FBI also. Don't even let the workers know what's up, 'cause I trust them and all that, but if one of them gets knocked who's to say they won't give you up to get off. You gotta be on them P's and Q's."

As I went on and on and on about how careful Trigger would have to be to make this whole thing work, it seemed that he'd been taking it all in very seriously. He knew how much he'd be responsible for and I trusted my nigga with that. If I had to put this kind of shit in anyone's hands, it would be the Trigger-man's. Especially with what he was leaving in NY waiting for him, I knew for a fact that he wouldn't be careless in taking on this project; even with very little help from home. This is what it had to be, until that day came where we hung it up. When all of this was over, we could all buy some land on some tropical island and chill. We'd just have to see.

The day after that was supposed to be Trigger's first day back in court with Judge Marilda Rosenberg fully prepared to dive in headfirst. Unfortunately for the unsuspecting judge, there wouldn't be any more deliberations for her to referee. This would be the beginning of the mu'fucking end for Mr. Peter Beckford. Once Trigger became a no-show that first morning, there was a warrant issued for his arrest. The judge would set two more court dates before she would officially declare him a fugitive of the law. Once this happened, I got the call I'd been nervously waiting for.

"Hello."

"Hola, Sr. Spits. I think we have some things that we need to speak about concerning your organization, no?"

"All right, cool, Mr. Ortiz. Where and when?"

"I'll come to you."

Now, that was a bit frightening to hear Romero Ortiz, the king of drug trade in Puerto Rico, saying that he's coming to me. The dude never left that island as long as I knew his ass, and now he was coming to see me? What for? Did he only make personal visits when he wanted to make sure a hit was properly executed? Did he want to send the message that I wasn't untouchable and that I could get it just like everyone else? I didn't know what to think after hanging up the phone with him. I just told myself to be ready for anything, and cross any bridge once I got to it with both guns blazing. My destiny would already be written, so all I had to do was play my position and let the chips fall where they may. I got a call later that evening from one of Mr. Ortiz's associates informing me that he would meet me at a tapas restaurant in SoHo, named Pintxos. I would meet him there at 7:30 sharp the next evening.

When I arrived at Pintxos, it was six o'clock. I wanted to get there early to scope out the area, and look for anything out of the ordinary. I went down Washington and up Hudson Street, then across Canal Street, then over to Vandam Street. I covered every inch of the entire area. I drove up, down and around those streets over and over again until I'd memorized every last thing, from the timing on the streetlights, down to the color the bums had on. When I felt comfortable enough with my surroundings, I pulled back up to the restaurant where I was probably going to meet my death. I bypassed the valet parking and found a spot around the back in case I had to make a sudden exit. I was prepared to my fullest ability. It was time to meet with Mr. Ortiz.

"I'm here to meet an associate of mines…a Mr. Romero—" I said right before the maitre d' cut me off dead center of my sentence.

"Right this way, Senor Spits," he said as he led me to Romero's special table. "Mr. Ortiz left specific instructions to show you to his table until he arrived. He'll be here shortly."

"Thank you," I said with uncertainty in my voice.

He wasn't here yet? Why would he be late to a meeting that he'd arranged? With all of these things racing through my head, I was beginning to regret even coming at all. Then, I realized that I had no choice. If I hadn't come because I thought that I would be killed, that would just give him a reason to kill me anyway. One way or another, I had to be here.

"Good evening, Senor Spits," Romero said in suave voice as he stood in front of the table. "Did you find this place all right?"

"Yeah, it was no problem. I come here all the time," I said sarcastically. We both gave a chuckle, and then it was time to get down to business.

"Senor Oberman has informed me of your situation here in the States, Senor Spits. He told me that one of your associates got himself into a pickle."

"Yeah, but we have a contingency plan all ready to take effect now. He's not an associate either, Mr. Ortiz; he's family. Everything is under control."

"Yes, I'm sure everything is under your control. But, you should understand my dilemma if you and your institute were to be placed under extreme surveillance by law enforcement. I would like for you to reassure me that our relationship will not be tarnished due to all of this legal basura."

"I feel you, Mr. Ortiz—"

"Please," he said, interrupting before I could finish. "I've told you on numerous occasions that you need not call me Mr. Ortiz. That sounds so formal. We, Senor Spits, are colleagues. Call me Romero."

"That's cool, Romero. I was saying that I'd never do anything that could possibly affect our relationship in a negative way. My first and only priority is to preserve our business interests. You have my word on that."

"Good. Now we can discuss your plans for our future establishment located in California."

"What?" I asked with bewilderment. "How did you—"

"Listen, Senor Spits," he said with a condescending smile on his face. "I have eyes and ears everywhere. You should learn not to underestimate the people that you do business with. I'm sure that you wouldn't be pondering using another connection for this infrastructure. That would be most disappointing, as I'm very excited that we are expanding our businesses to the West Coast. Do you understand?"

"Yeah, I got you in my radar. The fact that you had been informed of our new venture doesn't make me uncomfortable. You just caught me off guard; that's all. I'll try and make sure that doesn't happen again, but I had no intention on cutting you out. Besides, I have no other connections."

I was starting to figure out that this meeting had nothing to do with Trigger's trial. That may have been of some importance to him at some point in time, but that was the furthest thing from his mind, now that he'd found out about us expanding to Cali. With all that "we" and "our" shit he was talking, Trigger's issues had absolutely nothing to do with it. He just wanted to make certain that I knew that he knew what we were planning, so that I wouldn't try and cut his greedy ass out. I don't know how, but he'd found out. I also didn't know how much he'd already known, so I told him everything. No detail would be left for his imagination. He would be no threat with this information anyway. Shit, ain't no cop gonna give him a shorter sentence for giving little ol' me up. If anything, it'd be the other way around. For anybody that gets their hands on Senor Romero Ortiz, I'd be the last thing on their minds.

When our meeting was done, I left the restaurant with a sigh of relief. I'd imagined all the worst that could've happened from this situation, but I'd never imagined that all that prompted this meeting was plain old greed. When I left there, I went home and called Gin.

"What's up, Gin?" I asked once she'd answered the phone. "Listen, pack a bag, nothing heavy. We're going to California in the morning."

CHAPTER 9

When Spits first told Ginger about his plans for California, she'd become very nervous. She'd still been contemplating his suggestion for them to go away, but had yet to make a decision. Now everything was moving so quickly. Before she knew it, he was spitting directions and locations at her before even asking her if she felt okay going. Spits automatically assumed that she'd want to be with him, no matter what. He was right about her wanting to be with him, but she couldn't help second-guessing the flight.

"I don't know about this," Ginger said as they stood in line to board the plane.

"What do you mean?" Spits asked. "We're already here, Gin."

"I know, but I'm having second thoughts."

"Listen, this is business. I don't have time to play around. Now, I told Trigger that once I was out there to set everything up, that he could come. I can't let anything fuck that up, Gin. Trig's depending on me."

"Okay, Daddy," Ginger said, finally relaxing a bit. "Just promise me that you won't let anything happen."

"I promise," he said, immediately making her feel much better.

They boarded the plane and everything was moving according to schedule. The flight attendants went through all of the safety precautions, and then the pilot informed the passengers that they'd be approaching the runway shortly. When the aircraft left the terminal, Ginger grabbed on to Spits' hand and held on tightly. Once it was on the runway, she put her head back and shut her eyes. Spits had never seen Ginger behaving so fearfully. The look in her eyes made him uneasy, but he tried making her feel better by maintaining his composure. As the jet started down the runway slowly and then faster, Ginger's grip on his hand grew tighter and tighter. An instant fear of dying came over her as the plane left the ground, but once it was in the air, she took a deep breath and calmed herself down. The pilot came on to inform everyone of the estimated time of arrival. He also informed everyone that the seatbelt light would be going off so that they would be free to use the facilities.

"See, Mommy," said Spits. "I won't ever let anything happen to you. I promise."

She looked into his eyes, and recognized the sincerity in his voice. "I believe you."

"I can't wait to get to Cali so you can meet my sister. I think you two will get along real nicely."

"I don't know, Daddy." Ginger was nervous about meeting her. "You know, I can be a real bitch sometimes."

"Shit, you ain't lyin' either," he said with a chuckle. "If anybody, I know that's a fact. You don't have to worry about her approving of us, Gin. She's gonna love you."

"We'll see."

The rest of the flight was smooth and the turbulence was kept at a minimum. By the time the flight was over, Ginger hadn't even realized the minor bumps in the landing as the plane approached LAX. Spits had put her at complete ease. The only person that could've put Ginger in that frame of mind was him, and no one else. When they exited the plane, they collected the few bags that they'd checked, and were on their way. They immediately caught a cab to Rachel's apartment complex. When they got there, their arrival was met with open arms.

Ginger and Rachel hit it off immediately. As soon as they entered the apartment, all it took was a compliment to Rachel as to how nicely she'd decorated her place, and that was it. They went on and on about color schemes, sale prices, different fabrics, and whatever else two women could converse about. You would have thought they'd known each other for years. This would work out perfectly for Spits, as he didn't need either one of them interrupting in the business part of this trip. They both had an idea of what was involved, but that didn't mean he welcomed their opinions. Spits waited for nightfall before making the call that would set this plan in motion.

"Hello," said the voice on the other line.

"Yeah, is Red there?" Spits asked.

"Yeah, who's this?"

"Yo, tell him it's Spits."

"Hold up a minute, dog," he said, putting the phone down. "Ayo, Red. It's the homie Spits on the jack for you, blood."

"Ayo, homeboy," said Red as he excitedly picked up the telephone receiver. "What's up, fool?"

"Ain't nothin, son. I'm here now, so it's about to go down. You gonna be ready?"

"Oh, it's on, cuz. I'm ready for whatever, straight like that."

"Yeah, yeah. That's what I like to hear. Well, I'm over here at my sister's crib right now, but I don't want no meetings over here. You know, I'm trying to leave this spot untainted."

"Oh, that's cool with me, homeboy. Where you want to hook up?"

"I don't know. This is your hood, dog. Where's a good place to get a beer and chill?"

"Well, we can kick it up in Armadillo Willie's over there on Camino. They got some slammin' ass ribs up in there, dog."

"All right, I'm with that. Meet me there in about an hour."

"Cool. I'll be there."

After they'd hung up, Spits went to take a hot shower to relax before he left. He had a lot on his mind, and he didn't want anything to be left open. If anything fucked up, Trigger would feel the repercussions ten-fold. Aside from Trigger, so many people's livelihood depended on his actions. With all of the fun it was to still being a teenager and have so much at your fingertips, it took all the strength in the world to stop yourself from running around just capping people for no reason. It took an adult's mind-set to control all of the bullshit that surrounded Spits' lifestyle. He was controlling it now to the best of his ability, but it would only be a matter of time before he just flipped also. But for now, he was the most calm and collected mu'fucka you could meet.

"What up, son?" Spits inquired as he pulled into the parking lot of Armadillo Willie's.

"What's happenin', fool?" asked Red, unable to conceal his happiness to see Spits again; even though it had only been a short while since he'd been there. Red had anticipated the moment for what had seemed like years. It had only been a few months since he and Spits had first met, and he couldn't wait for the day he'd be back. He knew what would come shortly after his arrival, and he was ready for it. "Long time no mu'fuckin' see, nigga," Red said as Spits got out of the car to give him a pound and a hug.

Red was a husky nigga. He weighed about two hundred-sixty pounds and stood about five-nine. He'd gotten the name Red from his father. He was some badass that was deeply affiliated with a gang out there called the Bloods and was infatuated with the color red. Red gave Spits a bear hug that could've temporarily cut off his blood circulation. It wasn't hard to tell that he was sincere. From the moment they'd met, Spits had known that Red was someone that he could trust his life with.

They first came across each other outside the Galaxy nightclub on Haight Street in the Bay Area. Through a cat Red knew in Rachel's apartment complex, he'd heard about Spits and that he was all about money. Red was that down-for-whatever Cali nigga, and Spits had been looking for people in his sister's complex like him. Initially, Spits just wanted someone real enough to make certain that nobody fucked with his sister without being dealt with, but everybody liked making money, you know? Red wanted to get at Spits but didn't want to just come across like a fan, so he played the cut. It wasn't until some niggas from a rival gang were heard to be plotting on Spits when Red saw his opportunity.

Red just happened to be in the Galaxy while Spits was there. Spits walked past him as he exited the establishment, and Red noticed that he had two niggas following him that didn't look too friendly. When he finally made it outside the club to see what was up, they were already creeping up behind Spits as he fumbled to get the car door open. Before Spits knew what was going on, Red had the drop on them. After a brief gunfight that forced an unarmed Spits to duck for cover behind a dumpster, they'd taken off running. When it was over Red and Spits introduced themselves, and became a unit for the remainder of his trip. Spits had given Red his word that once he returned, he would bring fortune and he was ready to honor that promise.

"Yeah, whatever nigga," Spits said, returning the love that was received. "It's been too long, huh?"

"What's going on, man?" asked Red.

"Ain't nothin, son. You ready to get this paper, my nigga?"

"Always ready to get that paper, dog. Always!"

"Well, it's time now, son. Things are about to be for real. Let's go in here and get some food, so everything could be straight for when my nigga Trigger gets here."

They went into the restaurant and immediately requested a table in the back for privacy. The place wasn't crowded at all so they could also have some silence while they spoke. They went through every last detail three times over before Spits was comfortable that the information was burnt into Red's brain. The first detail that was discussed were the locations. They wouldn't go out on the street at all here. They'd deal directly from apartments that were rented strictly for work. Again, Spits figured if these fucked-up ass apartment complexes housed all of the addicts, then they'd house the dealers as well; just like in the park in '96. The next detail would be labs. If they were going to steer clear of suspicion, they'd use hotel rooms for stash spots. It wouldn't be wise to have the drugstore in the same place as the stash spot because you didn't need all that traffic where all of your work was kept. Of course the hotels would be affiliated with TB, but that wouldn't at all be public knowledge. They'd also adapt the same delivery process they used in New York. The next detail was the money. Ultimately, all of the money left after payroll would be in a safe that only Trigger and

Red had access to. It would stay there until it was time for packages to be sent home to New York. Red would exclusively handle the work to keep Trigger away from a direct connection. He was the front man and Trigger was his dictator. With the perfect plan set in motion and assistance from Tone and Mr. Ortiz, Spits had all that he needed to ensure that this expansion was successful. This shit would be perfect. He could call Trigger immediately. He stopped at a payphone on the way back to Rachel's place.

"Yo, what up, son?" asked Trigger as he answered the phone with anticipation. "Everything all good out there?"

"It's all good, dog," responded Spits. "Listen, you gotta be at LaGuardia Airport at ten o'clock sharp. Your flight leaves at eleven-thirty. All you have to do is show your ID at the front desk to check-in. They should have an electronic ticket for you under the name Nathaniel Evans. There should be no problems, right? I mean, Mr. Ortiz did send one of his guys with all of the papers you need, right?"

"Oh, yeah," said Trigger, reassuring him that everything was going according to plan. "The shit look mad official, too. I'm tellin you, ain't nobody gonna know the shit's a fake ID."

"Oh, okay. That's great. I had a little convo with my man Red. Yo, son is ready to die for the Family already, kid. He's on some dedication shit, for real. Besides that, you know he's always like thirty deep. He's going to be a good deputy."

"Word? That's peace. Yo, I can't wait to get out there, son."

"I know, son. I can't wait until all of this is over either. Listen, I'm about to motor. Me and Gin gonna see what we can get into tonight. I'll see you tomorrow, son."

"All right, God. Peace."

"Yeah, my nigga, peace."

Once their phone call came to an end, Spits hung up the receiver of the payphone and felt a bit of serenity pass through his body as he breathed in and out slowly. Everything was moving on schedule, and the confidence Spits had in himself came creeping back slowly, but surely. Soon, he'd be back to the extent of his controllability and arrogance as he felt he was yet to be defeated. When this mission was completed, there would be no stopping the Time Bomb Family. Of course, he would no doubt come across some speed bumps in his race to the finish line, but any real hustler could just move right through those.

After a minute of thinking to himself, Spits went back to the apartment to scoop Gin for a night on the town. They would go out for dinner, and then to a nightclub for drinks and dancing. As this was the first time Gin and Spits had actually gotten some sort of a vacation together, they had an immeasurable amount of fun that night. In all of the times they'd gone to nightclubs in New York together, they'd never imagined how much they enjoyed one another's company. Partying was different back home. They usually went out to get all dressed up and blow up the spot, basically to impress everyone they knew would be there. They never went out and just enjoyed themselves. It was purer away from home. Here, they didn't have to be image conscious, or put on a show. All that they were concerned with were each other, and nothing else.

Spits made sure to show Ginger the best time of her life so that she'd never be skeptical about another vacation idea. Also, he knew that starting the next afternoon, when Trig arrived, it would be all work and no play. Keeping that in mind, Spits woke up early the next morning, despite a hangover, and took Ginger out shopping.

They proceeded to the Great Mall of the Bay Area. Once inside, they hit the BCBG outlet, Nine West, the Off 5th Saks Fifth Avenue outlet, Donna Karan and Christian Dior. When Gin suggested they go to Mikasa to pick something up for Rachel, Spits recommended they split up and meet at the Outback Steakhouse for lunch. Ginger agreed and they parted ways. Although Spits gave off the impression that he'd gotten too tired to go on shopping, he'd been a bit deceiving. He wanted to surprise Ginger with a little something from Tiffany & Co. When they finally met up at the Outback, Spits already had a table for them. After they ordered, he laid a little box on the table. Her face lit up when she saw it, as she knew exactly what it contained. She loved those little blue boxes with the white ribbon. If she knew Spits, and she did, he'd gone all out for her. When she opened the box, she found a gleaming platinum bangle bracelet with 103 round brilliant diamonds in it that totaled 3.45 carats. She absolutely fell in love with it as soon as she laid her eyes on its beauty. She looked up at the love of her life with glossy eyes and simply said, "I love you, Daddy."

Just then, Spits got a call on his cell phone.

✪✪✪

"Peter Beckford," beckoned Judge Rosenberg. "Please stand and face the jury."

Trigger did so with no hesitation, and he suddenly became very ill. He got a sharp pain in his stomach and sweat started to form from his forehead. His hands started to shake uncontrollably as he wiped the sweat that had built up on his brow. Up until now, Trigger hadn't once regretted any of the decisions he'd made that would bring him to this point. He knew that how he'd chosen to live his life was wrong, but he'd never once thought that he could've made a difference. Now, with his life left in the hands of twelve strangers, he'd finally had those thoughts. It was now when he would develop a conscience, and actually feel some sort of remorse. But, unfortunately for Trigger, it was too late. He'd now be held responsible for all of the bad things he'd done. Now, he would pay his debt to society with interest.

As the bailiff handed the jury's verdict to the judge on a small piece of paper, Trigger felt like the room's temperature had risen to 130 degrees. Judge Rosenberg read the verdict on the paper to herself and nodded to the jury, signaling that she was ready for the verdict to be read aloud.

When the juror began reading the verdict, his voice seemed to get lower and lower until it sounded like a subtle whisper. Trigger closed his eyes and all he heard was silence. Then, he heard the word that he had been praying he wouldn't…GUILTY! It seemed to have come out of the juror's mouth in slow motion and it echoed over and over again in Trigger's ears. GUILTY… GUILTY…GUILTY. His head sunk into his chest and he felt tight all over.

"Peter Beckford," began the judge in a bold and emotionless tone. "You have been found guilty of the charges that were brought against you, by a jury of your peers. For these crimes, you are hereby sentenced to serve a term no shorter than twenty-five years, and not exceeding the span of your life, in a maximum security prison."

Trigger screamed out loud, and when his thunderous yells came to an end, he found that he had been in his bed and the whole terrifying scenario had only been a terrible nightmare. The only things that were authentic were the nervous twitches, the sharp pain in his stomach and the sweat on his brow. He inhaled a deep breath and blew it out slowly to calm himself. He attempted to roll over to get some more sleep, but his attempts had failed due to a sharp feeling he had in his stomach. So he reluctantly got out of bed and proceeded to get ready to leave. Trigger hadn't been comfortable enough in New York to get a good night's sleep since that morning the courts saw the last of him, and he was more than ready to leave. On his way out of the door, he grabbed the two small bags that he'd packed for his move, and he was on his way. When he got outside, he spun around slowly to take one last good look at the place he had called his home for so many years...the Bronx. He looked up at the sky and realized how beautiful the day was. When you'll probably never see something again, you take a better look at it and it doesn't seem the same. The sky seemed more pure. He didn't see the Bronx for the piss hole that he'd seen it as before. He recognized the exquisiteness in the building designs and the perfection of its imperfections and knew then, that he would miss it.

When he was ready, he started toward the cab that was waiting for him across the street from the building. All of a sudden, in the corner of his eye, he saw a navy blue Chevy Crown Victoria with dark tinted windows creeping from around the corner on the left. In the opposite direction, he spotted a black Astro van turning the corner unhurriedly two blocks down. Something told him that it was about to go down. He felt the streets getting hot underneath him. His hands started to shake. He wanted to just lunge into the direction of these pig mu'fuckas with both hands gripping .40 cal. Desert Eagles shooting uncontrollable fire. He was ready to go out blazing. One by one, he would take them all out, 'til every last one of those bitch-ass niggas was dead and gone. *Let's do it*, he thought to himself. "Let's get the shit over with. Come on!"

As the vehicle approached, still at a very slow pace, Trigger got the ground firmly beneath his feet. With a smooth movement, he managed to reach behind his back for the .40 caliber he had tucked into his pants. He had only intended on carrying the pistol halfway to the airport before disposing of it somewhere along the way. In fact, he almost didn't bring it along, thinking to himself that he was just being paranoid. It was a good thing he'd shrugged off his second thoughts and went with his gut feeling. Now, it was time and he would be ready.

When the car pulled up, it stopped in front of Trigger and the passenger side window came easing down. "Do you know where I can find Mace Avenue, sir?" the guy in the car asked.

Trigger took a deep breath and let out a sigh of relief. "Yeah, just make the next two lefts and go straight down. You can't miss it," he said, pointing in the right direction.

He inserted the pistol back into his pants and entered the cab still waiting for him patiently across the street. He got into the backseat of the car and it pulled off. "Oh shit!" he said out loud as he turned back toward the building he'd just exited. The cab pulled away as that black Astro van was pulling up. When it stopped, the doors flew open and what looked like federal agents came charging out of it with MP-5 fully automatic mini-machine guns in hand. They flooded the apartment building in search of what had just slipped through their unknowing fingertips. It was already looking like a good day for Trigger. He made it to the airport early enough to check in and get breakfast before his flight. When he reached Los Angeles, the infamous "Red" that he'd heard so much about was there to pick him up. He figured Spits meant for them to get acquainted as soon as possible. That was the reason for him sending Red to pick Trigger up. It didn't matter to Trigger though. As long as this mu'fucka knew who was the boss, they would have no quarrels.

Red took Trigger to Rachel's house. Trigger and Rachel had met a few times while they were both younger, when she used to visit New York.

They exchanged hellos, and Trigger showed his gratitude for her letting him stay there. They spent a minute catching up, and then he called Spits.

"Yo, who dis?" Spits asked, answering the phone showing aggravation as if the person who called was interrupting.

"What up, my nigga?" said the voice on the other end.

"Trig?" asked Spits with excitement.

"Holla at me, dog. Where you at?"

"My nigga, I'm over here at the mall turning this bitch upside-down. They ain't gonna have shit left when we done, dog. How long you been here?"

"I just got here a minute ago. Your boy Red came and got me from LAX."

"Yeah, I told him if I wasn't back in time to go ahead and do that for me. So everything went down according to plans?"

"Well, I wouldn't exactly say that, but I'll fill in all of those blanks when you get here. How long you gonna be anyway?"

"I'll be there in a few. We about to have some lunch and then we'll be out."

"All right, God. I'll see you in a minute, then."

"Yeah, nigga. One."

"Peace."

CHAPTER 10

"Are there any new developments on the Beckford case?" asked the FBI's Assistant Director to the two agents that were assigned the case.

"No, sir," responded Agent Cassett, nodding his head with hopelessness.

"The bastard just disappeared off the damn face of the earth," added Agent Clifton, showing his aggravation by slamming his fist down on his desk.

"Pardon me, Clifton," said the Assistant Director.

"Excuse me, Mr. Chistov, sir," he said, retracting his previous outburst. "I'm sorry, sir, but we have nothing to report regarding the Beckford case as of yet."

"Well, as long as you both are aware that regulation of drug traffic in this country is our number one priority. Flagrant violators of this directive, such as this Peter Beckford and this Michael Banner character, have to be made examples of. We must send a message to the underworld that illegal drug trafficking will not be tolerated in this country."

"Yes, sir", said both Agent Cassett and Clifton at the same time.

"He can't hide forever," added Agent Cassett. "We'll get him sooner or later, sir."

"Well, as you were, gentlemen," he said as he walked away.

Anatoliy Chistov, Assistant Director of the FBI, was one of the most passionate figures in the Bureau regarding eliminating narcotics trade in the U.S. He was born in St. Petersburg, Russia, and had only spent a small portion of his early childhood there. He'd come from a small family that had very little, and when his father suggested to his mother that they move to "America, where the streets are paved with gold," she couldn't have been more excited. But when they'd arrived, instead of the golden opportunities they'd expected for themselves and their son, all there was were drugs. Still surrounded by poverty, starvation, and the daily grind of the struggle, their self-pity got the best of them and they surrendered to the streets in the form of heroin. Anatoliy grew up in Brooklyn, New York in a predominantly Russian community, and saw his parents and their friends slowly deteriorate from drug use. He vowed to his father, while on his deathbed, that he would rid the streets of this horrendous menace. He'd since climbed the Bureau's ladder until he'd become Assistant Director; exclusively specializing in narcotics.

Special Agent Phillip Cassett and his partner Simon Clifton had gotten this assignment directly from the Assistant Director due to their evident passion for criminal justice. Phillip and Simon had first met in training camp and immediately clicked. Their relationship had soon extended further than the workplace, and they had become very good friends. They were quite pleased to find out that they would be assigned to the infamous *Time Bomb Family* case and were eager to show their supervisor, Assistant Director Chistov, that their feelings regarding criminal justice didn't differ from his own. They both respected his views and methods while they worked alongside him. Being that they shared the same vision, they all adopted a high amount of respect for one another. Although sometimes confusing that with a comfortable friendship, they'd maintained a professional relationship.

"It seems as though Anatoliy won't rest until the Time Bomb Family, and all of its members, are comfortably locked away behind bars for a long, long time," said Agent Clifton to his partner.

"Yeah," responded Agent Cassett. "I feel the same way."

✪✪✪

While everything seemed quiet back in New York for the Feds, the party had just begun on the other side of the country—in California. The new West Coast chapter of the Time Bomb Family thought that a little get-together at my hotel room was in order. We'd spent the last three days preparing for this one, and finally it was here. Early that morning, Tone had arrived with the first package. He was exactly on time and everything was going down according to plan. Actually, Tone had been one step ahead of me, bringing more than what was expected of him. I had only proposed that we ship ten kilos to start everything off, but Tone had taken it upon himself to bring fifteen. Plus, to congratulate our new deputy and his lieutenants, Tone had brought six .40 caliber Desert Eagles. The surprise was met with a warm welcome and Tone felt the gratitude. We'd spent the rest of the day cooking and bagging. Now, it was time for celebrations and congratulations as tomorrow would be a lot of work.

"Yo, listen up," I said, standing on a chair as I addressed all the Cali niggas of enough importance to be at the engagement. Besides me, Tone and Trigger, there was Red, and the five dudes that he suggested we appoint as lieutenants. "This is it, mu'fuckas. Today marks the beginning of the mu'fuckin' end for all of us that used to be broke, that used to be hungry, that had to rob and steal for paper, that thought that there was nothing in this world made just for us. Your niggas right here are all that matter; that's it. Nothing else will ever be more important to ya'll mu'fuckas than all of your niggas. Can't no bitch, or no cheddar, or no fucking punk-ass rat mu'fucka goin' turn you against your crew. If that's the way you feel, then you can be down with us. We are the TIME BOMB FAMILY! No team will beat us, ya'll feel me?"

"Yeah, yeah!" they all screamed in unison, nodding in agreement. My words weren't being taken lightly. My speech wouldn't fall on deaf ears.

"Look at me," I continued. "Look at my mu'fuckin' right-hand man Trig. Look at us together. Ain't nothing ever gonna break that up, and that's from the heart. Learn that who ya'll niggas call your family, will be just that and nothing else...family! Now, let us toast." We toasted to "To Dom P's and palm trees" and all began sipping our champagne together.

✪✪✪

"Yo, hurry up, Reggie!" said Boogie nervously. "What the fuck's taking so long?"

"Shut the fuck up, nigga," Reggie responded. "I told you I got this, all right?"

Boogie was short and light-skinned, but where he fell short in height, he made up for in weight. He weighed about two hundred and thirty-five pounds, standing at about 5 ft. 7 in. Reggie was tall and brown-skinned. Although he was a rather slim dude, he was very well-built, though it seemed that his features were dwindling due to his most recent experimentations with drugs.

"We gonna get caught, man," said Boogie with fear in his voice. "If they find us here, man, they'll kill us without a second thought. Fuck it, I'm out of here."

"I got it," said Reggie as he finally picked the lock on the door he was kneeling in front of.

Boogie turned back around. "It's about fuckin' time."

"Shut up, nigga, and come on."

As they entered the house through the back door they'd just picked, they quickly went directly for the closet. They walked past the stereo on the floor, and bypassed the television set sitting on the kitchen table, and hit the closet first. It seemed as though they knew exactly what they'd been there for. In fact, they *did* know exactly what they were there for.

Reggie and Boogie didn't know it yet, but they'd just committed the only breaking and entering misdemeanor charge that could possibly earn them the death penalty. You see, the house they'd just broken into wasn't just any house, and the people that rented the space weren't just any normal tenants. They had just picked a lock on a door attached to a house that was being rented by the Time Bomb Family. Just the breaking and entering portion of this could be considered means for a lynching. If they only knew the magnitude of danger they were in, just being in that house, they might not have been as dim-witted.

"Is this it, Boogie?" Reggie asked.

"Yeah, that's where they always used to keep it," responded Boogie.

They stood there for a second in the front of the closet doors and only could imagine what would be waiting for them on the other side. When Reggie opened the doors, he banged around until he felt the portion of the wall that was hollowed out. A plank off of the wood panel that covered the interior of the wall slid from its position and the inside of the wall was exposed. They both just stood there in amazement when what was behind that plank was revealed. Staring up at them was a little over fifty thousand dollars in cash and two kilos of uncut cocaine, plus three G-packs already cooked, cut, and bagged. Their eyes lit up as they began shoveling the cash into a pillowcase they'd brought for their findings. When the cash was securely tucked away in the pillowcase, they each took a kilo of the coke to carry in their coat pockets along with the baggies of crack. When there was nothing left, they were gone. As quickly as they'd appeared, they'd disappeared with pillowcases full of cash and their coats filled with coke and crack. They fled the scene thinking that there would be no repercussions for this heinous act. Yeah, right!

✪✪✪

After we'd set up shop on the Cali side, the next few days were a complete success. We moved more product in the shortest amount of time than we'd ever moved; especially in a new spot. It was like the fiends were waiting out front of the spots for us to get there. We lined them mu'fuckas up for what seemed like blocks to get a hit. After the samples were done, it took not even fifteen minutes for the first sale to come. After that first sale was dealt, it was all over. Fiends were coming back three and four times with more and more customers. It didn't stop until they'd almost depleted their entire stock of prepared product.

The success meant that it had finally become time for me to return to the Bronx. Now that I felt comfortable enough with Trigger and the new West Coast enterprise, I was ready to leave him all of the responsibility and go back home. Only if I knew that it wouldn't at all be as peachy in New York as it was in California. There would only be more work for me when I reached home. The life of a drug dealer was the furthest thing from the "*easy way out*," for real.

The night before I left, Trigger and I engaged ourselves in a lengthy conversation about life, responsibilities, and how only one's choices would determine their destiny. The conversation was meant to prepare Trigger for what he was about to embark on, but I soon realized that he'd already been prepared for this kind of accountability. In fact, he'd been ready and willing for a long time now. Now, he had the opportunity to show off his skills.

We left each other with a pound and a hug. We knew it wouldn't be too long before I came back to check up on things, so everything was real relaxed. Ginger and I went to the airport and caught a flight back to New York, after a two-week long vacation/business trip.

"Even though I'm glad me and your sister and I clicked so well, I was starting to get a little homesick," Ginger told me during the plane ride home as she laid her head on my shoulder.

"Yeah, I feel you," I responded, kissing her on the forehead. "I kinda miss the grime, myself."

We were both happy to be returning home; especially with the memories we could both take back with us. The trip had taught us both a little bit more about each other, and now we could see each other just a bit clearer. It only made us closer. The time was well-spent, but it was time to go. This had also been the longest time I'd spent away from work with only little contact with back home.

When I arrived, I hadn't realized that no one knew we were coming back, so I didn't set up any transportation for us from the airport. We hopped in a yellow cab and went to Ginger's house where I'd left my truck. When she was settled in, we parted and I went to my apartment to unpack and take a nap before coming back out later in the evening.

Not even two hours into my nap, my phone rang. It was Vision and he had news that wouldn't allow me to return to the comfort of my sleep. Vision informed me that we'd been robbed of over fifty grand in cash and almost a hundred thousand dollars' worth of coke and crack. When I was fully awake and realized what I'd just been told, I jumped out of the bed and began to yell into the phone receiver at Vision.

"What?!" I yelled uncontrollably. "Where the fuck was everybody at? How in the fuck do you let a nigga steal from us, the Time Bombs?"

"Calm down, dog," said Vision, trying to bring me to relax my anger. "I ain't the enemy, son. Don't kill the messenger, ya na'mean."

"My bad, dog," I responded with a more relaxed tone of voice. "How did this shit happen?"

"Some mu'fucka broke in through the back way, and shit. They knew exactly what they were there for, too, 'cause they didn't touch anything else. Nothing was overturned or disturbed. They went straight to the closet, and emptied out the inside of the wall."

"Oh, okay," I said, now better understanding the situation. "So, they knew where the stash spot was and all that, huh?" I asked to myself rhetorically.

"Straight up, son. I spoke to Ponch so him and El are going to look into the shit. It won't be long. You know mu'fuckas can't keep they mouth shut out here. Anybody that's one hundred thousand stronger overnight won't be able to keep it to himself, ya na'mean?"

"Word, I feel you, dog. But fuck that shit, son. I want everybody on this shit and nothing else."

"That's cool. We got a meeting scheduled in about 45 minutes."

"Where at?"

"Over on the Block."

"I-ight, then. I'll meet ya'll there."

"Yeah, my nigga. Peace."

"Peace."

When I hung up the phone, I sat there and thought to myself for a little while. I was trying to play the situation back in my head. I couldn't quite fully grasp the concept that someone had actually gotten over on me. How the fuck did they know where to go? Could it be some worker mu'fucka who robbed me and just made it look like a break-in? Could it be some nigga that just didn't quite make that cut and decided to hate on the rest of the family? A thousand questions went through my head after I received this news. It just didn't make any sense to me that these types of things were possible. This occurrence let me know that I wasn't exempt. I could get it, too, just like everybody else.

The meeting was scheduled for eleven o'clock. It would be imperative that everyone show up, as this meeting was incredibly important to me along with the other family members. When I arrived on the Block, I could spot in the shadows of the buildings El Don, Poncho, Ceelow, Little Jay, Vision, plus a few other key workers, all occupying the steps in the front of the building that I'd grown up in along with Cee, Trigger, and Pop. With all of them taking slow sips from plastic cups containing a mixture of Hennessey and Alize, called "*Blood Passion,*" no one could reflect a bit of happiness or contentment. They all just stood or sat there, with a blank and empty facial expression, looking as if plotting.

The address of the building was 666 East 224th Street. It was peculiar, but that was the perfect numbers for the building. It spawned some really devilish mu'fuckas, and the younger generation of hell dwellers would be ten times worse, but that's a different book altogether. Anyway, this was "*the Block.*" To us, it was the foundation. No matter how far this game took us in life, it was always just mandatory that we return once in a while. Until we owned our own houses on that exotic island somewhere in the middle of the Atlantic, it wasn't that hard for us to stay away. In fact, when it came time for us to get our own apartments, we all moved to other parts of the Bronx, except for Cee. He moved two flights upstairs from the apartment that he'd grown up in, where his mother and little brother still resided. Maybe he thought he would be selling out by moving anywhere too far from the Block, or maybe he just didn't think he was good enough to live anywhere else. In any case, it was time to get down to business.

After parking across the street from the building by a hydrant, I got out of the truck and entered the cipher of the rest of the Time Bombs. We all exchanged pounds and Cee handed me a cup of Blood Passion he'd prepared for me. I began to sip along with the others, and this began the meeting.

"So," I said to start everything off. "Let me know something. Who the fuck is these niggas that got enough heart to steal from us, and where the fuck they at, right now?"

No one said anything. They all simply stood there nodding unknowingly, until Little Jay broke the silence. "Exactly how much did these mu'fuckas get, anyway?" he asked.

"Almost a hundred and sixty thousand dollars," answered Cee.

"Shit," said Vision. "Somebody's gotta die, ya'll."

"You damn right," I agreed. "So, as of now, we don't know anything?"

"We don't know shit, dog," answered Poncho honestly. "Somebody gotta leak something sooner or later, though."

"Yeah, better sooner than later," I added. "We can't have the street saying that it ain't nothin' to take from the Time Bombs. We gonna have to put these streets under pressure."

"Pressure bust pipes," added Ceelow.

"Yup, and it's time to apply some," I continued. "These mu'fuckas out here gonna know not to ever fuck with something or someone that's part of this crew. Our first priority is find out who, and where these mu'fuckas at with balls big enough to steal from us, and that's it. I got fifty thousand for the cat that brings me their heads. Let all ya'll mu'fuckin' workers know what the deal is."

Everyone nodded in agreement while I went on further, and the focus grew deeper and deeper in their faces. They were to know that they had a family, and that they were a part of something bigger than a street crew that dabbles in narcs. The Time Bombs was a movement that needed to be represented properly. When you're part of a family, you have to be willing to do whatever is necessary to protect it. If any of them had anything to do with it, after this occurrence, there would be no more instances where the dedication of a Time Bomb soldier would be questioned.

CHAPTER 11

"Leave some for me, nigga," said Boogie to Reggie. "That's all we've got left."

"Shut the fuck up, Boogie," countered Reggie. "And how the fuck you smoke up three thousand dollars' worth of crack in just a few fuckin' days, anyway?"

It had been almost a week now since Boogie and Reggie had broken into one of the houses that were known Time Bomb stash houses, and they'd been too preoccupied with the findings from their heist to even bathe or change clothes. When they were through emptying out that hollowed-out wall, they'd rented a hotel room on Burke Avenue and Boston Road, named "*The Paradise,*" and never once had seen the light of day since. They didn't even eat. All they did was smoke, and smoke, and smoke.

Boogie and Reggie hadn't known each other long, but if you're as much of a dickhead as Boogie was, you could make a lot of friends when you're telling a bunch of rock-heads that you could get access to unbelievable amounts of crack. Boogie and Reggie both hung out at the same place when smoking their poison, and when Reggie heard Boogie talking his shit, he'd taken him very seriously. He'd put him under pressure until he'd told him everything he knew. Boogie told Reggie about when he used to be a part of the Time Bomb organization, right up until they'd found out that he was a user as well as a seller. Before he'd parted ways with them, he knew enough to get over on them at least once. He'd just been too afraid of what might happen to him if he ever tried anything. For good reason, too; until he'd met Reggie. Reggie had convinced him that no one would find out, as long as they did it correctly, and that was enough for him. No one but a fuckin' crack-fiend would even imagine double-crossing a Time Bomb, and he was the one stupid enough to think that he could get away with it, too.

"What?" asked Boogie. "What the fuck you mean 'how did I', like you wasn't right here with me, Reggie. Half of that smoke is in your lungs, nigga."

"Whatever, nigga," said Reggie, dismissing his statement. "Like I said, how the fuck we only got this last little bit of this shit left, man?"

"I don't know, man," said Boogie with confusion in his voice. "It seemed like a whole lot more than that when we took it."

Before the words were even completely out of his mouth, he looked up at Reggie with distrust. He thought to himself that they couldn't have possibly smoked up all of that crack-cocaine in only six days. If this was all that was left over from the entire supply they'd stolen, there had to be something going on that he didn't know about. He started to suspect Reggie of foul play. He stared at him with a look in his eye that could've burned a hole in the wall. Reggie was so involved in the pipe that he'd been inhaling so deeply from, that he didn't even realize how angrily Boogie had been gazing at him. When he finally did look up, he noticed the fire in Boogie's eyes.

"What the fuck is wrong with you?" he asked.

"Fuck you, motherfucker!" yelled Boogie as he charged toward Reggie, lifting him out of his chair and slamming him up against the wall. "You shiestie bastard, you stealing from me?"

"What?" Reggie asked with uncertainty. "No, I ain't stealing from you, nigga. What the fuck are you, crazy?"

"Yes, you are, nigga! Don't fucking lie to me!"

Reggie, finally realizing that there was no reasoning left in Boogie, fought to push him off. When he wouldn't let go, he lifted his hand and swung down, smacking Boogie in his face with the back of his hand. Dazed from the impact of the slap, he loosened the grip he had on Reggie enough for him to push him off and hit him with a closed fist across his jaw. He hit him twice more before Boogie curled up on the floor crying. When Reggie saw Boogie burst into tears the way he did, he started to feel sorry for him. He took his share of the loot they had and left without saying anything to him.

✪✪✪

This whole incident left me in a slump of confusion and doubt. The next few days hadn't been the best of times for me. I spent most of the time with my younger brother, along with my mother in the new house that I'd just recently purchased for them on the North East Side of the Bronx. It had three bedrooms, an attic that we'd turned into a bedroom for my brother, and a basement. It wasn't as far away from the city as I would've liked, but my mother insisted on continuing her job until her pension came through, so I kept it within the five boroughs. If it were up to me, she would've been somewhere in Florida without the stress of the city, but that would have to wait for whenever she decided to retire. It took a while, but she'd finally agreed to move out of the apartment we'd rented for the last few years. It was too hard for her to believe that she didn't have to struggle and starve for ends to meet anymore. All she knew was hard work, and nothing else. It was healthy for her to have something that she could call her own. I made sure no one knew about this place either; not even Ginger. Not that I didn't trust her, but if anyone ever wanted to get at me through my family, they'd be almost impossible for the average dude to locate. Plus, if anything ever *did* happen to me, I had a safe built into the basement floor with five-hundred thousand dollars in cash inside that only my mother knew the combination to. She was set.

When I needed to escape though, that's where I would go just to bring me back down to earth. Spending time with my family made me reflect and that, in turn, kept me level. I could only stand so much of the streets before I would just become a part of it with no feelings, second thoughts, or plans for bettering myself. I needed to have a little of both to keep me where I needed to be with myself. As this would be my little getaway from the world, I even built myself a small production studio in what was the shed in the back yard. It wasn't anything too fancy, but when I needed to pound out some sounds and make music, it could be done there just to relax me. That's where I was when I got the call.

"Yo, who dis?" I spat into my cell phone receiver.

"Yo, what up?" said the voice on the other end. "It's Vision."

"Oh, what up, my nigga? Everything good?"

"No doubt, playboy," he said with a hint of excitement in his voice. "Matter of fact, it's better than good."

"How's that?"

"I got that info about that thing."

When I heard that, I knew instantly that he'd found out who it was that had broken into our spot. Now I was excited, and I couldn't wait to hear the mu'fucka's name.

"Say word," I said, gripping the phone tighter against my ear, making sure I didn't miss a word.

"That's my word, God," he said, confirming my assumption. "You remember that kid that used to be a worker for us, but kept coming up short on his packs?"

"Who, that nigga that started smoking woolies, and shit?"

"Yup, that's him, that fool ass nigga Boogie. As for our old friend, don't even sweat that kid. He's not among the living anymore. I took care of that fiend mu'fucka myself. The only thing is, while he was crying and begging me for his life, like the bitch that he is was, he confessed that it wasn't entirely his idea. He claims some other so-called, thug-ass-crack-fiend-nigga named Reggie made him do it."

"Reggie?" I asked, not recognizing the name. "Who the fuck is this dude?"

"I asked around a bit. He's a nobody, but I got him in my radar. I think it's time to go check the kid, and see what he got to say about this shit, ya na'mean?"

"Yeah, no doubt, my nigga," I said, now biting my bottom lip with anticipation. "I feel you, one hundred and ten percent, for real."

"So I'm going to be on the Block. I got this shorty that wanna start bubbling for us, so I want to see what she's working with. What time we gonna link up?"

"Let's see, when I leave here, I'm gonna go ride the Avenues and pick up some paper. I'll be over by the Block in about an hour or two."

"All right, that's cool. I'll be here. Yo, don't forget to silence them things, feel me?"

"Yeah, my nigga. I got you. One."

"Peace."

I left my mother and little brother with a hug and a kiss, and they couldn't have imagined in a million years the crazy things I had going through my head at that point. As I entered my car, I immediately called Little Jay. He had a package waiting for me that I was saving for a couple of days now, since we'd had that meeting on the Block. When I hung up with him, I would be heading past Magenta Avenue to make a pick-up, then over to Burke, then back up to the Woods. When I had enough paper, I slid in and out of highway traffic on the Cross-Bronx Expressway to head over to Castle Hill Avenue, where Little Jay was waiting for me. I made a left turn off of the highway, then a right on Gleason Avenue and drove down halfway into the block where Little Jay rented the basement of a house. When I pulled up, he was already waiting out front with a black briefcase in hand.

Little Jay reminded me so much of myself that I tried my best to come across as a positive role model for him. If he followed behind all of these dumb-ass niggas in the streets, then he wouldn't ever accomplish more than what they had. I wanted for him what I had. Ever since we'd put him down, he'd done nothing but express his love and dedication. The name, Little Jay, obviously came from his physical features. He was about 5 ft. 3 in. tall, but he would go blow for blow or buss his gun in a second. He was half black and Puerto Rican and had a curly Afro.

"Yo, what up, son?" I said as I put the car in park. "That's my shit, right? Ain't nobody fuck with it, right?"

"Nah, it's just me in here," he said as he approached. "Honestly, I was wondering what the hell it was, but you know I ain't gonna fuck with your shit."

"Oh, okay. Well, I just got the word from Vision about that little job that everybody was supposed to be on. This right here," I said, taking the case from him. "This is what would have gone to you if you was the nigga that found out first."

I opened the case and saw Little Jay's eyes light up as he saw what was inside. There were two chrome-plated .44 caliber Desert Eagle hand-cannons with two clips both filled with hollow-head slugs. To mystify him even more, I opened up the knapsack that contained the cash that I'd just collected, totaling fifty thousand dollars. Fifty grand in cash looked like a whole lot more than it was and I purposely exposed Little Jay to this to make a point. If my intentions were satisfied, he'd know what was rewarded to hard workers. He could take this as a lesson learned.

Finally, it was time to meet Vision. I was nervous with anticipation. When I turned the corner on to 224th Street, off of White Plains Road, I spotted Vision sitting in his white SL500 Roadster with some broad bent over at the passenger side window. As I pulled up, the gleam from the CL600 I was pimping quickly shifted her interest to my direction of the street. She stood straight up and all I saw was the ass. The bitch had an ass like a fuckin' horse, with long legs, too. She had a chocolate complexion, a thick frame, and a pretty face with big brown eyes and big lips. She was appropriately dressed in a baby T-shirt with blue jeans. She looked like she just knew, she was a dime, but I could tell she was a bird though. When I pulled up beside Vision, and told him to hop in, I saw her face light up.

"Who this bitch riding your dick?" I asked as he got in.

"Oh, that's my new gangsta bitch, Simone," he said with pride. "Yeah, looks like it'll work out with her. She's for real, dog."

"Yeah, i-ight," I said, disregarding his statement. "Peep this."

As I reached into the back seat for the gift I had for Vision, here comes Simone interrupting us to be nosey.

"Are *you* Spits?" she asked with a confident grin that suggested *I could have you if I wanted.*

"Yo, Vision," I said without even acknowledging that she'd spoken. "This is business, my nigga. Tell this bitch to widen the grip."

Her facial expression switched to *I didn't want you, anyway* and she assumed her position back on the corner, after sucking her teeth and rolling her eyes.

When I opened the briefcase, his eyes lit up as well. He started rubbing his hands together as if he couldn't wait until he could use his new toys.

"You know what I like, God," he said as he lifted one of the pistols from its position in the briefcase. "I didn't know you was coming through like this."

"That's all you, baby."

"Oh, word?" he asked with even more excitement in his voice. "Say word, my nigga."

"Word up, kid. Consider that a gift for a job well-done."

"*Good lookin', son!*"

"Ain't nothing, dog. You deserve it. I got some cash for you, too, ya na'mean? I'm sayin' though, tell me how it went down, kid."

"Oh, you mean ya man Boogie?" he asked as if he couldn't wait to tell the story. "Peep the drama, kid. I finds out from the streets that some bitch-ass nigga is up and down the Ave talkin' all this *'the Time Bombs is soft'* shit. Come to find out, this is the dude that broke into our spot, and his dumb ass is still in the mu'fuckin' Bronx. So I goes to pick up the kid Frenchie from over there on 219th Street, 'cause he got a call from some bitch that tells him that our boy Boogie is on 228th Street right over there by the library. I left my car there, and we jump in his whip. The whole fuckin' time I got the Tec-9 sitting on my lap, ready to let them things go, ya na'mean?"

"Word?" I asked, feeling his energy. "Proceed, my nigga."

"Yeah," he continued. "So we finally get to where he at. While we pulling past 226th, we spot the cat coming towards us but he turns down 229th, so we cut down the 8th to cut him off."

"Come on, nigga," I said, interrupting him. "Hurry up and get to the good shit already." My attention was fully piqued.

"Just be easy, God…I got this," he said, easing his way back into the part of the story where he'd left off. "So, when we made that right-turn on Lowerre Place, the look on his face was worth a half-a-mill, kid. He was sooo shook. I cracked a smile and winked at him, and that's when he took off running. Frenchie jumps out the whip to go after him and I speed down the street to cut him off. I pull up on the curb in the front of him and Frenchie grabs him, pushing him on the floor. I jumps out the whip with the big boy Tec in my hand, and I could've swore this nigga pissed on himself by the way he looked. *'Click-clack'*…French cocks the nine-milly and puts it to his face. As soon as I got in arm's distance of the nigga, I swung the Tec from over my shoulder and cracked the shit out of him. *BONG! BONG*, I hit him again with the banger and the nigga starts crying and shit, tellin' me all kinds of bullshit about how some other nigga gassed him up to do it and how it wasn't his idea, blah, blah, blah. When I heard enough of his shit, I started dumping on him. *BOOM! BOOM! BOOM*...I must've put nine shots in his chest, before Frenchie grabbed me and shoved me in the hooptie."

"Damn, son!" I said, extremely pleased with how the story climaxed. "I wish I was there, yo. That's my word, I wish I was there. That shit was gangsta."

"*For real*," agreed Vision with a small chuckle.

"So, umm...what's up with this dude, Reggie?"

"Oh, *Reggie?* This mu'fucka is not a threat, whatsoever. This bitch Simone said she knew the nigga. She made me promise to put her on if she gave me the low-down, so I said whatever. I found out mad shit about the nigga, though. He used to be down with them niggas from the other side a while back, until this asshole started selling dummies to make extra money on the side. When their reputation started to get fucked up because of his bullshit, these niggas beat his ass right there on the Ave to let everybody know that they wasn't fuckin' with him no more. Peep how he used to wear these jeans with his name written down the front of them, right...so these niggas made him strip butt-ass-naked, and then hung his jeans from the light-pole."

They both gave a chuckle when Vision told that part of the story, then he continued.

"He fell off after that though, and now he's all strung out on crills. His life is lost once *we* catch up to him, though. That's my word. I'm gonna put one of these slugs right here in the back of his head."

Just as Vision finished, a black Chevy Impala turned the corner and came to an abrupt halt, pulling up on the curb sideways on the other side of the street. Before I could even blink, an arm gracefully extended from the window. When the arm was completely extended, everything became silent. The whole entire block just stood still and, frame by frame, the scene started moving in slow motion. I felt a calming sensation come over my whole body, and then a large jolt of energy, as this faceless arm, pointed directly at where Vision and I were sitting, started to send shots at us wildly.

"Get low!" I yelled as I grabbed Vision to push his head down.

I opened the door on my side, got out of the car and started to return fire while I kept behind the car for cover. I shot into the driver's side door of that Impala until my clip was empty. Without reloading, I grabbed the other .45mm I had with a fresh clip to quickly reengage myself into the battle. Shots were still firing from the window of this Impala, but I couldn't get a clear enough headshot. Just as I was about to deplete my back-up ammunition, Simone came running from around the corner with a little 380 in-hand. She busted three shots into the car window from the passenger side. When I looked up, she had already come around to the driver's side, peeking into the window with her pistol in the air ready to let him have the other four shots she had left in her clip. The gunfight had ended just as quickly as it had begun. Nothing was left but two cars full of holes and a street decorated with gun shells.

When I came around the other side of the car, I noticed that Vision was still curled up in the front seat. I reached into the window to shake him to see if he was okay, and his body just loosely swung around lifelessly to my direction and stared up at me with dead eyes. Before I realized that he was gone, I opened the door and pulled him out of the car to see if he had any vital signs. When I finally came to the realization that he'd already passed, I let one single tear run down my face before I rubbed it clear and attempted to focus my energy. Again, I would bury the emotions deep inside myself. My second reaction was to take it out on the mu'fucka that did this to my cousin. I ran over to the car where the gunshots had so wildly come out of and opened the door. When I saw that the passenger was still moving around a little, I dragged his ass out of the car and onto the street. With sweat running profusely down my face, I turned him over to look him in the eyes. I knelt down and put the gat to the top of his head with blood still leaking from his neck and his chest and cocked the hammer. I took a deep breath and all of the memories I had of Vision came rushing to my head. Inside of two seconds, my mind filed through all of the oldest memories I had of him up until the minute before this bitch-ass nigga came around the corner and made the worst mistake of his life. I wiped the sweat from my brow and stood up over top of him. Everything around me fell silent as I eagerly anticipated the pleasure I would receive from emptying the rest of my clip in this nigga's head. Then, when the trigger clicked with no loud boom, I realized that I had no more bullets left in my pistol, but I could do nothing but continue pulling the trigger over and over again. When I finally came to my senses, he was already choking on his own blood, trying to breathe. Without my help, he finally lost consciousness and died. He would be meeting up with Vision in his afterlife now, and that's where he belonged.

Finally, the sounds of the street came back when Simone, hearing police sirens getting closer, grabbed me and forced me into the passenger side of my Mercedes before hitting the gas and fleeing the scene. I didn't completely come to my senses at all for at least another few hours. When Simone had put enough space between us and the crime scene, she told me that it was that nigga Reggie who had just taken my cousin's life. I guess he'd found out what happened to Boogie and could only imagine the things he'd told us. He knew that it would only be a matter of time before we got in his ass, too, so he decided to set it off first. Oh well, he was a fuckin' goner now, so his ass got what he deserved. It made me feel just a little better to know that he was gone now, too, but that didn't make up for the hurt that I felt for Vision. He was there from the beginning, and now, he was dead. What would I tell his mother? How would I explain to her that she'd never see her son ever again? That day would be recorded as one of the worst days of my life. I'll never forget my nigga, Vision; may he rest in peace.

CHAPTER 12

"Yo, pass that weed, nigga!" Spits said to El Don as he took one last pull from the spliff before passing it off.

As El blew a tremendous amount of weed-smoke through his lips and nostrils, he suddenly had a thought that came to him like the meaning of life. He'd spent so many hours contemplating the solution to the problem at hand, and now he'd figured it out. His facial expression began with confusion, and then his eyebrows lifted up higher on his forehead as his thoughts began to take form. Now, he could suggest the perfect action to take to set everyone's mind straight. He looked up at everyone present, each for a couple of seconds before the next, and said, "Yo, we should just murder all of that mu'fucka's friends and family members." He waited for everyone's response to the bomb that he'd just dropped on their upset attitudes, but he received no feedback whatsoever. Everyone simply paid his comment no mind and went on drinking and smoking, and reminiscing about their dog, Vision.

Today was a dark day for anyone that knew Vision, as today was the day that he would be laid into the ground six feet deep, never to be heard from or seen again. It had already been four days since that tragic event that had taken Vision from his family and friends, but the memories of how it all went down were still as fresh in Spits' mind as if it were only four minutes. No one out of the Family had taken the occurrence worse than Spits, but everyone felt the helplessness the same. If there could be an end to justify the means that would be the only thing that could shed any light on the whole situation. After smoking massive amounts of weed and drinking even more liquor, the only thing any of them could come up with was to "murder all of that mu'fucka's friends and family members." Two plus two will almost always equal four.

This occurrence had brought together some of the dirtiest niggas the Bronx had ever seen. Once the news had hit the street that the "God," Vision, got murdered, mu'fuckas just started coming out of the woodwork to pay their respects. If anybody had the love of everybody all up and down the Avenue, it was him. When the ceremony was over, and they'd finally put him to rest, these were all of the niggas that were left. Out of all the hustlers, murderers, pimps, hoes, fiends, stick-up kids and purse-snatchers that had shown love, the only cats that remained were the niggas he could've called "*Dogs for Life.*"

As Spits took a look around the smoky park where they occupied the numerous benches by the playground on Burke Avenue, he began to analyze the individuals present. All in separate groups of three or four, they all reflected. They thought of the years before Vision's prison term when they were all growing up together in what seemed like a never-ending war. They reflected on the years of junior high school, where they would have to throw punches for each other to secure an untarnished reputation. They thought of the years of high school where they had to send shells to let niggas know that they were not to be fucked with. The trips that they'd taken out of state to buy and sell guns—where not all of them would return from—wandered through certain individuals' minds. They thought of the years that Vision was upstate doing his time when he could've easily snitched on half the fucking Avenue to get off. They'd all taken care of him when he was up North, and he'd chosen to roll with Spits and the rest of the Time Bombs when he'd come home. Maybe he thought that, with his little cousin growing up to be a man, this was his way of making up for the time that was taken from them. Besides that, from the pen, he could hear nothing but the way the Time Bombs were shutting shit down. Now, he was gone and everyone seemed incomplete in that they didn't have any way to rectify the situation.

"Yo," El Don continued. "I'm tellin' you, we should just merc all of them niggas, dog!"

"What the fuck you talkin' about, nigga?" asked Spits.

"You ain't even hearin' me, son," he answered. "That nigga already dead, feel me? He can't get it again, but somebody's gonna be held responsible for his actions."

"I feel that though, bruh," added Poncho. "Fuck it!"

"Word!" agreed Ceelow.

As El Don, Poncho and Cee continued, they started to pique the interest of the niggas who Spits and the rest of the Time Bombs called *"The Older Gods,"* because it was them—if no one else—who'd started niggas off getting money on the Block. Among the grimy of the grimy were Eddie (Green Eyes), B., Supreme, Essae, Dre, Ralik, Takwan, Monster, Crazy Lou, Treshawn, and Wise. These niggas all did their fair share of murdering, hustling and jail terms, and they were completely fearless. The way they looked at life was, "whatever's whatever," so no matter what niggas wanted to do was cool with them…"whatever's whatever"…

At first, it seemed like El's suggestion was the furthest thing from logical but as he went on, it seemed more and more feasible. Then, Essae asked the question, "So what's up then, lil' niggas? Ya'll ready for all that gangsta shit?"

"Word up!" added Dre. "'Cause these mu'fuckas are poppin' the most shit over here."

Essae was a big, bald, brown-skinned cat. The cat stood about 6 ft. 5 in., and weighed about 280 lbs.; all muscle. He'd used the time he'd spent behind bars—like most did—and had come home swollen. He looked like he could bench-press a fucking house. From his standpoint, he couldn't even imagine little frail-body niggas like them even being a little bit serious about all the killer shit they were talking. He'd learned from being upstate that putting the average nigga under pressure would make him tell on himself. Besides that, he just liked fucking with people, but El wasn't having that.

Once the situation was put on blast, everyone fell silent to the conversation and listened. El took immediate offense to the comment Essae had made and replied, "What? I'm not a shit-popper, dog. I'm about whatever, too, nigga."

"We could do this right fucking now," Poncho added. "I don't give a fuck either."

"I-ight, cool out, lil' homies," said Essae, realizing that Don and P. weren't playing games.

"I like these niggas," commented Dre.

Dre and Essae went back as far as grammar school, but they hadn't gotten really close until they'd coincidently met up with each other while serving time in Comstock Correction Facility. They'd previously been acquainted, but hadn't had the opportunity to grow as close as the prison system made them. Now, they were inseparable and commonly shared the same opinion regarding the street. Dre was about 5 ft. 10 in. He was the pretty-boy type, but sometimes they're the ones that buss their guns the quickest. That's the category that Dre fell under. "So, what's good then?" Dre asked. "It's been too long since the Bronx has been hot, anyway. Ya'll wit' it?"

Everyone else's attention to the shit that they were talking fell short at that point. It seemed as though they were the only ones taking each other seriously…very seriously! The rest of the night went by without anyone making any reference to their conversation. They all just went on smoking and drinking. They stood out all through the night and well into the early morning. Just as the sun was about to come up, Spits gave thanks to everyone's support and made his way home.

Late into that morning Spits was awakened with a hangover and a throbbing headache from all of the alcohol he'd consumed the night before. After an attempt to return to the peace of his sleep failed, he reluctantly lifted his heavy body out of the bed. Following a quick look out of the window, he knew that the rest of the day wouldn't be a good one. All that was seen out of the window through Spits' eyes was the darkness from the night before. All he could see was Vision's coffin being slowly lowered into the ground as his closest friends and family threw roses in, hoping that he could rest in peace. He wasn't recovering from this incident with any success at all. He got into the shower to try and wash his pains away.

✪✪✪

"You ready?" asked Essae of El Don and Poncho as they sat in the back seat of his truck.

"I was born ready, dog," responded El with confidence. "Let's do it."

"All right then," added Dre. "It's apartment 602, up there on the sixth floor. Ring the doorbell, and when they answer on the other side…" Dre continued until Poncho cut him off.

"We got this," said Poncho. "Don't even worry about it."

✪✪✪

"Aunt Nes, where did you say that photo album was again?" asked Dwight to his Aunt Nester as he walked out of the kitchen toward the living room.

"On the top of the wall unit in the living room, baby," answered Nester loud enough so that Dwight could hear her. "That's where I kept all of those old pictures of my baby Reginald."

"Oh, here they are," Dwight said to himself as he found what he'd been searching for. It had been up there for so long that when he finally got it down, he had to blow it clear of all the dust that had accumulated on it. After that, he would bring it to Nester for them to view. They could both sit beside each other at the dining room table as she showed him the pictures, and then he would listen to her tell stories about when her son Reginald was just a baby boy.

Dwight hadn't spent much time with his aunt for some time now. He simply figured that she'd want some company and support due to the drama that their family had just experienced. She'd just lost her son to the streets and that led her to beg and plead with her only nephew to lead a positive and religion-filled life. The more and more she spoke to him about religion and education, the more he started to realize that she might have had the right idea; but as they say, "the street kept callin'."

By the time Dwight returned to the dining room where his aunt had been waiting, she'd already begun to weep as she thought of her son. Dwight quickly laid the album on the dining room table and bent down to give her a hug. She grabbed on to him as tightly as she possibly could and let the tears flow down her devastated and frightened facial expression into his shirt. They kept this position for a while until she was ready to let go.

✪✪✪

"Can one of you please tell me how these TB scum-bags can turn a street corner into a battlefield and leave zero evidence for us to make some kind of arrest?" yelled Assistant Director Chistov. "Please, tell me you have something, Agent Cassett!"

"No, sir," responded Cassett firmly. "We're still waiting for the word from ballistics about those shells. If we can get the specifics about the weapon or a clean fingerprint, we can run them against the ones from the first shooting to see if there is a match."

"What about you, Agent Clifton!" yelled Chistov. "What do you have?"

"Umm…" he said before the Assistant Director cut him off.

"Is that all you have to say?" he asked condescendingly. "Umm…? You'd better have something better than that. This type of crap just doesn't happen…not on my watch, it doesn't. Now, you can't have a massive gun battle leaving two people lying dead on the floor without a trace. What's going on, Clifton?"

"Sir, we've gotten some leads to follow for possible eyewitnesses from the crime scene. All we have to do is rattle some cages, sir."

"Listen," he began as he stood up out of his chair and leaned over his desk. "Please, don't insult my intelligence with your BS about 'eyewitnesses,' okay. Since when has anyone ever fingered an employee from this organization? What do you suggest, that we get Michael Banner to participate in a line-up? The poor bastard that identifies him will come home to find his family dead, or at least that's what he'll think will happen."

"Well," Agent Cassett responded. "We do still have our informant. We've actually found that he's in fact directly connected to one of the dead bodies from the crime scene. Agent Cassett and I agreed to allow him a sufficient chance to come to us; given his present situation we shouldn't be waiting for long, sir."

"This whole entire situation just gives me a pain deep in my stomach when I know for a fact that Michael Banner and the rest of those low-life TB characters were immediately responsible for this blood-bath, and that we can't make anything stick to his ass."

✪✪✪

"Yo, who dis?" asked Ceelow as he picked up the phone near his bed as it woke him from a peaceful sleep.

"What's poppin' today, dog?" asked Spits to Ceelow.

"Ain't nothin', my nigga," answered Ceelow. "Why, what did you have in mind?"

"Whatever's clever, feel me?" responded Spits, stating that he'd finally be down for whatever. Cee and Spits hadn't seen much of each other since the incident, and Spits was finally showing some advancement. "If anything, I'll holla at you a bit later. I got some things to do, and then I'll be checking the spots up in *The Woods*'"

"That's cool, dog," responded Cee. "Just come get me before you do that. I'll be here."

"All right, dog…One!"

"One."

✪✪✪

"Listen, don't forget to take the stairs in the back," shot Essae to Don P. as they exited his Suburban truck. "I'll be waiting with the engine running, ready to get the fuck outta here, so don't bullshit."

"We got it, nigga," snapped El Don, showing his frustration. "How many times you gonna repeat the same shit over and over again?"

"All right, lil' nigga," said Dre. "Hurry the fuck up then."

Don P. entered building number 1648 of a housing project located in the Soundview area of the Bronx with the intention of reaching closure for the sake of Vision. When they were inside of the building, the broken lock on the door let them bypass the intercom system. They walked down a graffiti-filled corridor toward the piss-infested elevators and took one to the sixth floor. Once out of the elevator they made a right, walked down the hall and made a left at the end. When they found the door that they'd been looking for, they revealed two chrome-finished pump-action shotguns. They both pumped a shell into the chamber and got ready to blow. Once Poncho got the signal from El that he was ready, he rang the doorbell and they both waited for the response.

✪✪✪

"It's gonna be okay, Aunt Nes," said Dwight to his aunt as he patted his aunt on the back. "Everything is going to be fine. The police will find those bastards. If not, I will."

"No!" she responded strongly. "I don't want you to end up like him. I don't want them to take you away from me, too. You're all I have left, baby. I don't know what I might do if I lost you, too. You hear me?"

"I hear you, Auntie," responded Dwight, putting his head down on her shoulder. "Don't worry about me."

Nester got up out of her chair and took a deep breath. She took a paper towel from the stack on the table and wiped her face clear of the tears, and then she began wiping Dwight's shirt clear of any moisture. When she felt a little better, she insisted that they go back into the living room to view the pictures. Dwight followed her into the living room and they sat on the couch beside each other. She opened the book and immediately felt her son's presence with the first page shown. She pulled the plastic back and removed a picture of her and her son at his first birthday party. She was holding him in her arms, giving him a huge kiss on the cheek.

"This is a picture from his first birthday," she said, showing it to Dwight proudly. "You weren't even born yet, baby. You see his face? Can't you just tell that he knew how much love I had for him? Every chance I got I let that boy know how much I loved him. I would've done anything for my baby boy."

"I know, Aunt Nes," Dwight said for assurance. "I know."

She turned the page and the pictures basically took them through the entire course of her son's life. From one page to the next, she ran through the good and bad times they'd shared. From tears to laughter, and from pride to shame, that album told the story. From his birthdays, to his graduations, to his senior prom, nothing was left untold. Dwight's intentions were good, but the stories had in fact made him a bit tired. When he let a yawn out, she took it as a sign that she'd had gone on for too long.

"I'm sorry, honey," she said to Dwight. "Was I rambling?"

"Oh, nah," Dwight replied, trying to make her feel comfortable. "I'm enjoying this."

"Let me get you something to drink, baby?"

"Thank you, Aunt Nes."

"I'll be right back, baby." As she got up, she made a right out of the living room toward the kitchen when the doorbell rang.

"I'll get it," hollered Dwight as he stood up to answer the door.

"No, you just go and sit down, baby," said Nester as she turned around toward the front door. "It's probably just some Jehovah's Witnesses. I'll get rid of them and get you that drink."

As Dwight went to take his position back on the couch in the living room, Nester went to answer the doorbell. When she got close enough to the door for her voice to be heard, she yelled, "I'm not interested!" When there was no response, she took a glance out the peephole. *BOOM, BOOM!* Two loud echoing sounds resembling gunshots came from the hall in front of her that shattered the door and left it dangling from the hinges. The two shots fell directly upon the chest of Nester and flung her body six feet before she hit the floor. As she lay there lifelessly, Dwight came running from the living room and dropped himself on the floor beside her. He began crying hysterically as he could not yet figure out what had just happened. All he knew was that his aunt, whom he was just listening to talk about old times, was now lying motionless in his arms with her eyes pointed directly upward. He didn't know what to do. He looked up at the door or what was left of it and got a slight glimpse of two men standing on the other side.

"Yo, come on, mu'fucka!" yelled Poncho to El Don as he motioned toward the stairs. "What the fuck are you waiting for?"

Despite the numerous yells from his brother to get his attention, El couldn't budge from his stance. He took a glance through the huge holes that they had just put in the door and saw a face that was somewhat familiar. He lifted the shotgun back up from his side and cocked it for another shot, just to be thorough. He didn't want to leave any witnesses. Just then, Poncho grabbed him.

"Come on, you crazy mu'fucka! That bitch is dead; let's go!" he said as he pulled him away from the door.

"But, wait..." spat El as Poncho shoved him into the staircase for their getaway. They launched their bodies down the six flights of stairs and out of the back door where Essae and Dre had been impatiently waiting. Before they could even get the car doors completely shut, Essae hit the gas and they were off. They sped from the crime scene and never once looked back.

When the murderers that had just taken his aunt's life vanished, Dwight finally came to the realization that his Aunt Nester was gone. When he regained his composure, he called 9-1-1 and reported the shooting with tears still running down his distraught face. Once he'd calmed down a bit more, he made one more phone call that would serve his despair as a suitable strike back.

✪✪✪

"This investigation had better take a sharp turn in our direction, gentlemen," insisted Assistant Director Chistov. "These types of inconsistencies aren't acceptable behavior for the Federal Bureau of Investigation. Have I made myself perfectly clear?"

"Yes, sir," responded Agent Cassett.

"As God is my witness, sir, we won't rest until every last one of the Time Bomb Family is either behind bars or dead and buried," added Agent Clifton.

When Assistant Director Chistov was satisfied with his clarification, he walked away giving agents Cassett and Clifton room to breathe. When he was gone, they shot each other a concerned look. Things had gone from bad to worse and there wasn't anything that they could possibly do. They shared a sigh and attempted to shrug off the event and hope for the best. With any luck, there would be some kind of development. All they could do was hope for something to fall into their laps. At the exact point in time where they thought they'd exhausted every option, they got the phone call that they'd so eagerly been waiting for.

CHAPTER 13

YEAR — 2000

"Yo, what the fuck took you so long, man?" asked Ceelow, as he walked away from where the Doberman had been patiently awaiting his release from a holding cell in the South Bronx. "I was in here sweating my ass off waiting for you, nigga."

"I deeply apologize," replied William, trying to catch up to him. "But, it isn't the easiest task to get a judge to grant bail when you're charged with murder, Mr. Loew; especially with all of the evidence they have on you. Not to mention my track record with your organization. It's like pulling teeth, Mr. Loew."

"Whatever, nigga," responded Cee. "Anyway, the streets are where I need be, and now all I need to do is find this punk ass mu'fucka that ratted on me."

"I'd highly recommend that you don't do anything while you're out on bail that could jeopardize your trial. As it is almost impossible to build a defense around so much evidence pointing in your direction, I don't think it's constructive for you to start a war in the streets while awaiting a hearing."

"Listen, mu'fucka, you workin' for me," responded Cee, now stopping and pointing to emphasize his position. "Just do what you do, and I'll do what I do, nigga!"

The Doberman, though thoroughly insulted, made no comment. He simply shrugged off Cee's statement and allowed him to continue to dig himself deeper in the hole that he was already in. What was the use? He'd just opt to go on the run and end up like his friend Peter a.k.a. Trigger. *What a shame*, he thought to himself.

Cee exited the criminal courthouse on 161st in the Bronx with one thing in mind: to find the reason that he was there, and to body that mu'fucka. Some poor soul would have to pay dearly for the complications they'd caused, and they had no idea.

Back in the tranquillity of the Bronx Park, Spits had dozed off sitting on that bench waiting for things to liven up. Normally, it would be nothing for Spits to grind all night long until the sun came up, but it wasn't the same anymore. Four years ago seemed like forty, and he didn't have it in him to be that hungry, grimy mu'fucka he used to be. The fact of the matter was he'd grown up too fast and now he was feeling the outcome of all of his hard work at such an early stage in his young adulthood. Spits had endured more ups and downs by the early age of twenty than most would have had if they lived to reach two hundred.

"Excuse me, Mr. Spits?" said a man attempting to wake him up. "Are you awake?"

"Yeah, yeah," Spits uttered, still half asleep. "What you want…dimes? You want twenties? What you want?"

"Are you awake, Mr. Spits?"

"What the fuck you want?" he yelled, now fully awake but a little confused as to where he was before he'd fallen asleep. Then, after regaining his whereabouts, he saw the guy reaching into the inside pocket of his coat, so he tried to get the drop on him. It looked to Spits as though the guy was about to pull a gun on him, so he quickly pulled his first and aimed it dead center of the guy's chest. Looking into his eyes and away from his hand, he hadn't realized that all the man was doing was reaching for the money he needed to purchase a dime bag. When Spits saw the fear in his face, he reevaluated the situation. The guy quickly put his arms in the air, revealing the ten-dollar bill he had in his hand. He suddenly came to his senses and lowered the pistol, laying it on his lap.

"My friend Sonny told me that you had some good shit," the guy said, still frightened from the occurrence. "I was just trying to give you my business."

Spits hastily shrugged off what had happened without an apology and made the sale as promptly as possible, then sent the customer on his way. When he was gone, Spits shook off what happened and told himself once more, "I've gotta get the fuck out of this game, man…soon!"

YEAR — 1998

"Yo, ain't shit like the drug game, son," Spits said to Ceelow as Ceelow sped over the George Washington Bridge in his navy blue BMW 528i. They were on their way to the Mercedes dealership in Paramus, New Jersey to get a birthday gift for Ginger. "I love this kinda shit," he continued. "When you can just bounce and get your wifie a little Benzo for her birthday, that's when you know, kid. I ain't never going back, dog."

"I feel you, son," agreed Ceelow. "That is some hot shit though, for real. Only if I had a broad that I could trick on, and shit. But, it's like, I be meeting mad bitches out there that be worth that kind of shit, but then I be like, 'ain't no bitch worth that kind of shit.' You feel me, son?"

"Honestly, I don't know what the fuck you just said, but whatever, nigga," responded Spits before he started to laugh hysterically. "Whatever-the-fuck-ever," he said, still laughing hysterically.

When they reached the Prestige Mercedes-Benz dealership, the salesman that Spits had used a number of times before immediately recognized him and greeted his entry. Everyone in the dealership much-admired Spits as they knew that when he came through, he would never leave empty-handed. Today, he'd be looking for a brand-new cherry-red SLK 320 fully loaded. When he was satisfied with the interior, exterior and options, he arranged to get the car delivered that evening with a big red bow, to a location that wasn't familiar to Cee when he heard it. That was his other surprise, but it brought the curiosity out of Cee.

"You holdin' out, or something?" Ceelow asked as they left the dealership.

"What you mean, son?" responded Spits as if unaware.

"I mean that address you gave them, son. Don't act like you don't know. What, you got a new crib, too?"

"I don't know what the fuck you talking about, dog," he said, sticking to his original story.

It didn't take long, but Spits finally admitted to Cee that he'd bought a new house for himself and Ginger to live in together. It was supposed to be a secret until Ginger found out but now Cee and Spits were the only ones that knew. It was something that he'd previously said that he wouldn't do, but they'd grown so much closer to each other. He felt like it was the right time.

Planned for later that night, Spits had organized a block-party for his and Ginger's family and friends—which basically meant everybody. Ginger and Spits were definitely a well-known couple in their community. The love that they showed everybody was most appreciated and returned ten times over. Even though all of the girls were jealous of Ginger, and all the guys were afraid of Spits, they got an unmeasured amount of admiration from the hood.

They did it up on the Block better than anybody else could've ever thought to do it. It was truly inspirational. They had barbecue grills set up along 224th Street, with professional cooks controlling the flames under barbecue spare ribs and chicken, T-bone steaks, hot dogs and burgers. The speakers were set up on the roof of 666 so that the music could be heard for blocks, while DJ Supremacy handled the wheels of steel. The streets were barricaded so that they could set up tables and to give the kids room to play in the street. They had garbage containers filled with ice to keep bottles of beer, soda and champagne cool. Balloons decorated the building walls, and banners reading "Happy Birthday, Ginger" were hung in key locations to make everyone aware of the special occasion.

The little girls were playing Double Dutch, while the little boys bothered them. The ladies were all gathered around in groups to gossip and talk about each other, while the guys drank beers and played dice in the courtyard of the building. When the music stopped, everyone's attention was centered on the street. When a white stretch limousine turned the corner, it was obvious that Spits and Ginger were about to make their grand entrance. The limo trickled down the block slowly while everyone watched on in anticipation.

"What would she be wearing?" the ladies asked themselves.

This nigga is doin' it, the fellas thought to themselves.

When the pearly-white stretch Mercedes-Benz reached the front of 666, it came to a halt. The DJ put the needle to the wax and all that could be heard at first was the static at the beginning of the record. By the time Jigga's voice came on, everybody knew exactly what song it was.

"Yo, take the bass-line out...

Spits stepped out of the limo first, dressed extremely low-key sporting only a crispy white T-shirt, a blue pair of Iceberg jeans, white on white Nike Uptowns and a Yankees fitted cap.

"...All right, now let it bump."

Ginger stepped out, surprisingly also dressed casual, wearing a fitted Yankees T-shirt and a denim Iceberg skirt, with her hair in braids. When the song dropped, everyone sang along.

"It's a hard knock life for us...It's a hard knock life for us...Instead of treated, we get tricked...Instead of kisses, we get kicked...It's a hard knock life!"

Everybody started going crazy all at once. The entire block felt the energy that Spits and Ginger generated when they arrived, blowing up the spot as usual. Everybody was having the time of their lives, and it was greatly appreciated and well-deserved, just as expected from an event that Spits had planned.

This is the kind of thing that should be organized at least once every summer for everybody to unwind and have fun, just to escape the daily grind and give back to the community. Besides this block party, Spits and the rest of the Time Bombs had regularly funded bus rides to Six Flags Great Adventure, Dorney Park, various ski resorts and shopping outlets such as in Reading, Pennsylvania and Woodbury Common. As much enjoyment as they took from providing so many opportunities for the youth in their community to experience things they didn't have a chance to experience, the positive was almost always met with an equal amount of negativity. With their popularity growing in the hood, the hate for their organization was growing just as much, if not more. They had no idea, but the Federal Bureau of Investigation—among others—had been making an attempt at building an extremely error-proof case against TB for some time now. And now, with their most recent merriment, the fire that grew so deep into the Bureau was only fueled.

If Spits would've only paid a little bit more attention to the company that he kept, fed, and entertained at the block party, he would've come across a few of the Bureau's best. From the train tracks on White Plains Road, they took pictures of the whole entire event. From the street, they could actually co-mingle with the hoods that secretly controlled the inner-workings of the TB organization. That day was a very structural day for the FBI. With the background they'd obtained on their own, plus the assistance they'd gotten from haters and snitches alike, they'd really been making some headway. The only thing now was to catch some of the organization heads dirty, so they still had their work cut out for them.

After partying all night on the Block, Spits had gotten too exhausted to even remember that the night's events weren't completely done. Now that it was well after midnight and Ginger's birthday had officially begun, it was time for him to give her the presents that were waiting for her in Marlboro, New Jersey, where their new house stood. Although it had slipped Spits' mind where they were supposed to end up at the end of that night, it's a good thing the limousine driver didn't forget. Spits had it worked out with him from earlier in the day what they were going to do and where they would end up, but the "*Donnie P.*" had his mind twisted. When they entered the vehicle, the driver took it upon himself to deliver them to their final destination. With the both of them asleep in the rear of the limo, Spits didn't wake until they were already merging onto the Garden State Parkway from the NJ Turnpike. From the Parkway they would hit Route 9, then Route 18 to get to Route 79 towards the Matawan/ Marlboro exit. Spits grew more and more excited with every corner that was turned. Every stop sign made the anticipation grow deeper and deeper into his gut.

"What's she gonna think?" he asked himself. "I hope she likes it."

When Spits saw the limo pulling into the driveway of the two-story detached, contemporary, Colonial split-foyer home with five bedrooms, three-and-a-half baths and covering approximately 4,100 square feet, his dick almost grew rock hard.

As the limo-driver put the car in park and got out to open the door for them, Spits repositioned Ginger's face for a kiss. He tapped her lips with his own, and fixed her hair behind her ear. When she seemed to be waking up, he whispered to her, "Wake up, Gin. We're home, Mommy."

Ginger opened her eyes, squinting to adjust her vision to the dome light as the driver opened the door on her side. When she looked up, Spits grinned and said, "Come on, baby," as he smiled back.

They got out of the limo and the look on Ginger's face was worth ten times the $3.2 million Spits had dropped down on the house. After rubbing her eyes to get a better look at the surroundings that she wasn't at all used to calling "Home," a look of bewilderment fell over her pretty facial features. Then, a burst of energy seemed to flow through her body, as her eyes grew intensely larger and larger while her jaw dropped. She looked at Spits and then back at the house. After her body started to tremble a little, she grabbed on to Spits and let out a joyous holler while she held on to him for dear life. When their embrace came to an end, he opened the door to their new palace and simply said, "Welcome home, baby."

The doors opened up to a spacious foyer that led down two steps into the sunken living room simply decorated with a gray throw-rug with black and white designs, two plush black leather sofas facing each other and a few small white statues. The windows adjacent to the entrance almost completely covered the whole entire wall except for a pillar in the center, which contained the fireplace, and mirrors covered the walls on the side. The wood floors were made of a freshly polished oak, and the high ceilings had retractable windows. To the right of the entrance were stairs that led to the second floor, but just beyond that was the family room. Also decorated very lightly, it merely contained one long sectional couch positioned in front of a big-screen television. On the left of the main entrance was what used to be the dining room, now transformed into a game room with a pool table and a dart board. It was furnished with a small white leather sofa, barstools that were set up along the wall, and a white carpet covered the space. Just on the right side of the game room was the kitchen. In the master bedroom upstairs was a private bathroom decorated in white and black with a standing shower made completely of marble, an old-fashioned bath tub, and twin sinks with vanity mirrors. Beneath a king-sized bed covered with white silk sheets, a pure white carpet sheltered the floors. From the master bedroom, there was a terrace overlooking the pool and the patio.

By the time they got to this room in the house, the master bedroom, Ginger had no energy left to do anything but fall into the bed and wrap her body in the silk sheets. Spits began rubbing her neck, back and feet until she slipped away to dream land. When she was asleep, Spits slowly undressed her and got in the bed next to her. He lay naked next to her and wrapped his arms around her.

In the morning, she'd wake up bright and early from the tickle of his tongue on her clit. All night, Spits controlled his arousal, only poking her playfully in her back with a fully enlarged penis. When he couldn't take it anymore, he went underneath the covers and decided to wake her up the best way he knew how.

After making love for about an hour late into the morning, Spits left Ginger spread out in the bed to go downstairs to make breakfast in their new kitchen. He let Ginger rest herself until he was done cooking for them both: some scrambled eggs with cheese, sausage, toast and fresh slices of watermelon and pineapple. When they were done with their breakfast, Spits prepared Ginger's final surprise.

"Oh, shit!" he said, as if something had slipped his mind.

"What's wrong?" asked Ginger, now worrying what must've been disturbing Spits.

"Fuck!" he said, sustaining his frustration. "I didn't even fuckin' realize that the mu'fuckin' limousine driver was only supposed to wait for us until noon." He paused to take a glance at his wristwatch. "It's damn near three o'clock, and shit."

"Well, what are we going to do?" Ginger asked, now sharing his frustration.

"Awe, fuck it," Spits responded as a small grin peeked from his facial expression. "I fought it for as long as I could, but I guess you gonna *have* to drive now."

He placed the keys to her brand-new Mercedes-Benz SLK drop-top coupe on the kitchen table, and glanced up at her to catch her reaction. When she looked at the keys, she looked at Spits and began to smile endearingly. Her eyes filled with tears, and they began to run slowly down her cheek. She lifted the keys from the table and held them close to her heart with one hand. With the other, she gave a tug at Spits' T-shirt to pull him in close enough for a kiss. Ginger gave Spits a long passion-filled kiss with tears still running down her face. They hugged after that, and then Spits escorted Ginger to their three-car garage where her new car had been waiting the whole night with a big red bow tied around it that simply said, "Happy Birthday, Mommy."

She absolutely loved it. It was perfect.

CHAPTER 14

"Yo, what up, my nigga?" yelled Spits to a kid standing on the corner of 216th and Bronxwood Avenue.

"Ain't nuttin', King," responded "Pookie," one of the many loyal workers for the Time Bomb Family. "King" was a name that Spits was sometimes called by the younger generation of the TB Family as they referred to him as the "Kingpin."

Now Pookie was dark-skinned and had a frail frame. He stood about 5 ft. 11 in., and only weighed about 140 lbs. The only reason he was even considered to be put down was because the kid Little Jay had vouched for him. Little Jay was his older cousin, and he'd guaranteed that Pookie would be a loyal soldier. When he'd finally convinced Spits and Cee about his cousin, they let him work a spot that Little Jay ran for them. This way Pookie would be Jay's responsibility—one way or another—if something went down. It had only been about a month and a half now since he'd started, and he'd already expressed his dedication to the Family on numerous occasions.

"So, what's up? How's this shit moving out here?" asked Spits.

"Oh, it's been kind of slow since the morning rush, but it's moving though," answered Pookie. "It shouldn't be long before it pick back up."

"Oh, i-ight, that's cool. Where that paper at?" asked Spits as he shot him a smile and a wink.

Pookie paused for a split second as he was unsure of Spits' intentions for this uncommon visit, and then he went for the stash where he kept the money that was made before it was enough to make a drop. He walked down a small alley that separated a building and a private house until he reached the area of the alley that was kept for garbage. He tilted an old broken refrigerator to the side and reached underneath it until his search was satisfied. He grabbed the brown paper bag which held a few knots of ones, fives, tens, and twenties that totaled about $1,700. Pookie made his way to the curb where Spits patiently waited in his black S500 Mercedes while scanning the block for police. When he was standing beside the car he stuck his hand in the window and dropped the paper bag in Spits' lap. Spits took a peek inside the bag and when he was content with his findings, he looked back up at Pookie, who was standing there still a little baffled.

"So…" he began. "What's the occasion, King?" he asked, once his interest was piqued.

"Wha?" Spits snapped as he shot him a hostile look.

"I mean…" he stuttered. "I was just about to drop that off in another minute. I hope I didn't do nothing wrong."

"Don't fucking worry about that, nigga," answered Spits. "That's nothing for you to concern yourself with. Just tell Little Jay that when he's doing the count that he'll come up this much short and have him confirm that with me. You understand me, nigga?"

"Umm…" Pookie stuttered. "I'll let him know."

As the words were still fresh out of his mouth, he noticed that Spits' passenger wasn't familiar to him. According to Spits, they were only to do business around Family, and he had no idea who this dude was. He also wondered what had Spits on the jumpy side, when he was usually the calmest and most collected and relaxed nigga you could ever meet. When his mind told him to satisfy his curiosity by subtly attempting to introduce himself, he quickly and respectfully reconsidered. With Spits already in a "Fuck You" mind state, this would definitely push him to make a scene and possibly embarrass his ass right there in the middle of the street. With all of this going through the inexperienced and very unevolved mind of this youngster, he hadn't even realized that Spits, along with his mystery passenger, had blown from the spot already…oh well!

After a few blocks, Spits could no longer conceal his obvious uneasiness.

He took a glance at his passenger seat, and after a roll of his eyes, his top lip lifted on one side and he spat, "So what the fuck was you thinkin', nigga?" He paused for a second, seeming to have released his frustration, and then he yelled, "How much fuckin' trouble we went through?! All the fuckin' work we put in, you gonna fuckin' do some dumb shit like this! I can't fuckin' believe that you thought anything was important enough to jeopardize this thing of ours. What the fuck was that important to you…huh, Trig?!"

He had nothing to say to rebut Spits' comments. He'd practically shown up from out of the clear blue sky at Spits' old apartment building. Purely coincidently, an unsuspecting Spits just happened to be passing through his old neighborhood when he'd spotted what looked like his man Trigger in the courtyard of his old building. After a second thought, Spits shrugged off the occurrence, thinking that it couldn't possibly be true, even though something inside of him wished that it was. When he stopped at a streetlight at the end of the block, his wish would come true. Trigger came up on the car from the passenger side and excitedly banged on the car window to get Spits' attention. Although Trigger seemed happy to see him, Spits was completely displeased. He couldn't believe it. Before Trig could spit a word, Spits hurried him into the car and drove off nervously looking in his rearview mirror to see if they were being followed. Once in the car, Trigger attempted a long-time-no-see greeting, but was quickly detached from that mind state after noticing Spits' manner. The objective for Spits hadn't been the warm welcome that Trigger had anticipated, but to zigzag through the blocks to make certain they didn't have someone tailing them.

What made the situation even worse was that in the trunk of Spits' car, he had two kilos of cocaine he'd just picked up from a new connection. He was on his way to drop it off at his man Dave's apartment over on Tillitson Avenue and Boston Road where he could cook, cut and bag it up. With this surprise visit, he was faced with a dilemma. He had to either first make sure Trigger was on a plane back to California or risk making the drop. He couldn't trust any one of his workers with this package because of the intended secrecy of the situation. He didn't want it getting back to anyone from the Ortiz family that he may have been pondering a new connection.

That's when he decided that they would need to have some extra money available regardless of where this took them. And Spits only chose that particular spot because he knew that there wouldn't be anyone there to recognize Trigger. After they left the Block, Spits began rambling to himself as he tried to figure the best solution to this problem.

"I have to think," said Spits as he fumbled on his thoughts. "This shit is not happening. Nigga, you couldn't have picked a worse time to just show up like this."

"I had to, Spits," mumbled Trigger, finally responding to Spits' comments. "I just had to. It wasn't supposed to be like this though, son."

"Then how was it supposed to be then, nigga?" asked Spits. "This situation is fucked up; no matter how you put it."

"I couldn't even bring myself to try and have this conversation over the phone, as if that would've been any better anyway. I had to come out here so that it would be right."

"What the fuck is you talking about, nigga?" Spits curiously asked as he pulled over by a bus stop to give Trigger his full attention.

"I'm talking about..." Trigger began, unable to complete his sentence.

"What, nigga?!" Spits yelled impatiently. "What?!"

"I came here to tell you that..." Trigger continued before Spits cut him off.

"Aw fuck!" uttered Spits.

"What happened?" asked Trigger, still uncertain if he should continue.

✪✪✪

"Hey, Les," said Officer Albert Hargrove to his partner Lester Moore. "Are you ready or what, man? What's taking that greasy crap so long? We're going to be late again; now let's go."

"Aw come on, Al," responded Officer Moore. "Don't be so paranoid. And please, I don't need another health lecture. Spare me. We'll make it to roll on time, trust me."

"Trust you, huh?" asked Al sarcastically. "That's what you said the last time."

"Well, what would you like for me to do, starve?" asked Lester.

"No, I'd like you to be ready every morning with enough time to get breakfast," answered Albert.

"Well, I guess I wouldn't have to worry about that if I had a nice wife like yours that could cook me breakfast every morning, huh?"

"Well, I didn't say that," said Al. "But when are you going to get out there and find yourself a woman and settle down again? You aren't getting any younger, you know? You're only getting older and uglier."

"Oh, yeah? Why don't you settle down on this?" said Lester as he gave him the finger.

Officers Moore and Hargrove were two of NYPD's finest. This year made the ninth year they'd shared each other's company on the streets of New York, and they both hadn't expected to still be in such an undeveloped position this far along into their careers. Lester Moore came from a long line of successful and well-known police officers, and often felt the pressure of following in the footsteps of his father, his father's father, his brothers, uncles and so on. He was now forty-eight years old and already had fifteen years of the police force under his belt. In his earlier years of crime-fighting he'd possessed the fire in his eyes that could take a young police officer to heights such as detective, lieutenant and beyond. In fact, his relentless dedication to his profession would lead to his wife leaving him for another man. Ironically, this occurrence soon led to him losing that fire, and his career had been in a slump ever since. Lester stood about 6 ft. 2 in., with pale white skin. What hair he had left on his head had begun turning dusty gray, and he'd developed a healthy gut since his career as a cop had taken a turn for the worse.

Officer Albert Hargrove, on the other hand, was the younger, happier, and more focused version of Lester. He had a wife and two young sons at home that he loved with all of his heart. The only difference between him and Lester, at that age, was that he took every opportunity to show his undying love for his family. They understood that when he went to work, it was because he had to provide for them. Al stood about 5 ft. 10 in. tall and had a dark brown complexion. He was thirty-three years old and had become Lester's partner after only two years on the job. Although Albert was black and Lester was white, and they had completely different upbringings, it seemed as though their superiors had seen the connection in them and thought they could learn from each other.

Al and Les were currently two of the most dissimilar officers partnered together in the whole 47th Precinct but they'd once shared the same goals. They both had a passion for the law, and honestly got into the business of law enforcement to clean up the very neighborhoods in which they spent their childhoods.

"Look at that," said Lester as a black Mercedes passed through an intersection where they were stopped for a red light.

"What, the Mercedes?" Al asked. "It's sweet, huh?"

"Yeah, it's sweet," Lester responded. "Too sweet."

"Aw, come on, Les," said Al. He could see where the conversation was headed. "Could we please just go to the damn PD, and maybe show up on time for a change?"

"Doesn't that get to you?" asked Lester, expressing his frustration. "That motherfucker has got to be no older than eighteen, and he's driving a hundred and twenty thousand dollar luxury car. That doesn't shift you around in your seat just a bit?"

"Actually, no it doesn't," Al simply replied. "That kid was probably born into money, man. Just because his parents are probably loaded, it's not his fault."

"Born into money?" repeated Lester. "That's gotta be the most gullible shit I've ever heard. Wake up, Al, these guys have got to be into something illegal. Look at them."

"You know, you can't judge a book by its cover," said Al, showing his disappointment at Lester's comment.

"Call it what you want," countered Lester. "But if this was a book, it would be a crime story. This is the kind of shit that destroys our neighborhoods from the inside out. People see these scumbags and think that pimps and drug dealers lead a more fruitful life. And look, they think they can just park anywhere they want with no regard for those good honest people waiting over there for the bus to take them to work. Somebody's got to put these kinds of people in their rightful place."

"Oh, here we go again," Al mumbled.

✪✪✪

"I swear, everything always gets all fucked up all at the same fucking time," Spits cried. "First, you show up out of nowhere at the worst fucking time possible, and now this shit."

"Oh, shit!" Trigger hollered as he saw the police lights go on behind them.

"Yo, just be cool," Spits suggested. "I'm dirty right now."

"What?" asked Trigger.

"I'm dirty, nigga!" responded Spits. "I got a gat under the seat and two bricks in the trunk. Don't say shit. Just let me handle it."

"What the fuck you doing with two kilos of—?" asked Trigger before Spits cut him off.

"Shhh!" Spits said with a finger on his lips. "Just hold me down, nigga. I got this."

Just as Spits had the words out of his mouth, one of the police officers was in the street on his side of the car about to knock on the window. When Spits rolled down the window, he attempted to talk his way out of the situation while the other police officer came up on Trigger's side, shining a flashlight into his face and around the car.

"What seems to be the problem, sir?" asked Spits with the utmost respect. "Did I do some—?"

"Just shut up, okay, boy?" spat Lester as he glanced around the interior of the vehicle with his own flashlight.

The comment seemed to throw Spits out of his frame of mind. He completely lost focus and momentarily held a confused look on his face until he heard, "Who the fuck you callin' 'boy,' mu'fucka?" Trigger argued as he stared up at Lester, and then up at Albert, as if he should also be offended by the statement just made by his partner.

"Listen, youngster," began Lester, pointing his comments toward Spits as if giving him the opportunity to calm Trigger down. "Let's not have this get out of hand now. Tell this asshole to shut the fuck up or you'll both be headed through the system tonight. How would you all like that?" He paused for a bit to establish control of the situation. When Spits motioned for Trigger to relax, he continued. "All right now, hand over your license and registration and maybe you two can go home tonight."

When they both went back to their police car to review the documents they'd just obtained, Spits took a deep breath. He'd hoped that they would just concentrate on him and not Trigger, although Trigger wasn't making that easy for them to do. If they were to run Trigger's government name through the system they would find cause for searching them both and the vehicle, and then they would be fucked for real. "What the fuck is wrong with you?" asked Spits of Trigger. "I tell you I got a burner and two kees in the car with us and you jump out the window with this rah-rah with these pigs. Dog, this ain't no who got the biggest dick contest. Fuck that black and white shit. This shit is about green, nigga."

"You right," Trigger simply said, realizing that what he had said was wrong given their situation. "I wasn't thinking. My bad, son. You know I'm not even the type to come out of character, but I have a lot on my mind right now."

"Yeah, you're bad," Spits said. "Now if these bitch-ass niggas decide they feel like fucking with us, it's a wrap."

"What do you think?" Lester asked Al as they sat in their car behind Spits and Trigger.

"Don't even ask me what I think, Les," Al responded. "I didn't even want to waste our time in the first place."

"Did you see how that fucker reacted when I called his friend 'boy'?" asked Lester. "You know I don't talk like that; I just wanted to see how they would respond."

"Yeah, I gotcha,"Al said, still a little skeptical of his excuse.

"Maybe they are just some spoiled little brats like you said, huh?"

"Yeah, maybe."

"Let's say they're drug dealers. They wouldn't be stupid enough to fuck with us, right?" he asked, still trying to figure out what they should do.

"I would imagine not, Les," Al responded, still unenthused. "Would you mind if we got to the damn department now?"

Lester and Albert came to an agreement and evidently had nothing to hold Trigger and Spits on, so they let them go. When Spits pulled away from the curb with his freedom still intact, he didn't care about what Trigger had to tell him; not even a little bit. The next stop would be LaGuardia

Airport where Trigger would be on the next flight to California. Then after that, he would take his package to its destination.

As for Lester and Albert, the rest of their day would not be as satisfying. When they finally got to the police department, they had some guests that were not at all pleased with their delayed arrival. They were immediately escorted to their superior's office, Lieutenant Howard Fitzgerald, to discuss what they'd missed while they were busy with what had kept them from a critical visit from the FBI.

"We went over some very important details with these fellows from the Bureau this morning regarding a crime family that is known in the streets as the Time Bombs," said Lieutenant Fitzgerald as he sat across from Officers Moore and Hargrove. "It seems as though the numerous advances made on the part of the FBI in pursuing this criminal enterprise have fallen short of victorious. Now, they've collected a huge amount of evidence, including a living eyewitness who's willing to testify against them once they can put together another indictment. One of their members in particular who goes by the name umm…Trigger, was actually on trial a while back but jumped bail once it was discovered that they had the trial's judge on the payroll. As for Michael Banner, a.k.a. Spits, we just can't seem to make anything stick to him; he never seems to get his hands dirty."

"Excuse me, sir," interrupted Officer Moore. "Are these Time Bomb characters really that much of a situation? I've vaguely heard things about them but never enough to create this much attention."

"I'm sorry, Officer…Moore, is it?" asked Special Agent Simon Clifton. "These guys aren't to be underestimated, not one bit. If we were exaggerating the situation, then we would only be sending the message that we aren't capable of handling our own affairs, and that's not the case."

"He's right, Moore," added Special Agent Phillip Cassett. "Now, we're asking for the assistance of the NYPD. There's already an outstanding warrant for the arrest and seizure of Trigger, a.k.a. Peter Beckford. All we ask is that if you guys ever make a routine stop or find out something that we could use, make sure that we're informed immediately. At this point, we can't risk anything. This is a chart outlining the names of all the known members of the Time Bombs in order of importance with corresponding photographs. If ever you come across any of these characters, it is imperative that you treat them with extreme caution and leave no stone unturned. Do you understand?"

Both Albert and Lester nodded in agreement and began scanning the outline for future reference, but before they even completed the first line on the chart they couldn't help but to stare at two of the pictures right up at the top. Al and Les could do nothing but look at the pictures on the chart that belonged to none other than the infamous Michael "Spits" Banner and Peter "Trigger" Beckford with their jaws dropped halfway to the floor. What if…?

✪✪✪

"On the real, you gotta give me your word that you won't try no shit like this again, man," requested Spits of Trigger. "You almost gave me a heart attack, dog."

"All right, my nigga," Trigger agreed reluctantly. "My bad, son. I guess I just got a little homesick."

Trigger didn't want to say those words, but he was left with no choice. If it would ever be possible for Spits to trust him again, he'd have to agree to the terms of the situation and abide by the rules that were set in place. With the Family's best interests in mind, Trigger got on the next flight out of New York to California without even a mention of the news he thought was important enough to risk his freedom for. Spits was too nervous about another interaction with the police to carry on any kind of conversation. He finally relaxed a little more when once they were in the airport and the ticket was purchased. He ultimately told Trigger that under different circumstances, his visit would be welcomed with open arms, but also stressed how careful they would still have to be. Truthfully, Spits couldn't be happier to see his lifelong friend, but they had to take care of business before pleasure. It took all of Trigger's strength to get on that plane without telling his best friend of so many years what had happened in California between him and Spits' sister Rachel.

CHAPTER 15

YEAR — 2000

"Damn, what the fuck am I gonna do?" asked Ceelow to himself. "It's like all of our dreams are turning into nightmares."

Ceelow, after spending a week in jail with little communication with the outside world, felt at a disadvantage. His best bet would be going home from this experience to get his mind together. He hadn't yet put two and two together and he greatly needed to figure out his next move. Ceelow wasn't the type to sit around and figure things out; he was the type to buss his gun and figure it out later.

Ever since he'd caught that first body back in the park that night, he hadn't once hesitated when it came down to it. He took the position that was set for him to the heart. He was to secure every member of the Time Bomb Family; even if it meant that he had to take a loss. Whatever was necessary to provide a sense of security for his partners was all that had ever mattered to him. But lately he'd felt more on the defenseless side. So many tragic things had happened to the niggas he called "his family" that he couldn't prevent from happening. That gave him an empty feeling inside and he didn't know what to do about it.

Now, alone in his apartment on the fourth floor of 666 East 224th Street, he could be left to his thoughts. After a quick shower and a change of clothes, he spent the better half of this early morning on the fire escape that faced the back of the building. There he could watch the sun come up.

Ceelow was rarely without a drink so he sipped on a beer while he lit up a breakfast blunt to get his head on right. He smoked and smoked and smoked…until his thoughts came together like a puzzle. He still hadn't figured out who it was that had snitched on him, but his frustration made him blame the most obvious cause of all of his problems.

When he climbed back in his window, he stood there and stared at his bedroom. He stared at the walls that he had painted in his favorite color: royal blue. He looked at the floors where he kept carpet that covered the entire apartment spotless. He looked at his huge king-sized bed, made entirely of mahogany wood, where he laid his head every night. He looked at the wall opposite the bed where his 36-inch television sat on its stand, with numerous video games and DVD movies decorating the floor. He looked at his closet door which was half-open to display his large wardrobe. On all of these material items is where he placed the blame for his nightmares. For every bad thing that happened to him, he took it all out on his prized possessions. He let out a sudden roar of anger and lunged at his dresser where, with one punch, he completely shattered the mirror that was positioned on top of it. He snatched out every dresser drawer, emptying their contents on the floor. He lifted his mattress off of the frame and pushed it up against the wall next to it, sending the hanging picture frames flying. He then pushed himself to lift the television from its location before he threw it halfway across the room onto the floor. The screen exploded and the sound brought him back down to earth. He sat on the floor with his back up against the wall and put his head in his hands. Through his fingers, he saw a picture on the floor. It was of him, Trigger, Pop, and Spits that they took when Pop first got his own apartment. They'd popped bottles and sprayed each other with champagne to celebrate that occasion. It was a big step for them. They must've toasted to "Moe's, hoes and zeros" a thousand times that night and it was just the four of them. In fact, whenever it came down to it, it was always just the four of them. They always had each other's back one hundred percent. When he decided to call the only person left from this picture, he got Spits' voicemail. He left him a brief message, and then called El Don.

"Yo, what up, Cee?" asked El Don as he answered his cell phone. "Where the fuck you been at, nigga? You heard about all the shit that happened out here on these streets?"

"Nah, dog," Ceelow responded with a dead voice.

"This shit is for real out here, man," continued El, trying to sound like there was nothing wrong. "Niggas is getting popped left and right."

"Yo..." began Cee. "You ever just stab a nigga in the neck and watch him bleed to death?"

"Wha?" responded El, completely confused.

"You ever just poke a hole in a nigga's throat while he's asleep, and just sit there and watch him? Then when the nigga start coughin' up his heart, just ask the nigga if he's all right?"

"Yo, what the fuck you talkin' about, man?" El asked, still trying to understand Cee's line of questioning.

"I had to body some nigga on the Island the other day, just cause," he said.

"Just cause what, nigga?" El asked. "What the fuck were you doin' on Riker's Island? When did you get out?"

"The nigga tried to play me, son..." Cee simply stated. "He tried to play me! I just got out this morning. I'll probably spend the rest of my life in jail for the shit they got me for. Ain't no hope for me, dog; not if I don't find this nigga that snitched on me."

"The nigga that snitched on you," El said sarcastically. "Yo, son, just come through the crib so we can build about this shit. I don't want to have this conversation over the phone. I'm with Poncho. We got you, my nigga."

"All right then," responded Ceelow. "One."

"Yeah," El said. "One."

YEAR — 1999

Finally, the year was 1999. It was only August, and the streets had already heard about the Time Bombs' plans for the New Year's bash that would end the nineties and shoot every super-thug nigga in attendance straight into the New Millennium. Talks of expenses flooded the avenues of the Bronx as everyone asked themselves, "How much money would be spent on this shindig?" Some thought hundreds of thousands; others thought in the millions. With rumors in circulation that range from there being enough Cristal for every guest to have up to five bottles, to a performance by none other than the king of pop, Michael Jackson, everyone had their own predeterminations.

From the beginning, Spits just knew that this year would be their best ever. With money coming in from every direction, the Time Bombs as a unit had accumulated tens of millions of dollars. Besides the delivery service they'd started, they were represented on street corners all over the South and North Bronx. They had three apartments and a small house that they used for drugstores where they cooked, cut, and bagged up work. Everything was going greatly and Spits thought it could only get better, until...

"What you mean you goin' away for New Year's?" asked Spits as he screamed into the phone at Ginger.

"What do you want me to do, tell my mother that I can't go?" answered Ginger. "I don't see her enough as it is, Daddy. All she asked was that we spend New Year's together, with my family in Orlando. I have to, Honey. Things haven't been the same since we moved in together and you know how close we used to be. Please, don't make me feel like I have to choose between the two of you."

"Yeah, I know," admitted Spits. "But damn, New Year's? You will be here for Christmas though, right?"

"Yes, Daddy," Ginger responded as she grinned. "I promise I'll be here for Christmas with you."

"Damn," began Spits. "We got the hottest shit planned for this New Year's party, too!"

"Don't worry," said Ginger. "You won't even realize I'm gone."

"Yeah right," Spits said with a giggle and then a sigh. "Anyway, that means that we have to go all out for Christmas. What's up with Hawaii, or maybe the Virgin Islands?"

"You're crazy!" Ginger said.

"What?" asked Spits. "What's wrong with that?"

"Do you know how long the flight takes to get to Hawaii?" Ginger asked.

"Aw, here we go again," Spits said.

"I had to beg my mother to rent a car just to drive to Florida," stated Ginger. "I don't know if I could go twelve hours on a plane, Daddy."

"Aw, come on, Gin," responded Spits. "You're gonna be with me. Now, would I ever let anything happen to you?"

"Yeah, yeah..." responded Ginger, recognizing the premise of this conversation. "I know you won't let anything happen to me, but..."

"But what?" asked Spits cutting her off. "You can't say no."

"I'm not saying no...well, not yet anyway," answered Ginger. "But, I can't just say yes right now, either."

"Okay, Gin," said Spits, giving up hope. "I hear ya talkin'. I'd rather not talk about this now anyway. We're supposed to be celebrating. Now, hurry up and get ready.. I'll be home to pick you up in about an hour and a half. I won't be long. I just have to go past the Block first; then I'll be right over."

"Okay, baby," said Ginger. "I'll see you then."

Today was Spits and Ginger's five-year anniversary and Spits had the perfect evening planned. Ginger didn't know exactly how much work he'd put into it, but he'd made sure to tell her to dress her best or as he put it, "I'll look better than you." Spits had never once thought that he could ever find someone as perfect as Gin and as often as he could, he let her know how he felt. Now, five years had passed like nothing and it was time to remind her how he felt.

For Ginger it was the same thing. When it came time for her to give Spits his gift, she surprised him by showing up on the block to pick him up and treat him to a weekend in Atlantic City. They always had the best of times together and when Spits saw how much work Ginger had put in for him, he knew that when his turn came, it would have to be big.

When Spits reached the Block, he parked his car by a fire hydrant. As he hung up the phone with Ginger, he took a peek at his rearview mirror and saw Pop's mother coming down the block with a shopping cart full of groceries. It made him think of Pop. Seeing her always made everything that he'd felt and forgotten since Pop's death come back. That whole entire situation could have never reached closure in Spits' mind, as there was no way to avenge his killers. The only thing that could be done was to try and do for his family what Pop would have, if he were still there. Spits only wished that Pop's mother saw it the same way. She'd never liked Spits or any of Pop's childhood friends, and when they'd tried to reach out to her after his death, she couldn't bring herself to accept their help. She hated them even more now, as they'd taken the blame for what happened to her only son. Spits wouldn't ever be able to close that chapter in his book.

After a deep breath, he came back to reality and saw Cee pull up in his navy blue Beemer. Ceelow saw Spits and jumped out so that they could exchange a pound and a hug. "What up, my nigga?" Ceelow asked. "What's the occasion, dog? You lookin' all snazzy and shit. Ha-ha," he said, commenting on Spits' attire.

"Oh, you know," began Spits. "We're doing the anniversary thing tonight. I was just buggin' out about this nigga Pop again. When I saw Mrs. Black, I had to hold myself back from approaching her, you know?"

"Oh please," Cee responded. "Now you know that old lady got no love for us. All she goin' do is start that 'you're the devil' shit, and about how we need Jesus and if we don't start going to church and shit, we goin' to hell? I told you a long time ago, that shit is a lost cause."

"I know, but for Pop..."

"Yeah, I feel you," Cee said, understanding what Spits was going to say before he even said it. "But mu'fuckas is only gonna let you do but so much. You can't do for another mu'fucka what that mu'fucka won't do for they own self, feel me?"

"Uh-huh." Spits wasn't really capable of probing as to what the fuck Ceelow was talking about. "But anyway, what's been poppin' over here, son?"

"Same shit, same shit," responded Cee. "Ain't nothin' ever poppin' over here, son."

"Oh, okay," said Spits. "I just wanted to check up on..."

"Oh shit!" Ceelow exclaimed as his attention was shifted. It seemed as though an altercation was developing amongst some younger niggas across the street in front of 666. It looked like it was about to go down between these niggas Jacob and Winston.

Jacob was some little half-ass aspiring "pack-holder" nigga. Every once in a while Ceelow, or somebody like that, would give him a little something to make a run or to hold a gat when it was hot, and that made him think he was a hustler. Jacob was basically one of those niggas that would just sit there and stare at the older niggas getting money like that's all he ever wanted to do. It didn't help anything that they used to send him on runs when there was an emergency, but fuck it. When he reached the appropriate age and had some smarts with him, they could put him on, but for now he ran errands.

Winston was another one. He was young—not as young as Jacob—but he had some maturity about his character. He also had a little bad-boy image that he'd brought with him from Jamaica where he'd grown up. He'd come to New York to stay with family members when things had gotten out of hand in Kingston. Coming from a place like Kingston, Jamaica, where there was basically an ongoing war in the streets, would make any nigga think he was hard. He had a small clientele of weed-smokers that he dealt with to get his little money for sneakers and school clothes and shit; nothing major. When niggas were too lazy to walk or drive to get better product, he was always there with his nickels and dimes for sale. He wasn't a threat to the Block unless he started making shit hot, and as long as that didn't happen, he could continue to sell his weed without a problem.

Things started to get heated when Winston insisted that Jacob pay him the money he owed from the previous night when he'd "borrowed" a couple of dimes to smoke with his friends. Jacob told him that he'd get his money the next day, and when Winston came out, that was the first thing on his mind. He approached Jacob about the money he was owed, but he wasn't used to civilized mannerisms so that may have thrown Jacob; like Winston was trying to play him. Spits and Ceelow watched from across the street.

"Yo!" yelled Winston from the courtyard of the building. "Me want me money, ya hear?"

"Wha?" responded Jacob as he took immediate offense to Winston's tone.

"Me want me blood-clod money, pussy!" he repeated in an even more disrespectful tone.

"Man, fuck that," replied Jacob. "I ain't got your money right now. You goin' have to wait until I make some paper first." When Jacob had spoken his piece, he turned his back on Winston like the conversation was over and Winston didn't seem to like that one bit.

"Pussy! You want ramp with me?" he asked as he rushed Jacob from behind.

"What, nigga?!" yelled Jacob as he turned around pushing Winston away from him. "What's up, son? Fuck that, you wonna thump? Then throw up ya shits, duke. Let's get it on." He took off his sweater, revealing a scrawny chest and walked toward Winston.

"Flex, ya want flex?" Winston said. "You no know me a murderer?"

When Jacob got into his fighting stance to get ready, he balled up his fists and put up his arms really high, and then he bent his knees to get real low to the ground. He looked like he was joking but he was dead serious. When he was ready, he signaled for Winston to bring it. Before Jacob could throw a punch, Winston charged at him and kicked him dead center in his chest. The force of the kick wasn't much, but it was enough to push Jacob a few feet back. When he got his balance back, he had a confused look on his face like, *did this nigga just kick me?* Before he knew it, Winston was charging at him again with another kick to his chest. This dude Winston must've kicked him like eight times, with each kick throwing Jacob a few feet farther up the block. With each thump into his chest, Jacob grew more and more confused, then his confusion turned into frustration, and then his face turned red with rage.

Everybody on the Block—except for Jacob—thought that this was the funniest shit to ever happen in front of their faces. Even Spits and Cee were across the street from them, laughing like crazy. It was nowhere near serious—meaning neither one of them got hurt—but that can really hurt someone like Jacob's pride. The only reason he'd even reacted the way he did was because he'd felt that Winston had disrespected him in front of everybody. Now it was worse. Maybe Winston could have gone about getting his money another way, but that's how he was. He was just always naturally loud when he spoke and Jacob took offense.

When Winston was done, he'd kicked Jacob two building lengths up the block. When Jacob finally got up on his feet, he ran across the street where

Spits and Ceelow were standing and into the backyard of one of the houses. When he returned, he seemed to be concealing something behind his back. He jumped over the gate—only two houses from where Spits and Ceelow were posted, and pointed a little black .9 mm across the street at Winston. He let two shots go in Winston's direction that sent everybody that was gathered in the front of 666 fleeing and made Ceelow and Spits duck for cover behind a car. After letting one more shot go off, he ran away as fast as he could; as if he'd just caught a body. When Cee and Spits looked up to see if Winston had gotten caught, they saw him lying on the floor face-down. When Winston got up and brushed the dust off of his clothes—as if he wasn't at all fazed by the gunshots—Cee and Spits both laughed hysterically as they thought about what must've been going through Jacob's mind at that time.

"He thought he caught him, or something?" Ceelow asked. "Why the fuck did he run off like that and he's the one with the burner?"

"That's your boy, nigga," said Spits teasing Cee. "I don't know what the fuck is on that nigga's mind."

They both laughed for a minute with each other and then it was time for Spits to go. He still had to go all the way back home to Jersey where Ginger would be waiting; plus he had arrangements for a limousine to pick them up in exactly an hour. He would have just enough time to get home and make sure Gin was ready before they headed back out.

After speeding through the New Jersey Turnpike, Spits made it back home at exactly 5:45 p.m. The limousine was scheduled for 6 p.m. and Ginger had no idea what was planned until she saw the suit he had on. Spits was dressed from head to toe in Gucci and a fresh shave complemented the outfit perfectly. When he'd left the house earlier that afternoon, he was dressed very regularly in jeans and a white T-shirt. For the element of surprise, he'd never brought the suit home when he'd purchased it and had made arrangements so that he could pick it up from the Gucci store when he intended to wear it. After an appointment for a shape-up at his favorite spot on Allerton Avenue called Butter Cuts, he went down to 5th Avenue to the Gucci store. He changed in the dressing room and put the clothes he had on in a bag. When he left the store, Spits looked incredibly slick in this pitch-black three-button suit with a white shirt and a silver tie. From his sleeve, a perfect half-inch of cuff peeked out from under his jacket with platinum cufflinks appropriately engraved with his initials: "MS," for Mike Spits. Under that was a fitting Gucci watch with a diamond bezel in the form of a "G.".

When Ginger saw Spits, thoughts that she had overdressed for the occasion were quickly thrown from her mind. In fact, she thought that he still looked better than her, but she was often modest when it came to such things. She had on a sexy, tight, ankle-length black gown with a long slit up her right side that fitted her as if it was made especially for her. Her hair was done in Shirley Temple curls and her makeup was done perfectly in earth tones; just how Spits liked it. On her pretty little feet, she wore a pair of black open-toe shoes, with six-inch heels. Spits was speechless.

They kissed each other and they both respectfully commented on the other's appearance. When it was time to leave they walked to the door together. Upon reaching the front steps, Ginger lit up as she saw the white stretch limo that had been waiting for them at the curb. The driver opened the door for them and as they entered, Spits informed him that they were ready for their first stop. Ginger then began to get excited, thinking of what Spits had planned. After a ride through the tunnel and up the West Side Highway, they found themselves on 30th Street & 12th Avenue. Spits cracked the window enough for Ginger to see a sign that read: VIP Heliport. They exited the limo where a pilot was waiting to show them to the helicopter.

"Everything is set up just as you requested, Mr. Spits," the pilot said as he led the way.

"That's cool,"said Spits, as he took Ginger in his arms. "Let's do this."

They walked around a small building and through a gate that led to the heliport. After briefly instructing them about safety procedures, the pilot escorted Ginger and Spits onboard the aircraft. Once in the air, Spits revealed a bottle of champagne and they toasted to their love. The trip lasted about forty-five minutes to an hour. The pilot took them down the Henry Hudson River over to the Statue of Liberty where he circled a few times before heading over to the Financial District where the World Trade Center stood. After that, he took them farther north to where the Empire State Building was located, then past the Chrysler Building, all the while naming the landmarks as they flew around them. It was great. Spits had originally hesitated, due to Ginger's fear of flying, but minus the take-off and the landing, she said, "Everything was perfect."

When they landed, the limo-driver proceeded to Ginger's next surprise location. The spot that Spits had chosen for them to have dinner was the restaurant they'd gone to on their first date in '94, called Maroons, on West 16th Street. Upon their arrival, Ginger was somewhat surprised to see that Spits had reserved the entire restaurant for the portion of the night they were to spend there. Candles decorated the entire floor and all the tables surrounding theirs, where a fresh bottle of champagne graced the table. When Spits preordered the meal, he requested garlic shrimp for an appetizer, smothered pork chops for his entrée and the red snapper for Ginger's, and for dessert they had the applesauce carrot cake. When they were done eating, Spits gave the signal for the waitress, but instead of the bill, she came over to their table and placed a little black box on the table in front of Ginger. Ginger knew exactly what was in the box, and she looked as if she wasn't ready to open it. When the waitress just walked away without a word, Ginger didn't know what to do with herself. She looked up at Spits. She'd never, never seen him look at her so seriously before. She began to cry. She cried until tears began to form in Spits' eyes as well. She had never once seen Spits full of the kind of emotion he had in his face at this moment. She was at a complete loss, and she didn't know what to do. Her body was just completely frozen.

"I don't know what to..." Ginger said before Spits interrupted.

"Then, don't say anything. " He said. "You don't have to open it yet, Gin. I just want to see the look in your eyes when you do. It'll always be there for you, Mommy...just waiting. Feel me?"

"I love you, Daddy," she said as she let go of all the emotions that had just gotten stuck in her chest.

"Me too, Gin," he said plainly. "Now, let's get out of here."

CHAPTER 16

"What's there left for us to do, son?" I asked, as Ceelow and I each sipped on bottles of champagne in the VIP section of a popular New York nightclub called *The Tunnel*.. "We done did every fuckin' thing we set out to do. We did the cars and cribs...we got all these stupid bitches beggin' us just to get a cock-slap."

"Ha-ha, you can't be serious, nigga," Cee said with a giggle. "That's funny coming from *Mr. Commitment*. Ha-ha! Fuck that shit, son!"

I gave a moment to chuckle at Cee's comment, and then continued, "I mean we gave 'em the Benzes, the Porsches, the Beemers," I recalled. "We really did it up, son...but what now?"

"I can't call it, nigga," Cee responded. "But I know we ain't gotta do shit but keep on gettin' this money. 'Gotta get that paper, dog,' feel me?"

"No doubt, my nigga," I answered. "I guess that's what it's all about, huh?"

"Hell yeah, nigga!" Cee responded as his blood-shot red eyes grew larger. "2000 and beyond," said Cee as he lifted his glass for a toast.

I, too, lifted my glass and we toasted. "*Dom P's and palm trees.*"

As we threw back countless glasses of champagne, and choked on enormous amounts of weed-smoke, we sat there and celebrated life, and actually dancing hadn't even crossed our minds. *'Thug niggas don't dance.'* Only one song could demand that we leave the sanctity of the VIP section and enter the sweaty, melting pot that was the dance floor.

Funk Master Flex was on the turntables and it was just around 1 a.m. It had been a continuously live and entertaining evening, but Flex decided to liven things up a bit more; 1999 was a really good time for Hip-Hop classics, so he hit 'em with back-to-back head-bangers. He started with...

"Money, cash, hoes...money, cash, hoes."

Then, he hit 'em with...

"Holla, Holla...(all my niggas that's ready to get) Dollars, Dollars...(bitches know who could get 'em a little) Hotta, Hotta...(come on, if you rollin' wit' me) Follow, Follow...It's Murdaaahhh"

When Flex had our attention, all me and Cee had to hear were the first four words of this next record...

"Escobar season has returned."

When that shit came on, it was pandemonium. We made our way downstairs and as soon as we hit the floor, the hook had settled in time for us to go crazy along with everyone else and sing along.

"You could hate me now...but I won't stop now...'cause I can't stop now...you could hate me nooowww."

As the night progressed into the early hours of the morning, I completely forgot about the doubts I'd developed regarding the life that we were leading. My mind state had been heading in the direction of positivity, but that was quickly overthrown by expensive alcohol and potent marijuana. By the time I would have those thoughts again, it would be too late.

As our evening came to an end, the sun had already begun rising over the skyscrapers located in Midtown Manhattan. We stumbled out of the club and walked two blocks to 25th Street to where we were parked. From there we jumped on the West Side Highway to 125th Street to get a bite to eat at one of our favorite after-the-club spots called Jimbo's on 125th Street and Amsterdam Avenue. I'm tellin' you, no amount of money could ruin breakfast at those greasy, dirty, underground spots for us. It was just one of those things that you didn't grow out of; no matter what. We hadn't gotten so rich that we'd forgotten where we'd come from.

Once there, we got seats at the counter, right in front of the grill to make sure our food was prepared correctly. We both ordered cheeseburgers with a fried egg on the top, and a side order of fries—that was our special. While we sat there watching the cook close enough to make sure he was doing his thing, Cee snapped his finger and said, "Oh shit! I forgot to tell you."

"What's up?" I asked as I woke up out of the trance I'd slipped into, anticipating how delicious the burger would be.

"You remember that bitch-ass nigga Fish?" Ceelow asked.

"Yeah," I answered. "He fuck with that nigga AG, right? Didn't he get sent up a while back?"

"Yup that's him," said Ceelow. "He just came home not too long ago."

"Word?"

"That's my word, and this dude is already gettin' into shit on the Ave. Niggas told me that he just be posted up on the other side of White Plains Road all day and night like he waiting to pop off or some shit."

"Say word?" I said. "How long he been on the streets now?"

"The little niggas on the block say about two weeks, but I only saw him for the first time like two days ago."

"He say anything to you?" I asked.

"Nah, son," Cee responded. "I still think he's trying to figure out how much the Block is changed."

"It be like that though, son," I agreed. "But he's a dickhead anyway. It won't be long before that nigga end up gettin' sent back up."

"Yeah, well, he better realize that shit ain't the same since he left," suggested Ceelow. "You know me, dog. It's nothing to run up on a nigga and empty out one of them thangs."

"Yeah, well, let's see what's up first," I recommended. "No reason to heat the Block for no reason. He'll probably hang himself before long, you know?"

"Yeah, no doubt," Cee answered as our food was finally served.

By the time we left the restaurant, it was already past 7 a.m. We split up after that and we both went home. When I reached the crib, I hit the bed like a ton of bricks for a well-deserved rest. It had been a long night and I needed a little break before I started the rest of a long day.

I didn't wake up until early that afternoon. I hadn't intended on sleeping for that long but the booze and the weed had other plans for me. I had an appointment at 10 a.m. and I was already three hours behind schedule. I was almost positive that I would be late from jump, but I didn't want to be *this* late. I still had to get up and get cleaned up before I left. I took a quick shower and threw on a sweat suit. I then went into the safe I'd had installed in the bottom of my closet to make sure I had enough to pay for the trip I had in mind, and I was off. By the time I left, it was 2 p.m. I jumped in my car and hit the road. It took me approximately forty-five minutes to reach my destination on 34th Street and 9th Avenue. I was greeted upon my arrival by James Waters, my travel agent, and a twenty-minute discussion led to me parting with $42,000 in cash to cover the airfare and stay for my and Ginger's Christmas vacation.

I figured that when Ginger got a look at the brochures for where we would be staying, she wouldn't be able to resist. It would be perfect.

CHAPTER 17

After a frosty October and an even more arctic November, December had finally set in with a fierce and bitter chill. The snow that had accumulated in the streets of the Bronx would reach heights greater than fifteen or twenty inches. This year's Christmas season would be brutal for New Yorkers to endure. But as for the most popular and respected couple in the Bronx, Christmas would be represented in the form of white sandy beaches, palm trees and beautiful sunsets. The only chill that they would be getting would be from the mango daiquiris. Spits planned for himself, along with Ginger, to spend their Christmas in Hawaii at a plush, 3,300-square-foot, luxurious villa located in Maui. Only dreams could bring the images that could be found in this little part of the world. It didn't take long at all for Spits to convince Gin that they would have the time of their lives at this exquisite beach house property.

This heavenly dwelling would be equipped with five bedrooms—two of which were beach front—five bathrooms, a spacious living room with a fireplace, a dining room with an adjoining conversation area, gym, a heated swimming pool and Jacuzzi, and a full-service staff. Spits and Ginger would have all of these things to themselves for a period of six days and seven nights. This was something that Spits could only dream about doing with that special person and it was finally a feasible reality. He was going to take advantage.

While they were gone, the everyday grind would be left for Ceelow to handle, with the assistance of El Don and Poncho. It had been proven that the Time Bomb enterprise could be run responsibly in the absence of Spits so he would have no uncertainties about leaving everything in their hands.

It was now December 20th and Spits and Ginger were ready to start the rest of their lives with this single event.

"Are you nervous?" Spits asked Ginger as they rode to the airport.

"Well," Ginger began. "I would be pulling out my hair under normal circumstances, but, you make all of those feelings fade."

"Good," Spits simply said. "That's what I'm here for."

They chartered a private jet for the flight there that took approximately 12.5 hours; including a stop at LAX to refuel. The entire flight was without flaw. Ginger couldn't have been more comfortable than she was, lounging in the huge leather reclining seats while they were being served champagne and strawberries.

"*The only way to fly,*" Spits said as he noticed how much Ginger's perception of the air travel experience had changed since they'd first boarded an airplane. Even though she was still a little jumpy when it came to the taking off and landing part, she'd improved a whole lot. Her only beef was the light-headed feeling when it was time to de-board the plane.

They arrived in Maui just in time to see the sun setting over the clear blue Pacific Ocean. The colors the sun made the sky turn were unimaginable. Different shades of yellow, orange, red and purple. It was absolutely incredible.

Upon exiting Kahului Airport after claiming their baggage, they were met by a native Hawaiian holding a sign that read "'*Spits.*" The driver was instructed by Spits to take them to the Sandy Surf Villa in Wailea and following a short toured ride, they were pulling into the driveway of their new home for the next week. Upon entering the front door of this two-story dream-house, they were greeted by the staff—a butler, a cook and two maids—and then they were escorted by the butler through the entire space to familiarize themselves with the new surroundings. They were in complete and utter amazement as they went from room to room to room to room...

First they were shown the living area, which was fully equipped with huge sofas, chairs and ottomans made of oak, carrying cushions covered with cashmere. There was a big-screen television with a satellite connection and DVD. The floors were a glossy hardwood and were decorated with numerous Persian rugs that complemented the area nicely. They were shown the kitchen—which didn't interest either one of them as they wouldn't be spending any time there—and then they were shown the dining area which led to a patio area facing the rest of the island. The patio area also had stairs that led up the back of the house onto a small roof area that was used for a Jacuzzi. From this point you could see the entire island on one side, and never-ending stars reflecting off the ocean in the other. Then, they toured the bedrooms—each one bigger and more detailed than the last until they reached the master bedroom. The master bedroom contained a king-sized bed, his and her bathrooms, and a desk area with a computer, a small table with two chairs, and doors that led to the pool area which had stairs that led directly to the beach. When they reached there, the tour ended. Spits made arrangements for breakfast, and they would only take a quick shower before spending the rest of the night under the covers. The long flight had taken its toll and they needed to be rested for the following day's events.

In the morning, Ginger and Spits were awakened by the smell of freshly ground coffee and the brightness of the Hawaiian sun peeking through the curtains. When they were fully awake, they parted to their separate bathrooms to wash up before breakfast. When they returned, the maid was preparing the food so that they could eat while they lay comfortably in the huge bed. They climbed into the bed and sat up, making room for the bed-trays and when they were comfy, the maid revealed their meal. When the steam cleared they saw mouth-watering T-bone steaks, and scrambled eggs with cheese. On the side were breakfast potatoes, bacon, sausage and toast. The coffee was piping-hot and there were also glasses of water, milk and some Moet mimosas. At first, the dishes looked too perfect to be ruined, but that thought was quickly demolished as they began devouring this simply perfect meal.

"Whoa!" Spits simply said as he reached the limit of food he could consume. "This is the shit, for real! I ain't never felt as good as I do at this very moment."

"That's true," Ginger agreed. "I don't know where that cook came from, but we need to bring his ass back with us home."

"Fuck that!" Spits rebutted. "How about we just never fuckin' go back?"

"That would be fine, too," said Ginger as they both giggled. They knew that there was nowhere like New York they could really call home. Even though they lived in Jersey, New York would always be their home. They wouldn't ever forget that.

"Damn, Gin," Spits said as he saw Ginger getting back underneath the warm comforters. "I don't even feel like gettin' up to go anywhere."

"Me neither," approved Ginger as she pulled the covers up to her neck. "What did you want to do today, anyway?"

"Oh, I figured we could hit the shopping strip and go nuts," responded Spits as he cuddled with her under the covers.

"Okay, that's sounds like a plan!" Ginger said as her priorities were suddenly rearranged. "Let's go then," she said, jumping up out of the bed.

Spits let out a chuckle. He knew that was the easiest way to get her up and ready to go. The thought of shopping in a new town with a virtually limitless budget all of a sudden sounded way better than staying in bed all day. They both laughed and kissed playfully for a minute before getting ready.

They spent the remainder of the morning in and out of the many men's and women's shops, art galleries, gift shops, and jewelry stores in the Kahului Shopping Center. They bought all kinds of things ranging from figurines to swimwear. After hours of walking the entire length of the mall, they collected their bags and went to a restaurant called the Koho Grill & Bar for lunch. When they were done eating, they went back to the beach house.

Once there, they could shower once more before going back out to the beach. It was now a little past 5 p.m. When they reached the beach, the sky had just begun changing from baby blue, to yellow, and then light orange. They brought with them a bottle of champagne to drink as they watched the sunset. Spits popped the cork and poured two nice-sized drinks for them. They simply toasted to *love* and exchanged passionate kisses before slowly sipping on the bubbly.

When their bottle was just about done, Spits got up to get another. "I'll be right back," he said, making his way back toward the house. "I'm gonna go get another bottle."

When Spits was halfway back to the house, Ginger said, "No wait! Don't go."

Spits turned back around to see what was wrong, and Gin was just standing there, completely naked, signaling with her finger for him to return. All Spits could do was stare. "Damn!" he said to himself. "Is that for me?"

"Come here, Daddy," she said in a childish, bratty tone. "Don't you ever leave me!"

"Never," Spits said, walking back to her. "I'll never leave you."

When he reached her, she smiled up at him playfully, and as he approached her closer for a kiss, she pushed him away and sat him back down in the reclining beach chair he had just gotten up from. She stood up in front of him. She sat him upward and threw her leg over his shoulder. With both hands she pressed his head further and further between her legs until he could feel the heat from her insides. He kissed her clit, and then licked it. He teased it until it started to poke out from behind its lips, and then he wiggled his tongue on it fast, then slow, and then fast again. She started going crazy with anticipation. She wanted to cum, but she still wanted him inside of her. She grabbed the back of his head and pushed harder and harder until her body was jolting. She reached orgasm after orgasm while his tongue continued to tease her clit. When she couldn't take anymore, she threw him back on the chair. She made sure he was comfortable and then started caressing his chest. She took off his T-shirt and sat on his lap while she began kissing him more and more passionately. She kissed down his neck, and then down his chest. When she reached his stomach, she shoved her hand down his shorts and started fondling his penis as it grew larger and larger. She then forcefully snatched off his swimming trunks and took him into her mouth. When he grabbed the back of her head, she forced his hands to his side. She went slow, and then faster, and then slower again. She was driving him completely out of his mind. When he thought she was going to let him cum, she stopped abruptly. He could do nothing but stare at her as she teasingly smiled up at him.

"Take it from the back, Daddy," she said innocently.

He jumped up before the words were even completely out of her mouth and laid her down on the sand. Now, it was time for him to take control. He forcefully turned her over on her stomach and lifted her pelvis, making sure her back was perfectly arched. He took a moment in appreciating the sight, grinned for a second, and then forced himself into her wet, dripping pussy. The intensity grew with every stroke as she grew wetter and wetter. Spits had never felt this kind of intensity with her before. Maybe it was the pure white sand, or maybe it was how the stars reflected off the ocean. Maybe it was the silence and the privacy. Whatever it was, it was sending wave after wave of extreme sexual feelings through his body. As Ginger felt herself about to explode, she cried, "I'm gonna cum again! Don't stop, Daddy! Cum with me!"

Suddenly he was climaxing and with one last stroke, he was bursting over and over again as mind-boggling vibrations ran through his body with every drip and drop. When he couldn't cum anymore, he eased out of her slowly and they just lay there on the sand holding each other. They quickly dozed off right out on the beach for a couple of hours before Spits woke up and carried Ginger back up to their room. There, they would sleep into the late hours of the morning.

Tomorrow's agenda would be different from today's by far. Lucky thing they'd started early or they might not have had a chance to have as good a time as they were having.

CHAPTER 18

The next morning, Ginger woke me up out of a sound sleep. She had apparently gotten up before me and arranged for breakfast.

"Wake up, honey," she said, rubbing my back.

"What time is it?" I asked as I slowly woke up.

"It's already past eleven o'clock, baby," Ginger said. "You looked so peaceful; I didn't want to disturb your sleep."

"Thanks, Mommy," I said. "Did you have breakfast already?"

"Yeah, I had a little something to eat," Ginger responded. "I had the cook hook you up with something,too. I got you some sausage and eggs on a croissant, and some sliced fruit. It's right over there whenever you want it" she said, pointing at a tray sitting by the window.

"Good lookin' out, Ma," I said. "I'ma get in the shower right quick though. Where you goin' be at?"

"Oh, I'm goin' up on the roof in that Jacuzzi," she said with a big smile. "Are you coming up with me?"

"Oh, yes!" I said with vigor. "No doubt. Let me get washed up and I'll be right out after I finish eating."

"All right, Daddy," she said walking away. "Don't keep me waiting too long."

"I won't," I said. "Don't worry about that. Oh, and last night...that was the best ever, you freaky little girl."

"You're so nasty," she said playfully as she left the room with a little bit more wiggle in her butt.

"Uh-huh," I said, noticing she was trying to get my attention. "Keep it hot for me, Mommy."

When I got out of the bed, I stretched my body and went into the bathroom for a long, relaxing hot shower. I thought about all the things that had led to this point in my life. I was definitely at my highest right now. My life was definitely peaking, as far as experiences go, and I loved every minute of it. I almost didn't even want to call back home, just for the simple fact that I didn't want to be reminded of the daily grind that I would sooner or later have to return to. But something was calling my attention back to the Bronx. I had a bad feeling, and I felt no news was worse than bad news. When I got out of the shower, I called Ceelow for an update.

"Yo, what's up, dog?" I asked as Cee answered the phone.

"Yeah, what's good, my nigga?" he said.

"Oh, everything is good, dog," I answered. "This shit is some hot boy shit out here, for real, son. What's good in the hood though?"

"Ain't nothin'," Cee answered. "As a matter of fact, I think it's more bad than good out here."

"Why, what's poppin'?"

"Remember I told you about that nigga Fish?" Ceelow asked.

"Yeah," I responded. "What he dealin' with?"

"We goin' probably have to body that nigga, son," said Cee.

"Say word."

"That's my word, dog," responded Cee. "I'm tellin' you, this nigga's makin' shit too hot out here for these niggas to even make a sale. The police be posted up on the Ave, and shit, just waiting for some shit to go down."

"What the fuck happened since I been gone?" I asked confusedly.

"It's these niggas on the other side, dog," he began. "They startin' beef over the dumbest shit, just cause. Ain't gonna be too much more of this shit before we just have to body all of them niggas."

"Startin' beef?" I asked. "They ain't fuckin' with our workers, are they?"

"Oh, naw," Cee quickly responded. "They beefin' with niggas from the Valley, and shit. You know them Valley niggas run that side of the block now, since Fish got knocked. Since he been home, his old crew all of a sudden got heart now. Son, I would wreck each and every one of those bitch-ass niggas, son."

"Be easy, dog," I said, trying to calm him down. "Tell me what happened."

"All right," said Cee trying to get the situations in proper order. "You know Bullet, and Duff, and all them Valley Mob niggas, right?"

"Yeah."

"Well, they ain't even really been too vexed about Fish since he came home. They figure as long as he ain't tryin' to make no sales, he could live, you know? Him and that nigga AG be posted up in the liquor store all day, just chillin'. But for some reason, they decide they want to jump off for no reason. I peeps this nigga Duff goin' in the liquor store, right? I don't know what happened while he in there, but when he came out, this nigga Fish is backin' him down with the burner out. Now, everybody think it's about to go down, but he ain't tryin' buss him. He just swingin' it at his face, tryin' to pistol-whip him. Now, Duff ain't stupid, so as he backin' down off of Fish, he's leadin' him around the corner where Bullet and the rest of them niggas is. Fish, like a dick, just keep tryin' to hit him with the burner while Duff just duckin' and weavin'. Like two seconds after they get around the corner, that's when the shots start to go off. Everybody start running, and shit. Later on, I finds out that ain't nobody even get hit. Now these niggas is gonna be goin' back and forth with this bullshit forever, and sooner or later, it's gonna reach our side of the block. I'm about to just dead all of them niggas, and ain't nobody gonna get no money on they crew."

"Hold on, son," I said. "Them Valley niggas been cool from the beginning so the problem ain't with them. If anybody gotta go, it's that nigga Fish, and that nigga AG, and the rest of they bitch-ass crew, feel me?"

"Yeah, no doubt," answered Cee. "But you know how I gets down. I'll fuck around and do everybody dirty just on GP, like fuck it."

"Yeah, I got you in my radar," I said. "If anything, concentrate on that nigga Fish's crew. I never liked that nigga anyway. Just holla at me, and let me know what's goin' down."

"Yeah," he said. "I got you."

"One."

"One."

This whole thing with Fish left a weird feeling in my stomach from the first time Cee had put me on to him. I didn't know what it was, but I just wasn't feeling that dude. It wouldn't be long before he got his, though. Then I would relax. As for now, that nigga could sneeze wrong and get a hit put out on him. Fuck that!

When I hung up the phone with Cee, I decided to check my voicemail at the crib. Something was still leaving a pain in my stomach. As I scanned through the messages, one was from my mother, hoping that I had a safe flight and a good time. She made sure she wished the same for Ginger, too. She knew that one day, Ginger would be my wife, and she didn't disagree one bit. The next message was left by El Don, just asking that I call him back. The next message was left by someone much unexpected. When I heard his voice, I knew something was wrong. It was Red. He called to let me know that there was an emergency out there and that I needed to call him back. He said that it wasn't something that I should hear on a machine. When I heard that, all kinds of things ran through my head. My first thought was that Trigger had gotten arrested. My second thoughts contained worse circumstances, but nothing I could have imagined would have led me to believe what he actually had to tell me. I called him immediately.

"Hello?" said the voice on the other line.

"Hello," I said hurriedly. "Let me speak to Red."

"Who dis?" the person asked.

"Yo, this is Spits!" I yelled. "Is Red there or not, nigga?"

"Oh, I'm sorry, cuz," he replied. "Red said that you should be calling. He's over at the hospital right now. Let me put you on three-way."

Just as he said that, my heart stopped. I had no idea what was to follow. I thought maybe he'd gotten into some shit out there and had gotten shot. Or maybe it was Trigger that had gotten shot. I didn't know what to think and this insensitive asshole had just put me on hold before I had a chance to ask what the fuck was going on. When he clicked back over, the phone in the hospital was already ringing. When Red answered, I spit, "Yo, what the fuck is going on, dog? What you doin' in the hospital? Somebody hit you up, or somethin'?"

I kept asking questions back to back before he could answer and then he just said, “It ain’t me, dog.”

“Wha?” I asked confusedly.

“It ain’t me, dog,” he repeated. “I’m fine. It’s ...”

“What nigga!” I said, cutting him off. I was in a very volatile state right then and this nigga was not moving fast enough for me.

“It’s Rachel,” he finally said. “It’s not me. I’m over here in San Jose Medical with Rachel.”

“What the fuck are you talking about?” I asked now, even more confused than I was at the beginning of the conversation. What did he mean he was with Rachel? What would he be doing with her at work?

“Look,” he began. “Some shit happened with your sister, duke. She ain’t get a chance to tell nobody what happened yet, but she’s not looking good right now. She keeps goin’ in and out, but all she says when she can talk is, ‘Where’s my brother?’ She won’t even talk to her own pops. You gonna have to come out here or somethin’, homie. This shit is straight fucked, blood.”

I didn’t know what to say. I just sat there, staring at the wall with a perturbed look on my face. I was completely confused. This couldn’t be happening to me, not at the pinnacle of my happiness. I couldn’t believe it.

After Red yelled into the phone a few times to see if I was still there, he hung up thinking that we’d gotten disconnected, but I was just sitting there with the phone in my hand unknowing of what my next move would be. When Red hung up, the phone slipped from my hand and the sound of it hitting the ground brought me back to my senses. I just blinked and shook it off. I had to get into my problem-solving mode to get my shit back into proper perspective. All of a sudden, it came to me like a flash of light. I would have to go to Cali to make sure my sister would be all right. California wasn’t that long of a flight from Hawaii, so it wouldn’t even take too long to get there. I tried to think positively. Everything would be fine. It would take no longer than five hours to reach Cali, and when things were all good, I could just come back. Ginger would have to understand. I finally got up off of the bed and went up to where Ginger had been impatiently waiting for me in the Jacuzzi. She smiled when she saw me, but it took all of five seconds for her to realize that something was wrong.

"What's wrong, Daddy?" she asked.

"I have to tell you something that's not going to make you happy, Mommy," I said.

"What?" asked Ginger curiously. "Just tell me."

"I have to leave right now," I said.

"What?!" she said angrily. "Where do you have to go? And what am I supposed to do while you're gone?"

"Listen," I began. "Some shit happened with my sister in California."

"Oh my God," she said. "Rachel? What happened? Is she okay?"

"I'm not exactly sure of all of that shit yet," I answered. "But she's in the fuckin' hospital right now, and she just keeps asking for me."

"What?" she asked. "I don't understand. What do you mean? She won't tell anybody what happened?"

"All she does is ask for me," I responded. "I don't know what's going on. I was checking the messages on the house phone when I heard a message from Red that sounded urgent, so I called him up. He said he's in the hospital with her right now, and I don't know how serious this shit is. I have to go there and see what's going on. I'm gonna have to fix this shit."

"I understand, Daddy," she said, just like I knew she would.

"I mean, Cali is right there though," I stated, trying to make her feel comfortable with me leaving. "It's only a few hours to get there. If everything is cool, I'll be right back. You can even come with me if you want."

Although the offer sounded nice at first, just the thought of the flights there and back made Ginger think that she'd be pushing it. She'd just gotten used to flying, but she wasn't completely comfortable with it yet. Besides, this was time that Spits would need to spend with his sister alone. Not to take from her concern, but she felt that she'd be intruding in their personal family business. "No, that's okay, Daddy," she calmly said. "You go and be with your sister. She needs you more than I do right now."

With that, I was making arrangements to charter another flight from Maui to Cali. I was informed that there would be an aircraft available as soon as 5 p.m. From then, I would be in Cali by ten or eleven o'clock.

CHAPTER 19

The flight took approximately four hours and fifty-five minutes. It was 9:55 p.m. when the pilot landed at Livermore Airport. From there, it took approximately forty minutes in a cab for Spits to get to the San Jose Medical Center. When he got there, he asked for Rachel's room at the front desk. He got her room number and as the elevator doors opened on the fifth floor, he was immediately greeted by Red while he was sitting in the waiting area.

"Thank God, you're here, blood," Red said as he walked over to Spits to exchange a pound and a hug. "Long time no see, huh?"

"Yeah," Spits said, still feeling distant. "Where's she at, dog? Where's my sister?"

"Her room is uuh…right down here, homie," Red said after a slight hesitation. "She uuh…lost consciousness not too long ago. I gotta warn you though, homie, it ain't pretty."

Spits took a moment to study the look on Red's face once more before he'd entered the room. There was nothing on his facial expression that suggested his words be taken lightly. He was very serious. That in itself meant a lot, due to the crazy shit that Red had seen in his life. If this was a situation to be treated with sensitivity, then Spits would take it to the heart. He took a deep breath, and then turned the doorknob. Red closed the door behind Spits and positioned himself in front of it to make sure they wouldn't be disturbed.

What was on the other side of the door would immediately bring a glossy shimmer to Spits' eyes. He stopped at the doorway and lowered his head into his hands. When he could finally lift his head up he continued toward Rachel. The closer he got, the more upset he became. *Somebody's gonna die behind this shit*, is all he thought. Somebody would have to be held responsible for the bruises and cuts on his sister's face, for the casts that covered her right arm and leg, and for the bandage that wrapped her head.

Spits took her left hand in his and caressed it with his other. He promised her that whoever did this would be seeing their death sooner than later. He kissed her on her forehead and left the room in a rage. Upon exiting, the first person he spotted was Red. He lunged in his direction and held him up against the adjacent wall with his hand at his neck. With the other hand, he pointed between Red's eyes. "Who the fuck did this to my sister?!" he yelled. "The mu'fucka that did this better already be dead, nigga! I swear, he better already be dead before I find him. This was your responsibility, Red! You was supposed to make sure nothing happened to her!"

"Calm down, Spits," Red said as he attempted to reach Spits through all of the rage. "I don't know who did this shit, dog. I been trying to find that shit out since I been here, blood. All she did was ask to speak to her brother, and then she just lost consciousness," he said before pausing. "What the fuck was I supposed to do?!" he cried.

Spits let go of Red's neck and backed off until he felt the wall on his back, and then he just sat there on the floor.

"Are you Michael Banner?" asked a doctor that approached them while Spits sat on the floor.

"Yes," said Spits, now sitting with his head in his lap. "Who the fuck are you?"

"I'm Dr. Timothy Halsey. I've been treating your sister, Rachel."

He quickly jumped up so that the doctor could have his undivided attention. "Is she going to be all right?" he asked eagerly.

"Well, that's what I'd like to talk to you about, sir," he responded. "Would you mind it if we spoke privately?"

"Oh, that's cool," he said.

Dr. Halsey brought Spits down the hall and around the corner so that they could have some privacy and began by stating his deepest concern for his sister's health. He went on to say, "Your sister Rachel was in a very vulnerable state, Mr. Banner. She took a really bad beating, sir, and she's lucky to be alive at this point. She'd already lost a lot of blood by the time she was brought here, but we currently have that under our control. She'd suffered from a massive concussion from repeated blows to the head, and her sixth, seventh and eighth ribs were broken. She has a fractured triquetral and pisiform in her right wrist that could've come from her throwing up her arms in defense. She also sustained injuries to her tibia and fibula bones in her right leg that were caused by some sort of impact with a blunt object." He paused to let the information that he'd just provided sink in. He then continued, "Actually, Mr. Banner, had your friend not brought her here when he did, she probably wouldn't have made it."

Spits had nothing to say. He knew that the doctor was telling him this because Spits should know how much he owed to his man, Red. He took a moment to take it all in and then asked, "Will she be okay?"

"Honestly, Mr. Banner, sir," he began. "That information can't yet be determined, but at this point, I would say that her condition has improved since she arrived. She lost consciousness not too long ago, but that was caused by the hours and hours of surgery. She's been through a lot in the past two days, and all she needs now is rest."

Spits finally started to settle down. "Well, as long as she's going to be okay."

"Yes, Mr. Banner, I think as long as she gets the proper rest, I think she'll be fine," Dr. Halsey said. "Unfortunately, we couldn't do anything about her baby."

"What?!" Spits said confusingly. "What you mean, 'her baby?'"

"Oh, I'm sorry," Dr. Halsey said. "I thought you were previously informed. I deeply apologize, Mr. Banner, but your sister was three months' pregnant. The baby was lost. There was nothing that we could do. It was already too late."

Once Spits heard that, his brain just started going into overdrive. He hadn't even realized that his sister had been involved with someone, let alone had a baby on the way. There were too many blanks to be filled, like why would anybody have a beef with his sister? Something wasn't right. He wondered, "What could've made her keep something like this from me?" A thousand and one different questions ran through his mind that he'd have to ask her about after she regained consciousness. For now, all he could do was wait. He spent the rest of the night at her bedside waiting for her to wake up. After briefly apologizing to Red, he told him that he could head home if he'd like, but Red would hear nothing of it. He insisted on staying with him, in case he was needed. He made himself comfortable in the hospital lobby for the rest of the night.

After hours of pacing back and forth in Rachel's hospital room, Spits found himself sitting in front of her in a chair. He stared at her face all night and early into the morning. When Spits was finally about to doze off, he realized that her nose had started wiggling. This was the most she'd moved since he'd been there, and now he was wide awake again and giving her his undivided attention. A few seconds went by and her eyelids started twitching. Soon, she was blinking her eyes while she squinted to shield her sight from the bright lights that were now shining through the hospital window, as the sun came peeking out of the dark. Spits just smiled at her, silently cheering on her recovery to himself. He took a deep breath and held her by the hand to acknowledge his presence. It took a second of focusing for Rachel to realize that it was none other than her own little brother sitting in front of her rubbing her hand, and when she did, a smile crept from her facial expression, until the pain it caused brought her back to her distressed reality. All of sudden, she became conscious of her appearance, but was unable to adjust. She attempted to shield her embarrassment by turning away from his proud stares, but Spits simply chuckled it off and got up to kiss her forehead. He sat back down and she smiled at him. She felt much better, now that he was there with her.

"Can you talk?" he quietly asked.

She moved around her jaw for a second, and then uttered the words, "It hurts when I move my mouth."

"Don't worry about it," he reassured her. "We have all the time in the world to talk."

"No!" she said firmly. "We don't have much time. I need to tell you what happened."

"Listen..." He began rubbing her forehead. "You shouldn't be too active right now. The most important thing is that you get better. Everything else will have to come second."

"But, I can't..." she said before the sound of the door opening cut her off.

Spits got up to see who it was and once he got a good look, he said, "What's up, my nigga?"

"What's up, dog?" responded Trigger. He seemed surprised to see him. "When you get here?"

"Last night, dog," Spits responded. "Where you been at?"

"I just got home and checked my messages," responded Trigger. "That shit bugged me out when I heard this nigga Red on my voicemail saying that something happened to Rachel, so I came right over. Did she tell you anything yet?"

"Naw," responded Spits. "Matter of fact, she just woke up a second ago. I don't know if you want to see her like this, dog."

"Oh, come on now, son," he responded. "We still family, right?"

"All right, my bad, son," Spits said. "Just hold on for a second. Let me tell her you're here."

✪✪✪

When Spits returned to Rachel's bedside, she was just lying there looking up at the ceiling with a hopeless look on her face. He sat down in the chair next to her and said, "Trigger is here. You don't mind if he stays while we talk, do you?"

Her eyes opened up wider, and she looked as if she was conflicted about how she should answer. But before she even got a chance to respond, Trigger came from around the curtain. He smiled at her and said, "Are you feeling any better, Rachel?"

She just smiled and nodded.

"Listen…" he said with a concerned tone of voice. "You have to tell us who did this shit to you. I swear to God, I won't rest until we find these cowards and fill them full of slugs."

"Yo, calm down, dog," Spits said. "The most important thing is that she gets better right now. Family business first, and then we could take it to the streets, feel me?"

"No, he's right," Rachel said. "The only thing that I'm worried about right now is making the punk that did this to me pay."

✪✪✪

Back in the Bronx, even though the temperature read under freezing, the streets were about to get heated up real fast. With a short call from Cee to Don P., they were ready to make their move. This bitch-ass nigga Fish would see his last day on the streets. He went too far and now he would have to pay. It was reported to Ceelow late last night that Fish had attempted to strong-arm a worker for the Time Bomb organization. It was all Cee needed to wage an all-out war against Fish, and his whole crew—if they wanted it. Once Cee got the news, El Don and Poncho were the next to find out. Everybody on the streets knew that the Time Bombs were just not to be fucked with, and whoever didn't know would get a crash-course. Don P. were ready at all times to drop bombs for the clique so when they got the word from Cee, they were happy to offer their assistance.

El Don would provide backup for Cee, while Poncho would drive the getaway car. When Cee was ready, they met on the 224th Street and Bronx Boulevard, down by the park. If he was stupid enough—and he was—Fish would still be in the liquor store getting drunk, making it even easier for them to roll up without him getting the drop. They planned to drive up 228th Street and come down 224th Street. There, they could just make a right turn and be directly in front of the liquor store. Everything was going as planned. After pulling ski-masks over their faces, Ceelow and El Don hopped out of the hooptie and approached the front of the store.

Through the glass door, Fish spotted a couple of dark figures coming in his direction. Before he knew it, one of the figures was in the store with him while the other stood out front blocking the door. Inside of two seconds, a long black object came from behind the figure standing in front of him dressed from top to bottom in black. He thought he was dreaming, but he wasn't. This wasn't just a dark figure that had just appeared in front of him from out of nowhere, and it wasn't just a black object that was now pointing directly at his chest. Maybe if it was his imagination, he wouldn't have anything to worry about, but it wasn't. This black figure was Ceelow, and the object he had in his hands was a black 12-gauge shotgun. All he heard was the sound of a slug being chambered before he came to his senses, but by then, it was too late. *BOOM!* That was the last sound Fish heard before half of his insides hit the wall behind him. When he fell to the ground lifeless, Cee let him have it again just to make sure. *BOOM… BOOM!* He was gone now, and wasn't nothing bringing his ass back.

✪✪✪

Trigger and Spits just fell silent to Rachel's comment. Spits hadn't ever once seen his big sister lose her cool; and even though this is what Trigger had asked for, he himself was even surprised at the statement she'd made. They both just waited with anticipation for her to fill in the blanks that they needed for immediate action to be taken. She looked at Trigger in his eyes as she searched her memory banks for the best way to describe what had happened. Then, she looked at Spits to unconsciously assist her in her description. After another look at Trigger, she looked away—out of the window—and uttered under her breath, "It was a burglar."

"What?" both Trigger and Spits said at the same time.

"It was a burglar," Rachel repeated. "When I came home, I found somebody in the house. Before I even got a chance to get away or call the police, he was swinging a damn baseball bat at my head."

"Did you see his face?" Spits asked. "Did he look familiar?"

"Yeah," she answered. "I saw the bastard's face, but he didn't look familiar.

He was about five feet, eight inches, with long hair in corn rows. He had a brown skin tone, and he was wearing all black. That's all I remember." With that said, Rachel just paused and waited for a reaction. Spits reacted first.

"All right," he said. "That's cool for now. Don't stress yourself out behind this, Rachel, until you have enough strength to deal with this shit in your own mind. Let me talk to Trig right quick and I'll be right back." Spits got up and walked toward the door and Trigger followed close behind him, still not taking his eyes off of Rachel. When they were outside the door, he said, "Yo, you think you could find something out from the description she gave? I know it ain't shit, but we ain't got shit else right now, you know?"

"Yeah," Trigger replied. "That's just gonna have to be enough, I guess. I'm gonna see what the streets is talkin' about, i-ight? I'll call you here if I find out anything, cool?"

"Yeah, no doubt," Spits said. "You do that. I'll be here."

"Yo, it was good seeing you again though," Trigger said as they exchanged a pound and a hug. "Even under these circumstances, you know?"

"Yeah, I feel you, son," he said. "Let's see if we can't make the best out of a fucked-up situation."

When Spits and Trigger ended their embrace, Trigger was off. As the elevator doors were closing, Spits reentered the room where Rachel was. Startlingly, Spits returned to hear the sound of Rachel sniffling. When he came from around the curtain, she had formed a small puddle of tears on her pillow. When he rubbed her back to attempt to console her, her cries grew worse.

He said, "Don't worry. We gonna find this mu'fucka, and I swear he's gonna die for what he did."

When Rachel could no longer conceal her hurt, she looked up at Spits. She wanted him to just be able to read her mind without having to say what she was about to say, but he couldn't do that. She would just have to come clean. She softly uttered two words under her breath that got Spits' full attention the moment he heard them. She said, "I lied."

"What are you talking about?" Spits asked confusingly.

"I lied to you, Michael," she said, looking him straight in his eyes. "I never once had to lie to you, until now. I lied."

"What do you mean?" he asked. "You lied to me about what?"

"I loved him, Michael," she said now staring out of the window. "I loved him with all of my heart. I could've never imagined that he had it inside of him to do something like this. Never in a million years, Michael... never!"

"I don't understand, Rachel," he said. "You're starting to confuse me."

"I gave him everything," she continued. "And I guess it wasn't good enough. I thought I was going to die. He almost killed me!" she screamed with all the energy she could muster. "I told him I was pregnant with his child and he called me a liar. He accused me of cheating on him with another man. I thought he would be happy for us." She paused for a second, and then continued, "I thought you would be happy for us, but he didn't think so. He said you'd kill him if you found out."

As Spits sat there and listened to Rachel rambling, her words started to make sense to him. Everything that had happened started to come together like a jigsaw puzzle. Pieces of one story were being pulled from everywhere. All the things that didn't make any sense were starting to become clearer. *That's why...* he thought to himself. *And that's what made him...* he figured. Could this be the answer to all of these questions? He couldn't believe it. He started to reject the obvious. He went through a brief period of denial, and then rage filled his body. He needed to hear it in plain English.

"I wanted to say it right to his face," Rachel continued. "I wanted to scream, 'You bastard, look what you did to me!'...But I couldn't...I just couldn't do it."

"I need to hear you say it, Rachel," Spits desperately requested. "I need to hear the words."

"You know what I mean," she cried. "Stop trying to fight it!"

"Just say it!" he yelled, as a tear leaked from his bloodshot eyes. "Just fucking say it, goddammit!"

"It was Peter!" she yelled at the top of her lungs. "That's right! It was your best friend. Peter's the one that did this to me!"

Spits dropped to his knees and leaned on the bed over Rachel's legs and thought to himself, *How can this be happening?* He was just standing face to face with this punk mu'fucka, and he had the nerve to say that he was going out on the streets to find out who did this shit. His top lip curled up on one side as he thought to himself what he would do when they met face to face again.

Spits suddenly got up off of the floor and, in a menacing trance, he walked toward the door despite the numerous cries from his sister to come back. His mind brought him to the waiting room where Red was still sleeping. Before he knew what he was doing there, he was waking him up to ask if he had a pistol on him. When Red confirmed that he was holding, Spits demanded his pistol and the keys to his car. When Red complied, he handed Spits a pair of keys and a shiny, nickel-plated .8mm Beretta, and Spits started toward the stairway. After numerous inquiries from Red as to where Spits was going fell short of his attention, he followed him to the stairs to let him know that he was parked in space number 2036 on the second floor of the parking lot. Spits shot him a "Good lookin'," and instructed him to stay with Rachel until he returned. Red complied once again.

When Spits found himself at space number 2036, he was surprised at what he discovered.

✪✪✪

As Ceelow and El Don got back into the car, Poncho hit the gas. Everything went according to plans. Poncho drove calmly from the crime scene and went down 226th Street. He let Ceelow out of the car on 224th Street and Carpenter Avenue so that he and El Don could dump the car. Ceelow got out, leaving the shotgun in the back seat, and headed up the block where he would go home and change clothes before coming back out to see if there would be anybody talking to the police about the murder that had just taken place. By the time he got upstairs, changed, and then back out to the front of the building, about half an hour had passed. By now, the cops had reached the crime scene, and they were sealing it off from the crowd that had gathered. Almost everybody that lived in 666 was standing outside by now, asking each other what was going on. Cee posted up in front to make his own inquiries as to what had gone down.

"Yo!" he called to Winston. "What's all this shit about, dog?"

"Me no know," he answered. "A bwoy must've get shot up, seen?"

"Oh, for real?" Cee asked.

Just then, out of a car that had just come to an abrupt halt in front of the building came another dark figure. But this time the dark figure was coming towards Ceelow. This dark figure also had an object in hand, cocked and loaded. When the dark figure pointed the object, Cee realized that the dark figure was Jacob and the object was a .9 mm pistol. *POW! POW!* The sound left an echo in Ceelow's ears, and he heard nothing else. Everybody was scattering now. All it took was a blink of the eye, and Ceelow could now feel some sort of hot liquid dripping down the side of his face.

✪✪✪

When Spits confirmed that he was at the right space number in the parking lot, he found a blood-red Ducati Monster 800, with a matching blood-red helmet tied to the back seat. Spits quickly hopped on the bike and started the engine. He placed the Beretta in his pants behind him and rode off spinning the tires out. He had still been traveling in some sort of trance when he left the parking lot, and he didn't even know where he was going, but his subconscious was taking him exactly where he needed to be. He made left turns, and right turns, until he found himself on the freeway. He hit a small bump in the street and all of a sudden came back to his senses. He found himself behind a black Dodge Durango. He stayed behind it for a little while before taking a deep breath and pulling along the side of it. He crept up on the right side of the truck until he got a clear glimpse of the driver. Spits bit his bottom lip and his eyes began to bulge out of his head as he realized it was Trigger in the driver's seat. He sped the bike up and cut over in front of Trigger. Then, he slowed down on his left side until he was parallel with the driver's side door.

By now, Trigger's curiosity had been piqued, as he wondered *What the fuck is this dude doing?* By the time he figured it out, it would be too late.

Spits kept the helmet cover down, but kept looking over at Trigger to see if he had his attention. When Spits was sure he had Trigger's undivided attention, he faced him and lifted the helmet cover. The look on Trigger's face was worth a million in cash. When he saw Spits' screwed-up facial expression, his heart dropped down into his ass. He hit the gas but Spits wouldn't get left too far behind him. They climbed up to speeds as fast as 95 mph, but never once did Spits break eye contact with him. They locked onto each other's eyes for what seemed like hours. Every memory they had together went through their minds. They both thought about when they were kids, when they could only dream of experiencing the things that they'd experienced now that they were all grown. Nothing could hurt a man more than being stabbed in the back by someone that he could have referred to as a brother.

Spits' and Trigger's whole lives together flashed before both their eyes, until Spits reached behind his back and pulled out what looked like a bolt of lightning. The way the newly risen sun shone off the nickel-plated Beretta made Spits' hand look like it was completely consumed with light. He lifted the light, and still parallel with Trigger doing over 100 mph, he shut his eyes for the split second it took for him to pull the trigger. He let off one, two, three…four, five shots at Trigger, shattering his window into a thousand pieces and sending brain bits and blood onto the passenger side window and all over the interior of the truck. When Spits took one more glance into Trigger's dead eyes, he sped off. As what was left of Trigger's head fell lifelessly onto the steering wheel, his truck lost control and swerved into the median flipping over thirteen times before it came to a complete stop. Nothing could explain the tranquility that Spits felt as he rode off hearing the noise of Trigger's truck flipping over, while the wind blew on him. He had just committed his first murder and he didn't even consider giving it a second thought, even though he had just taken his oldest and best friend's life.

✪✪✪

When Ceelow felt that hot liquid, he thought for a second that he was the one that was hit. That thought quickly vanished when he realized that

Winston's lifeless body was lying on the ground next to him with the back of his head blown out.

Cee had realized that Jacob was finally taking revenge for the scuffle he'd had with Winston. Now Winston was dead, and all he died over was a fucking ten-dollar bag of weed. Jacob got Winston back for that day, but when he went fleeing, the gunshots didn't stop. They only continued as he attempted to engage himself in a gunfight with the police, of course making him the next to fall victim to the streets. It had happened so fast that if you blinked for too long, you would have missed it. Inside of sixty minutes, three people were dead in the streets of the Bronx.

Before Cee got a chance to make his own getaway, the police had already surrounded him. Now he would be going through the system, ironically not even for the crime that he'd actually committed that night. He wasn't worried about it, but he couldn't have picked a worse time to get arrested, with it being the end of the week, plus with all the following week containing the Christmas and New Year's holidays. Before he knew it, it could be a week or two before he got to see a judge. Cee would have to call Riker's Island home for a little while.

CHAPTER 20

"Did you hear about what happened in California?" asked Special Agent Cassett as he walked up to his partner sitting at his desk.

"Yeah," responded Clifton. "Peter Beckford, a.k.a. Trigger, was gunned down on Interstate 680 early this morning. The shit is all over the news. This whole thing is going to lead to a huge shit-storm. I can feel it."

"Well, I wouldn't normally say this, but I ain't too sad to see him go," Cassett said.

"The little fucker must've pissed off the wrong people out in California," Clifton said. "I wonder what he was doing out there to begin with."

Just then, one of their colleagues came over to where they were sitting and said, "Hey, fellas! The Assistant Director wants you guys in his office, ASAP!"

"Aw shit!" Clifton snapped. "You know we're in for it now."

"Yup!" Agent Cassett agreed.

When they reached Assistant Director Chistov's office, they were directed by him to be seated until he was done on the phone. They sat there with their backs straight up and their hands folded, as they waited for him to complete his phone call, which seemed like a more "politically correct" version of the chewing out they would be receiving. With every word spat at him from the other end of the phone, his face grew more and more twisted. He began staring at Cassett and Clifton with a fierce and vengeful look on his face. They knew for a fact that they would be in for it.

When Chistov finally hung up his long and drawn-out phone call, he began in a calm voice by saying, "I'm pretty sure you boys heard about what happened to Peter 'Trigger' Beckford in California not too long ago?"

They both nodded in agreement.

"You may have most recently been informed of his alleged involvement with another crime syndicate located in the Sunnyvale part of California?" He paused for a second, and then continued, "But what you probably don't know is that Peter Beckford has been living in California under the name Nathaniel Evans, and that he's probably been living it up out there since he jumped bail." He paused again, and then went on in a higher tone. "I cannot believe…that this Time Bomb Family is showing so much blatant disregard for the laws of this country, and yet they continue to be given the easy way out!"

"Well, sir," interjected Agent Clifton. "I think that many would agree that Peter Beckford got what he deserved, and that he wasn't granted the easy way out."

"Excuse me, Clifton," Chistov answered. "Did he stand trial?"

"No sir, but—" he said, before the Assistant Director cut him off.

"Did he serve time?!" he yelled at the top of his voice.

"No, sir," Clifton answered, seeing the direction of the questioning.

"Well," Chistov said firmly. "Then he got the easy way out! When I say I want someone to go down, then that's what I mean. Now, if that doesn't happen because we were too busy sitting on our asses, then we've lost, gentlemen…we've lost!"

"We still have the East Coast organization in our grasp, sir," Cassett reminded him. "We can still move forward with the plans that we have laid out."

"I'm sorry, but I'm a little bit concerned about our plans now," Clifton added. "If we're going to move, I think we need to move as soon as possible. I don't think, with his new development, that we have the option of waiting any longer."

"That's absolutely absurd, Clifton," Chistov said. "We will remain focused. We cannot screw this up, too, boys. We won't let another one of these career criminals slip through our hands. It's all we have now, and we will follow through."

✪✪✪

I got back to Ginger in Hawaii the next afternoon. After making sure once more that Rachel would make a successful recovery, I chartered the next available flight. As much as I wanted to stay with her, too many things were pulling me in the opposite direction. First of all, no one could even find out that I had gone to California with all of the things that had happened out there. It would be too easy to put two and two together. The only people that would ever know were Ginger, Rachel and Red. At that point, Red was my mu'fucka. I loved that dude for what he'd done for me. I basically owed him my sister's life, so he could be trusted with my life as well. On top of that, I'd spent almost two days of my vacation with Ginger out in California, and it was now Christmas Eve. Ginger would never have forgiven me if I'd left her all alone in Hawaii through the holidays when it had been my idea to go away. I had anticipated her feeling lonely and spending the entire time in the room alone, but I should've known that wasn't Ginger's style at all. When I got back, she was ecstatic to see me but she had kept herself very busy in my absence. She greeted my arrival at the door as I entered, and first inquired as to Rachel's condition. When I told her that everything would be fine, she went on to show me how she'd occupied her time alone. She led me to the bedroom, and as I walked in, it seemed like she had a shopping bag for every hour we'd spent apart. I simply smiled and kissed her on her forehead. I spent the remainder of the afternoon on the bed while she modeled all of the clothes and jewelry she'd bought. I would soon forget about all of the things that had happened in the past two days, but that wouldn't last long at all.

Ginger never knew of anything that had taken place while I was in Cali, and that's only because she didn't need to know. That's how it needed to be. I simply told her that some guys had broken into my sister's apartment and tried to kill her when she found them there, and that she'd be fine. It was true, except of course for the part about guys breaking into her apartment and her finding them there.

I just overlooked the part about it actually being my best friend, Trigger, that had done that shit to my sister, simply because she was pregnant with his baby and he was afraid of what I might do when I found out. His panic led to his death, and now I neglected to even think twice about what I'd done. I preferred to believe that it had been a stranger that had done those things. It was easier for my mind to conceive that as a reality. That bitch-ass mu'fucka deserved exactly what he'd gotten. He should've been a businessman instead of a fuckin' playboy. Fuck 'em!

As my mind began to wander from the fashion show that I was receiving, Gin started to realize that something clearly must've been upsetting me. She came over and sat on the bed next to me. She got her arm around me before I came back to reality. I attempted to shake off the ill feeling that kept my attention divided from Ginger, but it didn't go away. She kissed my cheek and that forced a small smile to my face.

"She's going to be fine, baby," she said, referring to Rachel. "You don't have to worry about that. She's a strong girl. Nothing can ever take that from her."

I wanted to tell her that Rachel's condition, although very important to me, wasn't the only thing on my mind. I wanted so much to relieve some of the stress I was putting myself through, but I wasn't able to bring it to the surface. It's better that she not know, is all I kept telling myself, but it was getting harder and harder to conceal the frustration. "I know, baby," I said, trying to lift some of the pressure she felt to cheer me up. "I only have one sister, though…you know what I mean?"

"I understand, baby," she answered. "But she wouldn't want you to be here worrying yourself, baby; especially when you're all this way from home. You know what?" she said, taking a peek at the clock on the nightstand. "I know what'll make you feel better. I was going to wait until twelve o'clock to give you this, but whatever. It's already a quarter after ten, so it's Christmas in New York already."

"Oh, yeah," I said, remembering that it was Christmas Eve. "I almost forgot all about that."

"Yeah, wait right here, baby," she said, leaving the room to locate the gift she'd bought me. She reentered the room with a box in her hand wrapped in red with a white ribbon. She handed me the box and I actually felt like a little kid again as I anticipated what might be inside. As I gave a tug at the ribbon, and pulled back the wrapping paper, I saw a black box that looked as if it contained jewelry, but it was too big and heavy for that. I looked up at Ginger suspiciously, and proceeded to open the case. When I opened it, there was a gleaming chrome studio microphone, with the words "Time Bomb Records" engraved on the handle in script.

I had only told her about my idea for starting a record label once in passing, and she'd remembered. I absolutely loved it. It was perfect. Ginger was good for making a shitty day seem like the best.

CHAPTER 21

When it came time for Ginger and Spits to return home, they had reached complete and utter tranquility. Everything Hawaii had to offer them was accepted by them one hundred percent. They had the best time possible in this beautiful villa in Maui but, unfortunately, they'd come to the end of their dream vacation and it was time to go back to work.

By the time they landed on the East Coast, it was a little past 11:00 p.m. From the airport they took a cab to their home where they found a truck in their driveway. Before they were completely pulled into the driveway, Spits realized that it was El Don and Poncho that were parked in front of his house in Don's black Toyota Land Cruiser. As soon as Spits realized who it was, he knew the only thing that could have brought them all the way out to New Jersey from the Bronx was the one thing that he had been avoiding the entire time he'd spent in Maui since he'd returned from Cali. They were immediately approached as they exited the cab with the news of Trigger's death.

"Yo, dog," Poncho began as Spits and Ginger approached the door where they had been awaiting his arrival. "I don't know if you know this yet, but if you don't, we got some bad news just recently from the West Coast. It's about Trigger."

"Something happened to Trigger?" Ginger blurted out before Spits gave her a look that suggested she leave them to talk amongst themselves. "Him, too?" she said, still baffled as she turned toward the door to enter the house.

When Spits and Don P. were alone, they continued.

"What happened to Trigger?" Spits asked as he made an attempt to express obvious confusion and concern. "He got knocked, or some shit?"

"Nah, son," El answered. "He's dead. Somebody bodied him."

"What?!" Spits said, raising his voice. He looked into the faces of the persons that brought this news to him. The information that they provided was so upsetting, they couldn't even return the glance. They were avoiding the eyes of Spits, and found themselves staring at the ground until it was safe to make eye contact. "I can't believe this is happening. Who the fuck did this shit? That mu'fucka gonna die. Who the fuck did this shit?!"

Although Don P. shared Spits' distress, they were even more hurt that they couldn't answer the question that could've possibly brought some light to a rather dark, fucked-up situation. It would've made them feel so much better bringing this news if they could also deliver news that whoever was responsible for it was somewhere leaking out the rest of his brains onto the floor. They wanted to say that they'd found out who'd done it, and that they'd been torturing his ass for the past two days waiting for Spits to come home to finish him off. They wanted to say, "Yeah, we got the nigga in the trunk right now, son!" But they couldn't do that. All they could do was stand there in silence staring at the fucking ground. All they could do was wait for Spits to break the silence. So until that happened, they just stood there.

Unfortunately for Spits, he didn't share the same distress and confusion that Don P. had regarding the news. He knew exactly who it was that had splattered Trigger's brains all over the interior of his truck, but he wouldn't be able to let them know that at this point. The events surrounding those tragic circumstances would never be revealed to anyone besides Rachel, Red, and Spits himself. There were things that nobody needed to know that led to Trigger's death, and that would eternally be between him and Trigger. It was nobody else's business.

When the silence was finally broken, Poncho said, "Yo, we got them niggas over there looking all over the place trying to find out who did this shit, but we haven't heard anything yet. That nigga Red said that this situation will take top priority."

Spits heard that and knew for a fact that if they were waiting for Red to give them an update about this shit that they would be waiting forever. "This bitch-ass nigga that did this shit will not live a day past the day we find his ass, you hear me?"

"No doubt," Poncho replied.

"Word up!" El Don agreed.

"Listen, we gonna have to talk about this shit later when my head is on straight, my niggas," Spits said, trying to quickly get rid of them before Ginger caught wind of this news before he had a chance to let her know. "I'ma holla at ya'll cats when I get a little settled, you know?"

"Yeah, I feel you," Poncho said. "This ain't exactly the kind of shit you want to hear coming home from vacation, and shit. Just holla, dog, and we there for whatever."

"Word up," El added. "All you gotta do is holla, son."

As Spits let out a deep sigh of relief that he was able to successfully complete his first confrontation regarding Trigger, he walked toward the door before he was stopped by Poncho's call. When he turned back unsuspecting of what was left unsaid, he found out that there was more that he didn't know.

"Yo, in case you ain't talk to Cee, ain't nobody seen that nigga on the Block in a couple of days," Poncho said. "He had put us on to a situation about some beef, and we handled that shit, but we ain't seen the nigga since. If you hear anything from him, let us know."

"All right then," Spits said. "One."

"One."

Spits used the five seconds it took for him to insert his key in the lock and open the door to try and figure out how he would explain what had happened to Trigger to Ginger. Although nothing had come to his mind yet, he opened the door anyway. Upon entering the house, he realized that those five seconds were wasted as Ginger had never left the front of the door and had been listening to the entire conversation. When she'd left them alone to come into the house, her curiosity kept her behind the door where she could hear what they were talking about. When she'd heard what happened, she'd taken a seat on the floor on the left side of the door, and had begun crying into her own lap. It wasn't until Spits heard her sniffles that he turned back to find her there. He bit his top lip and took a deep breath. As he walked back to where Ginger was sitting on the floor, she looked up at him and they shared a bewildered glare.

Ginger looked as if she needed further clarification. She needed for Spits to tell her what was going on in a way that made sense to her. Everything that was happening all at the same time was too much for her to handle. There were so many blanks in the story that didn't make any sense. There were so many questions to be answered. While her mind thought of different circumstances and scenarios to try and put these events together, all Ginger could do was stare at Spits with an incomplete look on her face.

The look that Spits returned was similar, but it wasn't the same. The expression that Spits wore on his face was more like suspicion. He thought that Ginger was only looking at him the way she was because she had figured out what had happened, and she was only waiting for it to come out of Spits' mouth. He thought that she had put two and two together and knew that Spits had something directly to do with Trigger's death. He felt a sharp pain in his stomach that would just get worse and worse. He was at a loss for words. There was no explanation that could justify his wrongdoing. He could do nothing but stare at Ginger with an incomplete look on his face.

"How did this happen?" Ginger asked.

Spits didn't want to answer too quickly because he was still not sure of what she had already put together in her mind. "What you mean, Gin?" he asked, so that she could further clarify her question.

"How could these horrible things be happening to everybody that is so close to you? And all at the same time?" she asked. "I don't understand how, first, this awful thing happens to your sister Rachel. Then, once that's under control, it's like…life just throws another curve ball your way. I feel so sorry for you, baby. I don't understand how so many bad things could happen to someone with a heart as good as yours."

All Spits could do was gaze into her eyes. Everything she was saying was coming from her heart. He'd had the complete wrong impression of her attitude. She wouldn't dare think anything negative about him. The only thing that was confusing to her was how he would be able to handle it. That's it. The thought brought a tear to his eye. Her words actually started to make him believe that he was the person she was describing. She loved him so much that the thought that he had anything to do with Trigger's death wouldn't even cross her mind. That's the level of dedication she had for him.

Although Spits was unable to control his first reaction to the statements that Ginger had just made, he knew that if she was going to recover successfully, she would have to know for a fact that he would be all right. In order for him to accomplish that, he would have to be strong and control his emotions. He wiped the tears from her face and sat next to her on the floor. He put his arm around her so that she could lay her head on his shoulder. There they sat for the next thirty to forty-five minutes, just thinking in silence. From there, they would make their way up to the bedroom for a well-deserved rest.

Early the next morning, Spits would be awakened by the sound of music playing in the bathroom. He got up and found Ginger in the shower.

"I didn't mean for you to wake up so early, honey," she said. "I found a message from my mother on the voicemail and she said that I should be on my way to her place as soon as I get back. We have a long way to go to get to Florida. Are you going to be okay, baby?"

"Yeah, I'll be cool, Gin," he answered as he washed his face. "You don't have to worry about me. I'll be fine."

"I'm sorry I woke you up, baby," Ginger said. "I would've only woken you to say bye when I was on my way out. I already called a cab to take me upstate."

"It ain't nothin', Mommy," he said as he brushed his teeth. "I'ma be i-ight, sweetie."

"I'd hate to leave you if you didn't feel better,"she said.

"Please." Spits shrugged off her comment and walked back toward the bedroom. "I'm going back to sleep."

"Wait!" Ginger said, calling him back. "I'm going to miss you a whole lot, baby. Give me a kiss good-bye."

They kissed and Spits made his way back to the bed after saying, "Have a good time, baby. And, umm…I'll be missing you, too…more than anything, sweetie. Love you."

CHAPTER 22

"Yo, you ain't heard shit from this nigga Cee yet?" I asked Poncho while in my car on the way to meet up with him and El.

"Nah," Ponch responded. "He must've bounced after that hit, or some shit. Maybe he thought it was gonna be too hot in the streets, ya na'mean?"

"I don't know about that, dog," I said. "Sounds kind of thin, you know. Why wouldn't he holla to let us know what was up?"

"I can't call it, dog." Ponch still was unable to satisfy my curiosity. "Probably he got a bad vibe, or somethin'."

"Bad vibe like what? What you mean by that? Ya'll niggas ain't never mention nothin' about that whole Roscoe situation, right?"

"Nah. I mean…I don't know. I ain't like you, dog. I can't just be around a nigga that I can't trust and be one hundred percent comfortable, and shit. I'm not the actor type."

"What?!" I spat as my temper started to rise. "Yo, we ain't never get to the bottom of none of that shit this nigga Roscoe was talkin'. Ain't no actin' over here, dog. He's still my man, you know? I ain't just gonna shit on him off the strength of some bitch-ass nigga that would've said anything to save his own ass."

"I-ight, fam," Poncho said, trying to calm me down. "Relax. All I'm sayin' is that I ain't trust that nigga since that shit went down. I don't know for a fact, but maybe that is why he just disappeared like that…ha-ha…if that's what's up, that mu'fucka's a bitch-ass nigga!"

"Yo, son!" I yelled. "Just remember that this shit here was poppin' way before you, nigga! Don't ever forget that shit!"

"My bad, nigga." Poncho tried to conceal a small nervous chuckle. "I was just talkin' shit, you know."

"Yeah, whatever! Just meet me at the spot, i-ight. One."

A few days had passed since Ginger and I had gotten back from Hawaii and things had just started to calm down as far as that whole Trigger thing, but you could tell that there was still some tension in the air. Besides the shit with Trigger, nobody had seen or heard from Ceelow in a week. If you let Don P. tell it, he either left 'cause he thought we was gonna do him, or 'cause he thought the streets was too hot. Either way, the shit just didn't make any sense to me. First of all, if it was something as mediocre as him fleeing from the heat in the streets, he would've known that he could holla at me to let me know what's up. Secondly, if I knew Cee like I thought, finding out that we was about to murder him would have just made him jump off first. One thing about Cee, he wasn't no bitch-ass nigga. That's probably what made Poncho act in a funny way with me. They must've thought I was scared of the nigga, or somethin'. Ever since that Roscoe shit had gone down, they'd been different. It was like I was just supposed to take him out with no questions asked. On some real shit, I knew that Cee was a hard-head nigga, but he wasn't stupid enough to think he could just take on the entire family. Just the thought of it sent a shiver through my spine. I wasn't afraid of Cee…but, I was afraid of what might happen if we had to get it on.

Well, now it was New Year's Eve and we were about to jump off this New Year's party without my nigga Cee, and that shit was stressing me the fuck out. Everybody that I started this shit with wasn't going to be with me when I thought it was my highest point. I felt like I was peaking, and it seemed like everyone that I loved wouldn't be able to enjoy it with me. Everybody that I once trusted with my life from the beginning of all of this shit wasn't with me, and I hadn't yet figured out how to deal with that. In any event, the show had to go on, so I had to adjust really fast.

When the time was finally near for the most anticipated bash of the year, there was a huge buzz on the street. With all of the rumors already in heavy rotation, we just knew that we would have to dead all of the gossip and blow everybody's expectations out of the water. Until the flyers hit the street to promote the festivities, no one could've imagined in a million years what the night would hold. Niggas got really hype when they found out the location and concept.

These dudes out here wouldn't have imagined where this shit was going to jump off. When niggas found out that it was poppin' off in the Times Square area of Manhattan, they said, "That's serious!" When they found out it was happening in the Marriott Marquis Hotel, they was like, "And these niggas is not playin'!" But when they heard that it was going down in The View, the rotating restaurant located at the very top of the hotel, all they could say was, "Whoa!"

Aside from the bangin' location, the whole theme of the party is what really made the shit live. I figured that the hottest shit in the world would be to have the dirtiest niggas in New York, in the middle of Times Square, at the top of the Marriott Marquis, looking the cleanest they've ever looked. So, I decided that this would be a White on White event. When the invitations got sent out, the heading read:

"Pure and Uncut"

The Time Bombs Presents, "I'm Dreamin' of a White New Year's"

✪✪✪

In order for you to enter the bash of the century, to end the century, you would be required to be dipped head to toe in pure white clothing. It didn't matter if you wore a full-length mink or a pair of shell-top Adidas, as long as it was clean, and as long as it was as white as a brick of uncut Colombian.

It was now 4 p.m., and I was on my way to meet up with Don P. to make sure that everything was going according to plans over at the spot. I told Don P. to meet me there just to make certain that I didn't forget anything, but this nigga Ponch was getting on my fuckin' nerves about Cee. They would just assume to think that shit was sweet, and I wasn't feelin' that at all. But, when it came down to it, all of that was neither here nor there. I had to focus on the situation at hand.

When I got to 1535 Broadway, I saw that El Don and Poncho had beaten me there. I parked in the front of the hotel and they greeted my arrival with pounds and hugs. As we were about to enter the building, Poncho, already seeing that I was a little troubled, attempted to apologize for the comments he'd made earlier, but I cut him off and told him to forget about it. I shrugged off the entire incident. I could understand, to some degree, Poncho's stance, but he didn't know Cee as long as I did. With that, he had to understand my position. If it were El that we heard was stealing from us, he would go to war against the Family just to have his brother's back. That's the way I felt about Ceelow.

Until we reached the top floor of the hotel, I felt a rumbling in my stomach. So much had happened that would've normally determined a negative outcome of this entire situation but now I had a "fuck it" attitude about the whole thing. At this point, I was expecting the worst to happen—if it hadn't already. When the elevator doors opened, we stepped out and what we saw put me and Don P. at complete ease. I could finally inhale deeply and breathe easy. Everything was exactly as I pictured it—for a change.

Immediately out of the elevator, which was located directly in the center of the building, there was a podium set up for checking invitations. It stood in the middle of the restaurant, in an area that was stationary, while the rest of the floor spun slowly around this section. There were also elevators along the side of the building that were used for floors below this one, but all of our guests would be entering through this area. Next to the podium was a case of stairs that led up into the lounge area. The rest of the restaurant floor was transformed from an elegant eating establishment to a Hip-Hop nightclub. We'd completely "hooded it out." The floor was kept clear of tables and chairs to be used as a dance floor. There were a total of three bars located throughout the space. There was one small bar in the lounge area and two large ones on the restaurant floor. Behind both bars on the dance floor I'd had them build small stages for some exotic dancers—nothing too crazy; they wouldn't even be topless. In addition, there were two small cages that I had built to hang from the ceiling of the dance floor that would also house exotic dancers throughout the night. On top of that, there would also be exotic dancers on the floor to keep niggas from holding up the wall. We had everything covered.

Upstairs, the lounge area was reserved for VIP access. This section was also stationary and you could view the rotating portion of the dance floor over a side rail. There would be lounge chairs, tables and sofas sporadically placed throughout the floor. It seemed to encompass enough space for all of our VIP invites. They could either relax up there all night and drink the complementary champagne and mingle among themselves, or go down to the dance floor and go crazy with the party people. When we were completely satisfied with how everything was set up for the biggest night of the century, we were off to get everything else ready.

After we made sure that everything was properly set up at the spot, me, Don and P. had our own separate responsibilities to take care of before we could actually go to the crib to get ready. I would be handling our security measures. I had to make sure that we had an appropriate amount of "thick-necks" to hold us down, so that we could feel comfortable in not having to buss our shit the whole night.

El Don was going to make sure that our chefs were properly equipped for the night. We had a split menu for our VIP invites that gave them a choice of Southern or Jamaican dishes. There was also a small menu of appetizers for whomever occupied the bar on the main floor.

As for Poncho, he would make sure that all of our dancers would be able to make it to the spot properly prepared for the evening and on time. He set it up for them to be picked up and brought to the party, twice throughout the night like a one-two punch. They would arrive in a convoy of Escalades in groups of ten. Their first drop-off would be early while everyone was still lined up to get in. When niggas saw them in couples hoppin' out of five pearly white Cadillac trucks, they would be even more hyped to get in. The next drop would be when the line was already moving as it neared midnight, and that would be the knockout blow. Niggas could mingle with the ladies as they came in to make them feel a little bit more comfortable and confident to have the best time possible throughout the rest of the night. That shit would be perfect.

It was now a little past seven o'clock and everything was going according to plans. It was time for us to head in our separate ways to get ourselves ready for later. Don P. would be by my crib to pick me up by 10:00 p.m., so I had more than enough time to get myself prepared. I had a stop-over on Allerton Avenue before I went all the way back home to finish getting ready.

When I reached home, I immediately got into the shower to try and wash away all of the anguish I had been feeling from earlier in the day. My early-afternoon pressures had been relieved and now I would need to be prepared for my late-night pressures. This event had been one my oldest childhood dreams and it was finally about to come true.

Even with this situation with Ceelow still fucking with my subconscious, I hadn't begun to imagine the worst. All I did was put any negative thoughts in the back of my head, and tell myself that he would be showing up at the spot that night like nothing had ever happened. It was nothing until I made it something. In any case, this single event would seal the nineties—and all of its complications—and mark a new beginning.

When I got out of the shower, I hurriedly went straight to the closet where I had my outfit for the night already prepared. I had the perfect garments put together for the party. I would be looking extremely crisp, and I could hardly wait. When I finally had it all laid out on the bed, I couldn't help but to gaze in appreciation. When I was fully dressed, I made two phone calls. The first was to the manager at the hotel to make sure he waited until there was a healthy line accumulating outside before opening the doors. He assured me that the line was even healthier than we had anticipated, and that they'd already opened the doors promptly at 9:00 p.m. By the time we got there, it would already be pretty thick on the main floor, but I didn't expect any VIP invites until after ten or eleven o'clock. The next call I made was to El Don to make sure that everything was going according to schedule. Again, I was left to relax and wait for their arrival, which would be in no more than twenty minutes. When I hung up the phone with El, I posted up in front of the wall mirror in my bedroom for a minute to make sure everything was just right.

From top to bottom, I had on a white Dobbs "Godfather" hat with a white ribbon, and matching feather. Under that, I wore a crispy white du-rag—just to thug it out a bit. I had on a white Dolce & Gabbana vest with white pinstripes, and a silk Gabbana button-up to match. On my feet, I appropriately wore a pair of Gabbana slide-in loafers, and topped it off with a pair of rimless rectangular D&G sunglasses. From my neck hung twenty carats of diamonds in the shape of our TB logo, and on my wrist I had an Oyster Perpetual Rolex with a diamond-flooded bezel and band. You could say I was just about ready.

El Don and Poncho were at my house to pick me up at approximately 9:10 p.m., and when the doorbell rang, I was nervous with anticipation. When I got to my front door, we exchanged pounds and hugs. They both had on white cashmere V-neck sweaters with white leather pants and matching white three-quarter jackets. They also each had on white Kangol golf caps and white on white Air Force Ones. When we were done complimenting each other's garments, they parted to show me what we would be pulling up to the spot in. when I saw the big-boy, bright-white Hummer H1 four-door wagon sitting by the curb looking simply remarkable, it was a wrap.

It wasn't until we were already halfway to the spot before I realized that we were in fact missing one more person. This nigga Little Jay was supposed to be riding with us to the hotel. "Yo," I called to Poncho over the loud-playing music. "What happened to this nigga, Jay?"

"Oh," he said, remembering that he was supposed to give me a message. "I forgot all about that shit. He told me that he wasn't gonna roll through with us tonight."

"So, he gonna meet us there, or somethin'?" I asked.

"Nah, dog," he answered. "I don't think that nigga's coming at all."

"What?" I said confusingly. "What happened?"

"I don't know," he responded. "He gave me this number for you to call so that he could explain all that shit."

Poncho handed me a cell phone number on a ripped brown paper bag and I called it immediately to see what was up with my little man. If anything, I wanted him to roll in with us, just to write it in stone that he was on top of the world with us. I wondered what could've kept him from that.

"Hello?" said the person that answered the phone.

"Yeah," I said. "Who's this?"

"You called me, nigga!" the voice on the other end of the receiver replied. "Who the fuck is this?"

Noticing the sound of the voice a bit gave me an idea of who it was. "Pookie?" I asked.

"Yeah," he said. "Who's this?"

"This is Spits, nigga!" I said as my temper rose a bit. "Where the fuck is Jay?"

"Oh," he said in a low tone as the thugness in his voice no longer existed. "My bad, Spits. Jay's right here. Hold on a second."

Little Jay got on the phone. "Yo, what up, my nigga Spits? Happy New Year, dog." He was acting as if nothing was wrong.

"Yeah, Happy New Year," I said, not yet understanding what was going on. "Anyway, what's good, fam? Why ain't you comin' through the spot? We 'bout to jump off the ultimate New Year's bash."

"Oh, my bad, dog," he said. "I'm not going to be able to make it, son. I would if I could, but I can't do it."

"Why?" I asked. "What's so important that it can't wait until later?"

"Well," he said slowly, easing his way. "The thing is...I'm on my way to Philly right now. Me and Pookie about to jump off our own thing down there. It's not like I wasn't eating or nothin' like that. It's just...lately, I been feelin' like I need to have my own shit, you know?"

"What you mean by that?" I asked.

"I just been feelin' like I want to run my own enterprise. Something that I could call mines," he answered. "Me and Pookie been talkin' about makin' this move for the longest, and...I figure ain't no time better than now... with tomorrow being the first of the month and all. These be the times when niggas get the most lax, you know, so it'll be perfect."

As Little Jay went on and on about his ideas for his own drug enterprise, he reminded me of myself a few years back. He had everything that he needed to be successful in this life. Although I would've wanted more time with him to mold him into a real "G," it was time for him to assume his own position behind the supervisor's desk. I should've known it would happen eventually. I couldn't have imagined myself working for someone else for too long either, before I would've wanted my own thing. I didn't have anything negative to say as I was positive that he already had everything worked. It seemed as though he'd put a lot of thought into this power move. He even had his own connection, and the price he was paying for weight wasn't that bad. When we finally hung up, I wished him all the luck in the world. I told him that he was a good protégé and that I hoped to hear from him soon. We would soon find out that we would be speaking to each other again quicker than we both could've expected.

CHAPTER 23

When Spits, Don and P. pulled up to the spot, it was looked like pure anarchy in the streets. The line to get in was still all the way around the corner, and it didn't look as if anybody was planning on giving up any time soon. Of course, the red carpet was extended to the curb when the gleaming white Hummer pulled up, and everybody knew exactly who it was. First, Spits jumped out the back seat, then Don and P. With Don and P. moving closely behind Spits, they literally had to push through all the girls that attempted to rush them on their way in. When they finally got to the elevator, it was about 10:20 p.m. They went straight upstairs to the VIP section and sat at the booth that was reserved for their party.

"This shit is jumpin'," Poncho said, referring to the liveliness of the party.

"Hell yeah," Spits agreed. "These mu'fuckas is goin' nuts. You seen the way them bitches was actin' in the front, son?"

"For real, though," El added. "I ain't think it would be packed like this, and niggas is still tryin' to get in."

After they went through numerous toasts to, "Dom P.'s and palm trees," and they guzzled uncountable bottles of bubbly, time started moving by real quickly. As they saw the midnight hour nearing, they fled to the center of the dance floor with bottles of champagne in hand. Before they knew it, there were only fifteen minutes left until twelve o'clock. As the tension grew, and the excitement reached the highest level, Spits began to anticipate the night's climax. Just then, he got a call on his cell.

"Hello!" he tried to yell over the sound of a few thousand people, all screaming at the same time.

"Hello," said the voice on the other end. "Can you hear me?"

"Huh?" he yelled. "Who is this?"

Before they got a chance to respond, the connection was lost and Spits shrugged it off and continued partying. It took ten minutes, but the resourcefulness of the caller finally paid off. His cell phone rang twice more before he heard it and answered.

"Hello!" he said even louder than the first time. "Who is this?"

"It's Gin," she said, now yelling also.

"Oh, what's up, baby? How's Florida?"

"It's all right, baby. It's just raining a whole lot. But I miss my baby...even more than I thought I would. But anyway, how is the party, honey?"

"Oh, it's i-ight," he answered. "But I miss you, too."

"What?!" she yelled. "I can't hear you!"

"I said that I missed you!" Spits repeated in a louder tone.

"I still can't really hear you, baby!" she screamed. "You're fading in and out!"

"I said...wait, let me find somewhere that's a little less noisy," he said, leaving the dance floor as he headed toward the back away from the party. He made his way through the crowd and felt an uplifting energy just from being on the phone with Ginger. It was just what he needed. So much that he didn't even give it a second thought to leave the party as it was about to climax. "Can you hear me now?" he asked as he entered a staircase in the back.

"Yeah, that's much better," she said. "Now, what were you saying?"

"I was saying that I miss you, too, sweetie," he said, with a grin forming in his facial expression.

Ginger simply returned a smile as if she were looking at him right in his face.

When Spits realized that he couldn't reenter the party from this stairway, it was already too late for him to catch the door. It was locked from the inside, as it was only supposed to be used as an exit. He made his way down one flight of stairs and left the staircase on the next floor down. When he got out of the staircase, the sight of all the people that had gathered in Times Square kept him at the window in the lobby for a moment. It was a sight like he had never imagined he would see. What looked like millions of people, all occupying the streets of New York for the same reason…to celebrate life. Spits watched in appreciation with no hurry as the party upstairs was obviously getting more and more live with every second that passed. He entered the nearest elevator with exactly thirty seconds left before the new millennium and went down. The elevator was made completely of glass and was directed toward the street where everyone was gathered. He pressed the button for the bottom floor and never once took his eyes off the sight that had him totally captivated in its splendor.

"Are you still there, baby?" Ginger asked.

"Yeah. I'm still here, Mommy."

"It got so quiet."

"I'm in an elevator. This shit looks crazy out here. You should see it. Mu'fuckas is jumpin' up on top of buses. Niggas is tryin' to break through the department store windows, and shit. This shit looks crazy, for real."

As the elevator made its way to the street level, the ten-second countdown had begun and Spits could see the New Year's ball begin to drop over the huge crowd counting along. Ten…nine…eight–every second was like a thunderous jolt passing through each individual in attendance. Seven…six…five–the eagerness grew more and more. No one really knew what to expect from the year 2000. There had been so many talks of Y2K bugs, a new world order, and the world coming to an end as everyone knew it, that as much as it was exciting, it was nerve-wracking at the same time. Four…three…two–before the last second of 1999, many could do nothing but close their eyes and wish for the best. Only few would actually witness the ball drop that last little notch before it lit up and everybody would scream, "Happy New Year!" Millions of prayers went out, and even more New Year's resolutions were promised. It was finally time to see what would happen.

As the elevator doors opened on the street-level floor, all of the elevator doors on the top level opened as well. And while Spits departed the elevator and made his way toward the nearest exit, the Federal Bureau of Investigation had made a total breach of his get-together on the top level in search of what had just simply vanished without a trace. The music went off and everyone could do nothing but stare in amazement as what seemed like hundreds of federal officers surrounded them with semi-automatic machine guns locked and loaded. Even as the ringleader of this organization was nowhere to be found, there was no way they were letting anyone else slip through their fingers. Almost everyone there would be going through the system tonight; whether they knew it or not.

"Happy New Year!" Spits could hear everyone screaming in unison as total strangers exchanged hugs and kisses in celebration. Under the screams was the sound of the horns blowing, as tons and tons of confetti flew through the sky. For most, this would be one of the best days of their natural lives. For Spits, similar feelings would be quickly destroyed with the news of events.

Simultaneously, all throughout the Bronx, police raids were being conducted to seize everything that the Time Bomb Family had worked so hard to build from the ground up. They had finally moved in and ripped the guts out of Spits and his entire enterprise. It was all surgical. They already had everything they needed to build an extremely strong case against Spits a.k.a. Michael Banner, but they wanted to make sure that everything was done with the utmost efficiency. They knew that if all they did was indict Spits that he could easily continue running the enterprise from prison. In order for them to be completely successful in their attempts to bring the TB Family to its knees, they had to get everything all at once. They'd waited until Spits fully stocked all of their drugstores with enough product to handle the first-of-the-month traffic. Also, as to not let anyone slip through the cracks, they'd waited until the major figures were all together at Spits' very much publicized New Year's party. They'd thought of everything. Well, everything except for Spits himself slipping right out of the back door while they went charging in the front. If nothing else, Spits was incredibly lucky Ginger had called him when she did. Otherwise, he would've been going through the system along with everyone else in his clique.

For Spits, it took a cab ride home to find out that they had been infiltrated. The mere presence of the authorities at his doorstep was enough to deter him from exiting the taxi. If only he could've gotten inside of his house before they did. Now, it was too late for him to empty out the safe he had in the closet that kept all of his savings. He simply kept it moving right through his neighborhood, and proceeded to the safety of his mother's house. There, he could get his thoughts untangled and figure out his next move. He called Don and P. first to see if the police had raided the hotel. When he received no answer, he painted his own picture of what had happened. He soon came to the conclusion that they must've gotten everything. Even if they didn't, it would be a minute before he was going through the hood to find out. It was easier to anticipate the worst, but in this case, the worst had actually happened. He had to put himself in the mind state that everything was already gone, and that he had to build whatever he needed from what he had.

He started in the most obvious of places. He called Mr. Ortiz to ask for some work on consignment. He needed some quick cash, and he didn't know any other way to get it besides hustling. If he thought that he could count on anybody, it would be Mr. Ortiz. Given the relationship they had, he thought there was a mutual respect between them. He would soon find out otherwise.

"Hola?" said the woman that answered the phone.

"Sí, el Sr. Ortiz, por favor," Spits said. "Usted lo puede decir es Spits."

"Un minuto, por favor," she said before putting him on hold.

After only a moment went by, it felt like an hour to Spits. He was incredibly nervous and he didn't know how he was going to explain his position. Then, he heard Mr. Ortiz say, "Ah, Sr. Spits. So good to hear from you." Spits just took a deep breath and felt completely at ease.

"Yes, Mr. Ortiz," he began. "I have a favor to ask of you. I should stress the urgency of my situation before I continue, just to let you know that only in an extreme situation would I ask for you to extend your hand."

"You don't need to stress anything to me," Mr. Ortiz said in a cold manner. "I already know the importance of your situation."

Spits was stuck. All of the positivity that he had turned into confusion. Now he didn't know where he stood. Ortiz couldn't possibly have found out what had happened so quickly. Spits had only just found out. How could he have known already? "I don't understand," he said. "What are you talking about?"

"You second-guess me still?" he asked. "After all we've been through, you still underestimate my intelligence. Did you think that I would not find out that your partner is on trial for murder?"

"What?!" Spits yelled. "What the fuck you talkin' 'bout?"

"Listen to me, Sr. Spits. I have always given you the respect that you deserve, but I don't think we can continue doing business if you're going to continuously spit in my face with no regard."

"I apologize, Romero," he said before he was cut off.

"No," Ortiz said. "I'm sorry, Sr. Spits, but we are no longer business associates. You can address me as Mr. Ortiz."

"I don't mean any disrespect," Spits began in an apologetic tone. "I'm just a little confused as to what it is you're talking about."

"If this is an attempt at humor, let me assure you that I am not amused," he responded. "You mean to tell me that you didn't know that your partner, Sr. Loew, has been in prison for the past week for murder. Unfortunately, this is just an illustration of your incompetence. It seems as though your partner got picked up during a routine sweep and when they analyzed his fingerprints, they matched the prints taken from a murder weapon found next to two dead bodies in the Bronx Park four years ago."

"How did you find this out?" Spits asked, still confused.

"Sr. Oberman informed me," he said. "I do have my ear to the street at all times."

As their conversation continued, Spits felt that he hadn't been making any progress. Mr. Ortiz knew every detail of the events that had been taking place in the hood. He even knew that Spits once tried another connection, but that it didn't work out. Even with that, he continued to do business with their organization completely off the strength of their past loyalty. But now, Mr. Ortiz figured his time was up. By now they've already had the best of times, and with this new development, he knew that it could only get worse. Romero's instincts were telling him that Spits and Ceelow were setting him up. He thought that they'd given him up to get Ceelow off, so he figured that a meeting where narcotics would exchange hands would only bring the authorities to him. even though that was the furthest thing from the truth, he wasn't going to risk what it would take to find out.

When they finally hung up with each other, Spits felt worse off than he did when they'd started. He felt at a disadvantage now with no resources. He knew now why Cee hadn't been around for the past few days but it still didn't make any sense. Then, it hit him like a ton of bricks. That must be how those mu'fuckas got the drop on my whole fuckin' organization, he thought. That bitch-ass nigga ratted on me to save his own ass. Don P. was right. I should've bodied that nigga when I had the chance.

Spits went through a number of different emotional stages at that point. He was running out of options really quickly and he didn't know what to do. When Spits finally reached the end of his rope and exaggerated every alternative, he made the one call for help that he could've never imagined he would be making before this day.

"Hello?" said the voice that answered the phone.

"Yeah, what up," Spits answered. "It's Spits. I need a favor, dog."

"What is it?" Little Jay asked. "Anything you need, king."

With that phone call, he set it up for Jay to send Spits the one thing that he could ask for without sacrificing his pride. He asked that Little Jay front him a brick to flip. He explained the whole story to him and with every word, Jay realized how lucky he was to have made the decision he did when he did. He was happy that Spits felt he was someone that he could call on for assistance. He had long been on the other side of these types of situations and Spits always held him down. It was his turn to do the same. He offered to send money, but Spits let his dignity get in the way. He wasn't comfortable with becoming a charity case before he made a valiant effort to get back on his feet. He'd done it before, and he'd do it again.

After a quick shower and a change of clothes, he left his mother with a hug and a kiss. He gave his little brother a pound and a hug and told them both that he loved them. He also told them that he didn't know when he would get another chance to visit because the police might come there to look for him. Spits and his mother both knew that this might come and they were prepared for it. From there he went to a motel on Gun Hill Road, named Friendly's, where he would rent a room and wait for Pookie to arrive with the package from Little Jay.

Spits lit up a blunt and smoked half of it before his exhaustion got the best of him. After a short nap, Spits was awakened by a knock on the door. He'd left instructions with the front desk that someone by the name "Pookie" would be asking for him, so that they could send him up immediately. He opened the door and seeing Pookie was like a lifesaver. He quickly pulled him in the room before nervously looking around to see if he'd been followed. When Pookie was inside the room, they went over the agreement.

"So, uuh…Jay said that you want me to stay until I finished bussin' down this brick," Pookie said. "That's what's up?"

"Yeah," Spits replied. "That's what's up. Just let him know that I'll get back at him when you get back to Philly. Let's get started. We only got a few hours before the morning rush."

Together, they broke down enough coke to make two packs of twenty-six. With this much done, Spits left Pookie to finish while he hit the streets. With everything as hot as it was on the streets, Spits couldn't imagine anywhere to hustle these packs. The Woods would be too hot. The Block would definitely be too hot. But it was the first of the month and he had to figure something out, and fast. Ironically, he ended up right back where he'd started. He couldn't think of anywhere else to bubble where they wouldn't be looking for him. So, there he was. He'd done a complete three-sixty. He didn't really feel the pressure until he took his position on that dark street in the park by the overpass. He stood where he stood the first night they'd hustled there. He glanced at the top of the steps, where the wall provided cover from the bullets flying at him that unforgettable night. He remembered the sound the car made as it peeled the rubber from the tires to get away. He looked at the sidewalk where they had them bitch-ass mu'fuckas face down on the ground. He distinctly remembered the seven shots that Cee had sent from that .9 mm. He remembered the look on Ceelow's face after he did it, looking as if nothing was wrong. He remembered the fun they'd had with the rest of that night, and the guilt he'd felt the next morning.

After only fifteen minutes, Spits was already growing more and more impatient with the traffic on the street, or lack thereof. He relit the blunt that he'd put out and inhaled deeply. "Fuck!" he snapped. "Ain't shit moving out here tonight," he said before blowing the weed smoke into the air and resting his head on the back of the bench.

CHAPTER 24

"Yo, this nigga Spits is gonna go crazy when he find out," said El to Poncho as they sat in court waiting for the judge to accept or deny their attorney's request to grant them bail.

"Word," Poncho agreed. "He can't say shit now. We gonna have to body that mu'fucka."

"For realm," El said. "Ain't no fightin' this shit. It'll be right there in the nigga's face. He won't have no choice."

The judge made his decision and granted them each a five hundred thousand dollar bail. Once the okay was given, the Doberman attempted to inform the judge that they were prepared to post, when he was interrupted by some kind of commotion in the rear of the courtroom.

"What?!" yelled a young brother sitting in the back before he stood up to leave. "Goddamn, bitch-ass, mu'fuckin' judge! This nigga gonna let these niggas get right back out on the street? I've had it with this shit!"

He stormed out of the courtroom with his arms swinging wildly and his face screwed. Don P. only looked in time to get a glimpse of the guy's back side, but they paid it no mind. The important thing was that they were about to get back on the street. Their first priority would be to find Spits and let him know what they'd found out about his boy Ceelow. It seemed as though the Doberman was just there a little earlier trying to get a judge to grant him bail. When the Doberman saw the perplexed look on their faces, he went on to inform them as to why he was being kept too tightly. When they heard that shit, they put two and two together to make five. It was obvious to them that Cee had snitched on the rest of the crew to get himself off, hence the simultaneous raids taking place all over the Bronx. Now, they were on their way home in a cab and Ceelow wouldn't know what had hit him when they caught up with his ass. They were so focused on that one goal that nothing else mattered, not even the car that was tailing them.

As the cab driver took the local blocks to get them to El's crib, they discussed what they would do when they found Cee. They spoke about cutting off a number of his limbs. They even thought about torturing him while they kept him alive to prolong his suffering. They went over every fucked-up thing you could do to a dude to make him feel it. One thing that real gangstas hated was a snitch. It was bothering them to know that they finally had a reason to body this rat mu'fucka, and they didn't know where to start looking for him. And then out of the clear blue sky, he drops right into their lap.

"Oh shit," El Don said as his cell phone started to ring. "You ain't even gonna believe this shit, dog."

"What?" Poncho asked as his brother answered the phone without responding. All he heard was him say, "Yo, what up, Cee?" It was like music to his ears. He didn't even know it, but he was smiling. He was genuinely glad to hear from him.

When El hung up the phone, the music just kept on coming. He told Poncho that not only did Cee think that they didn't know that he's the one that snitched, but that he was on his way to El's apartment right at that moment.

"Get the fuck outta here," Poncho said as El told him the best part of the story. "You can't be fuckin' serious."

"That's my word, my nigga," El responded. "We probably got like an hour before he get there, then we gonna break that nigga off somethin' real proper, ya na'mean."

"Yeah," Ponch agreed. "Hell yeah."

They reached El's building and hopped out of the cab in a hurry. They quickly entered the building and pressed the button for the elevator. When it arrived, they got in and pressed the button for El's floor and just as the doors were about to close, someone caught them and reopened them. A stranger entered the elevator and they proceeded upward to the fourth floor. It should have troubled them that this stranger didn't even press a button when he'd entered the elevator, but maybe they thought it was just a coincidence that he happened to be getting off on their floor. They should have also noticed the look on his face the whole ride up. They should have taken into some consideration his heavy breathing and awkward grin, but they didn't. They hadn't even noticed that they knew this nigga from somewhere. They hadn't realized how much history him and them had. They just continued trading torture methods to perform when Ceelow arrived. Maybe if they would have noticed one or two of these facts, they wouldn't have let the nigga get the drop on them.

As Don P. were about to exit the elevator, El got a funny feeling. He turned around to face this stranger and said, "Yo!"

That was all he got out of his mouth before he heard, chic-chic. Just like that, there was a huge shotgun poking him underneath his chin. He could do nothing but shut his mouth and peek down at the cannon that had just taken his breath away. He curled up his lip and looked his assailant directly in the eyes before spitting in his face.

"Oh yeah?" he simply said. He lifted the gun from under his chin and in one foul swoop, knocked the daylight out of El with the butt of the shotgun. He then pointed it in the direction of Poncho and made him carry his brother to his apartment and open the door. When they were inside, he made Poncho tie El to a chair with telephone wire. When he was securely fastened to the chair, still out cold, this stranger proceeded to tie Poncho to a chair as well. When they were both gagged and bound, they would find out how much history them and this stranger had together.

✪✪✪

"Ma, can you believe it's finally the year 2000?" Ginger asked her mother.

"It got here quick as hell, huh?" she responded.

"For real, right?" said Gin. "It's just messed up that the weather's so bad out. I really wish Michael could be here, though."

For the past week Ginger and her mother had been having the best time with one another during their trip to Florida. Her mother had missed how much they used to hang out before she'd moved in with Spits, but she didn't know how to deal with it before. This idea for them to go away for New Year's was the best thing she could've done to reach out to her daughter to let her know how she felt. She'd previously just hinted toward how much she missed her only child, but she also didn't want to drive her further away, so she kept most of her complaints to herself. In order to bridge the gap that was forming between her and her daughter, she'd planned for them to have this time just for themselves and it worked. Ginger and her mother were the inseparable pair they once were, and it made her feel exceptional. Unfortunately, it was now time for Ginger's mother to explain her ulterior motive for bringing her all this way from home.

"Baby," she said, getting her attention from the storm that had developed outside. "I have something that I need to tell you."

"What is it?" Ginger asked, not really giving her mother her undivided attention.

"I have something to tell you about Michael." She could feel the tension getting thicker the moment his name was out of her mouth.

"What do you mean? What about Michael?"

"I want you to know that I always knew what he was about. In the back of my mind, I always hoped that you'd do what was right. But I couldn't just sit around anymore and wait for that to happen."

"What do you mean, Ma?" Ginger asked, starting to worry.

Her mother took a deep breath and then continued, "I knew that he was nothing but a drug dealer for longer than you could imagine. Who did you think you were fooling, huh?"

Ginger began forming small drops of tears from her eyes. She made an attempt at hiding her emotions, but to no avail. "Well, what would you have wanted me to do? Was I just supposed to leave him?"

"Yes, that's exactly what you were supposed to do," responded Gin's mom. "Immediately after he endangered your well-being, and sacrificed your safety, you should have stopped seeing him, plain and simple!"

"Is that what you did?!" Ginger yelled.

Her mother said nothing.

"It isn't, is it? Do you know why?" she asked her mother. She waited for a second and then answered for her, "Because you loved him."

"That's right," she admitted. "I loved him. But where is he now? That boy is nothing but a two-bit hustler. He is nothing like your father!"

"You're right!" Gin yelled, interrupting. "He isn't anything like my father. He's still here. He'll never be anything like my father because he would never leave me…like my father left you."

"Don't you ever!" Gin's mother yelled with fire in her eyes. "How dare you?"

Ginger could do no more to hold herself back from letting her tears run. They began slowly, but then they ran as steady as a river. She couldn't even speak anymore.

"Well," her mother said in a softer tone. "All of that doesn't matter anymore. Michael won't ever get another chance to hurt you."

"What do you mean by that?" Ginger asked. "What have you done?"

"I haven't done anything," she said. "But I'm positive that you won't ever see Michael again and there isn't anything I could do about that; not even if I wanted to."

"Why?!" Ginger spat. "You can't do anything to keep me from him! He's going to be my husband!" She finally put the words together. She hadn't even realized what she'd said until two seconds after it was out of her mouth. She'd shocked herself, as well as her mother. They both just sat there in awe at what Ginger had just said. Spits had been waiting months to hear it, and he wasn't even there.

"Over my dead body!" her mother said coldly.

✪✪✪

El Don was awakened from the disturbing feeling of ice-cold water splashed into his face. He quickly assumed the manner he was in prior to being rendered unconscious. "You pussy ass mu'fucka," he said. "You gonna get ya shit twisted backwards as soon as I get loose. You better kill me, nigga!"

"Don't worry about that," he responded. "You ain't gotta worry about that at all, you little bitch-ass nigga." He approached El until he was within arm's reach and then smacked him with an open hand across his jaw. "You gonna get yours."

After smacking El once more with even more force and anger, he momentarily left them alone bonded to chairs in the middle of the living room. While he was gone, both Don and P. simultaneously began searching the room for a possible escape. When they found no visible escape from the torment this crazed unknown had in store for them, they searched their memory banks for potential diversions and again, they came up with nothing. They wouldn't let him see it, but they were actually growing somewhat afraid of what he was capable of; especially because they had yet to find out where he knew them from.

When he returned, he simply sat on a sofa positioned in front of them. He put his hands under his chin and rested them on his lap. He looked at Don, and then Poncho. Then, he looked back at Don. "Which one of ya'll mu'fuckas actually lit the match?" he asked the both of them.

They didn't understand. They just stared at him, and then at each other with bewilderment.

"Which one of you lit the fuckin' match?!" he yelled at the top of his lungs as his patience grew thin. "What, you don't remember now?"

An awkward calm fell on the room until Poncho broke the silence. "What the fuck you talkin' 'bout?"

"Oh, you don't know what I'm talkin' about, huh?" he asked. "Well, which one of you bastards killed Drew, and that nigga Pone then?"

"Drew and Pone?" they both asked in unison. They thought he had to be absolutely insane. "Who?" they said once again at the same time.

"Is ya'll mu'fuckas tryin' to piss me off?"

After a few more questions that didn't make any sense to neither Don nor P., they ultimately found out that this stranger was no stranger at all. In fact, they had coincidently bumped heads in the streets on a number of occasions, with him always ending up with the shitty end of the stick. Most recently, and probably what had pushed him over the edge, was when they were granted bail earlier that morning. He'd been sitting in the back of the courtroom when the judge had said the words, “Bail granted,” and he couldn’t even control himself. He’d stormed out of the courtroom abruptly and could no longer contain himself. Earlier than that morning, they were directly responsible for his aunt’s untimely and savage killing. They didn’t know it then, but this was the same Dwight that was on the floor cradling his Aunt Nester’s lifeless corpse after two shots came tearing through her door. As quickly as the chance was given to them to get rid of the only living witness to the murder, it was taken from them as Poncho shoved El down six flights of steps to make their getaway.

Just before this incident, he thought that someone representing their organization was to blame for his cousin Reggie’s bloody murder. All that was left was a clutter of shells surrounding his body, but he figured who was responsible. This feeling was only confirmed when he saw them through the holes in his aunt’s door. All roads were leading back to the Time Bomb Family.

Of course, he hadn’t even known about the events that had led to his boy Bobby’s a.k.a. Tec’s death but he’d subsequently blamed Spits. He’d spent the rest of the whole day trying to figure out ways to get back at them. The loss of his friend would also have to be taken out on Don and P.

“Ya’ll some bitch-ass niggas!” Dwight said in a loud tone before he paused to give a chuckle. “You heard? Ya’ll some bitch-ass mu’fuckas. Why the fuck didn’t ya’ll merc that nigga Ceelow when Roscoe told ya’ll that he was stealing from ya’ll?”

A surprised look came across the faces of El Don and Poncho. “How the fuck did he know about that?” they asked themselves over and over again but couldn’t complete the equation. It wasn’t making any sense yet.

“What?” Dwight asked condescendingly. “Was ya’ll mu’fuckas scared or somethin’?”

“Fuck you!” El Don yelled. “I ain’t scared of no-fuckin’-body, not even ya punk ass.”

“Well, ya’ll must’ve been scared if ya’ll let that nigga keep breathin’ after what Roscoe told ya’ll.”

“Fuck Roscoe,” Poncho bluntly said. “Fuck Ceelow, too. Let’s talk about your punk ass. Why don't you stop playin' this bullshit game and tell us who the fuck you are?"

"I'm the one that told Roscoe to tell ya'll dumb ass mu'fuckas that shit about Ceelow," he said as if he'd been waiting forever to tell someone. He then waited for a response, but there was none. "Is it startin' to make sense yet, dummies?"

When they could do nothing but carry blank looks on their faces, he knew that he had to continue.

"You see Roscoe was just some bitch nigga that owed me," Dwight said. "He was expendable, so I ain't care when ya'll niggas sent him back to his essence. I ain't get tight until I realized nothin' was gonna happen afterwards, ya na'mean. Now, does that mean that our boy Roscoe's death was in vain?"

"Why?" Poncho asked. "What the fuck made you want to fuck with us? What was worth how much work you put in to wage an all-out war against us?"

"What?!" Dwight yelled as his eyes grew larger. "What the fuck you mean?! You don't know yet? Maybe that summer night didn't mean as much to ya'll mu'fuckas. Maybe you can treat a double-homicide like a walk in the park."

"Hold up a minute," El said aloud as he began realizing where they'd first met. "That was you?" he asked.

"Yup," Dwight answered with a silly, but devilish, grin on his face. First, he felt a bit of contentment with the idea that they hadn't completely forgotten about that late-summer night in the park, four summers ago. But when El Don let out a chuckle, that feeling quickly transformed into a fit of rage. He got up out his seat and approached El with his shotgun cocked and pointed directly at his chest. "What's so funny, mu'fucka?"

El looked him straight in his face and said, "You's a bitch-ass nigga." El said it with so much conviction that it sent a shiver up Dwight's spine. "You mad 'cause you ain't have enough balls to jump out the fuckin' whip and get buck for your boys? You just a pussy."

All of the emotions that Dwight had felt after that night came rushing back to him. He hadn't spoken about that night once since it had happened. He was always afraid of what someone might say about the way he'd left his boys without any assistance. He was so sorry for his cowardly behavior but had yet to get an opportunity to express these feelings. After everything, he wished nothing more than to go back to that night. He wanted so much for a second chance. He knew that if only this one wish could be granted, that he could've changed the outcome of that night. It was his fault that Drew and Pone got killed, but he couldn't admit that to himself. He kept telling himself otherwise, but he'd later come to the realization that had he not left them alone the way he had, they might have had a chance. They might still be here today. He had no idea that this night would be a pivotal point in his life.

Immediately afterwards, he couldn't yet find it in himself to go after his friends' killers. It only made it worse when they got so big and well-known in the streets. The fear only grew deeper and deeper. Finally, he'd come to the conclusion that he'd be justified in getting back at the Time Bombs in otherwise non-conventional methods. In other words, he did what the average bitch-ass nigga not thorough enough for the game would do. He started ratting. His first experience with the Federal Bureau of Investigation led to the arrest of Peter "Trigger" Beckford, and the unfortunate death of Mikey "Pop" Black. Things started to look a little bit better for Dwight after that, but that all quickly came to a halt once Trigger disappeared.

Now, he could no longer play the background while they screwed up the numerous attempts they had to apprehend the key members of the Time Bombs to bring them down. With this final example of how incompetent the police were, he'd decided to take the law into his own hands. He couldn't sit back anymore and wait for them to settle his beef. Now, he was prepared to handle his own.

BOOM...chic-chic...*BOOM!* Dwight hit El with two shots in his chest at close range with the 12-gauge he was gripping. The first shot hit El with so much force that it pushed his chair over on its back. He then stood over him to give him the second shot and said, "That's for my Aunt Nes, you bitch-ass nigga!" When Poncho heard the first shot go off, everything else just went silent. His eyes grew larger and his face got so red that you could see veins bulging out of his neck and forehead. He couldn't contain himself. He tried with all his might to get free from the wire that had his hands and feet bounded but to no avail. His numerous attempts to get up simply looked like a pointless rage to Dwight. He looked at him and smiled, then smacked him across the jaw with the butt of the shotgun. "You want some, too?" he asked, and then stood up behind Poncho's chair.

"Yeah, mu'fucka!" Poncho yelled helplessly. "Let me out of this chair, nigga. Please, let me out of this chair and I swear on everything I love, I'ma buss you right in ya shit!"

Click-clack…Dwight cocked back a chrome .9 mm pistol, just like the one that Cee had used on his boys that dark summer night, and put it to the back of Poncho's head. "This is for Pone and Drew…you bitch-ass nigga," he said before pulling the trigger seven times. He put two in the back of Poncho's head for Pone, and when his body fell lifelessly over on the ground, he put five more shots in his back for Drew.

✪✪✪

"I can't believe that you could even say a thing like that, Ma," Ginger said to her mom as a river of tears continued flowing down her face.

"Well, there isn't anything that anyone can do about this now, baby," she said, trying to reason with her daughter. "Michael is going to be going to prison for a very long time, and all the money in the world couldn't stop that from happening."

"You're a liar!" she yelled. "That can't happen. He would never leave me."

"Listen to me, baby," she said as she walked over to console her only daughter. "It's already happened. The FBI picked him up at the Marriott Hotel in Manhattan last night."

"That's not true," Ginger said, still in denial. "How could you possibly know all of this?"

"I know because they told me, out of respect, to keep you as far away from that party as possible."

"What?" Ginger asked.

"They knew for months that they were going to move in on Michael, a.k.a. Spits, and the rest of the Time Bomb Family the night of their New Year's Party. Purely out of the respect they had for my dedication to the police force, was I informed of their plans ahead of time. If I could get through to you, it might not be too late for you to put this horrible person behind you and do what's right for you."

"I don't know what that means, Mommy," Ginger said helplessly. "I wouldn't know what to do without Spits. I love him with all of my heart, and I can't do anything to change that." She paused for a second. She cried, and cried, and cried until she could form no more tears. It was hopeless for her to even consider a life without Spits. She would rather die.

FINAL CHAPTER

As the afternoon hours set into the first day of the New Millennium, I was finally convinced. I knew now that I wasn't at all the same person that had begun this business only four short years ago. After all of the ups and downs, the good times and bad, I had gotten to a point in my life where I just didn't give a fuck about all of the same things anymore. My priorities got thrown all out of order that summer of '96, and now I had gotten in too deep to make a reasonable recovery.

As fucked up as everything seemed, it possibly went from bad to worse. My cell phone let out an indication tone that meant that I had a new voice-mail message waiting. It surprised me that I would even be getting a message, as my phone hadn't been receiving a signal all night. My first feeling was genuine happiness as I listened to the message, but as it continued, I suddenly became numb. A single tear formed from my eye as I decided that I'd had enough. All of a sudden, I felt all alone in the world. I felt like there was no one left for me to even imagine talking to about my deepest and darkest feelings. I was lost. That one tear would soon turn into more, and those tears would turn into an uncontrollable wave of emotions. Wave after wave of deep emotions would be buried for no longer. "Why the fuck is all of this shit happening to me?" I asked myself that question over and over again but found no answer. My life was lost. Years and years of burying my feelings deep inside me was now in control of my actions. This is when I called it quits, but as with most of my decisions, it came just a bit too late.

"What the fuck?" I said as I realized that I was being surrounded by what looked like an entire police department. As I turned to make a getaway in the opposite direction, more cars came rushing from underneath the overpass toward me. All I saw were jackets that said "POLICE" and "FBI" in big white letters, and all I heard were the voices yelling, "FREEZE!" and, "WE'VE GOT YOU SURROUNDED!"

This is it…this is where my song comes to an end…I guess it's just my time. Sounds like the most reasonable thoughts to have in this situation, doesn't it? Nope. None of that shit went through my fuckin' head at this point. All I could think about was going out. All of the people that I'd loved had either fucked me, or were dead and gone, or both. My life was fucking over, and I wasn't about to spend the rest of my days in a goddamn jail cell. Fuck that!

I grabbed the first mu'fuckin' pig that got close enough to me, and put my big shiny burner to the side of his head with a slug already chambered. I held him in front of me for cover as I backed down the rest of them. "Get the fuck back!" I yelled as their looks went from "we've got this under control" to a look that could only be interpreted as one thing…"we're fucked." I held him tight and close to my body with the gat planted firmly against his head, and without a second thought, *BOOM!* I splattered that mu'fucka's brains all over the sidewalk. I felt an indescribable burst of energy go pumping through my body and I was ready for more. When his lifeless body fell to the ground, I got low for the fire that would return. I made my way to a parked car where I knelt down for cover. With graceful and swift extensions of my torso and arms, I got up from behind the car to take aim and squeeze. On my right side I caught one of them tryin' to creep, *BOOM!* Then, they tried blindsiding me on the left…*BOOM…BOOM!* One by one, I picked them off. Aiming strictly for head shots with every squeeze of my trigger, I evened the odds and brought the ratio down to size. But, as the casualties grew larger and larger, my ammunition grew more and more thin. That's when I heard the best nine words I ever heard in my life.

"You bitch-ass niggas want it with the Time Bombs?!"

✪✪✪

"What the fuck?" Ceelow asked himself as he approached El Don's building. "What's going on here?"

As Ceelow turned the corner of Pelham Parkway and Bronx Park East, he saw what looked like police lights illuminating the whole block. As he approached the building closer, he realized that not only were there police cars, but there were ambulances and fire trucks as well. He didn't know what exactly was going on so he decided to enter the building through the rear entrance. When he got around to the back, he noticed that the smoke was coming from El's window.

Unfortunately, the lock on the back door prevented him from entering the building as quickly as he would have wanted to. He would have to wait for someone to open it for him. Luckily for Cee, he didn't have to wait too long. He saw someone approaching the rear exit in haste and he impatiently waited. When the doors finally flung open, he was rudely shoved from the person's exit path. When he turned to address his blatant disrespect, a curl of his top lip formed as he drew his weapon.

"You?" Ceelow said aloud.

"It's you," Dwight said before brandishing his own weapon.

They stared at each other in this position for what seemed like hours, when in fact only seconds had passed. Only one man would walk away from this unusual and exceptionally coincidental reunion, and neither thought that of the other individual.

BOOM! With just a blink of the eye, Dwight had hesitated only a split-second longer than Cee. The last thing he saw was black, and the last feeling he felt was the blood trickling down his forehead. He went down like a ton of bricks, and that was the end of Dwight. Ceelow wrapped up four years of mischief in only four seconds. That was the only missing piece of the puzzle, but unfortunately for Cee, he was still puzzled.

Alone with his thoughts, Ceelow made his way through the back blocks until he got to Bronx River Parkway on Allerton Avenue, and he had only one thing on his mind…finding Spits. Once he saw Dwight exiting El's building in such a hurry, he knew that he was the one responsible for all of the commotion. He also knew that in no way, shape, or form could he be allowed to continue breathing. When Dwight dropped, Cee just jumped in his car and flew. He went up and down the streets in search for clarity. His mind was racing again and he didn't know what to do. "How the fuck did all of this happen?" he asked himself. Of course, that was the million-dollar question that would take this story to start over from the beginning to answer. "This is fucked," he concluded. "Everything's fucked!"

Just as Ceelow was about to give up all hope, another gathering of police officers drew his attention to the Gun Hill Road exit on the highway. When he witnessed what looked like his boy Spits engaged in a massive gunfight with NYPD, he was left with only one option in the matter. With a simple suck of his teeth, he exited the highway and pulled his car over on the overpass before popping the trunk. He picked his weapon of choice and proceeded to the nearby steps for a clean shot.

"You bitch-ass niggas want it with the Time Bombs?!" he yelled as the scenario was reminiscent of their past experiences.

Ceelow was only doing what came naturally to him, just like Spits had once done. The only difference is that he didn't have to point like he had a gun, when in fact he had a big boy Uzi with a full clip in his grasps. He took the time to smile and wink at Spits before engaging in the gunfight, thinking only of the preservation of his family, and Spits used the diversion to reload his twin cannons before continuing the rampage.

Beneath the uninterrupted storm of the many thunderous firearms being discharged all at once, Spits could hear the smallest hint of laughter coming from behind him. The sound was so chilling that his focus was taken from the countless bullets heading in his direction. He paused for a second to take a look over his shoulder and what he saw sent a rippling chill through his body.

There was Cee, with his entire body vibrating from the recoil given from the Uzi, laughing uncontrollably. Although he was laughing on the outside, all Spits could see was the pain he was shielding. The menacing look in his eyes reminded Spits once again of that night they'd first graduated from small-timers, to career criminals. In a way, the events that had taken place on that one night basically wrote everyone's fate in stone. This was their destiny and they were living it out to their fullest ability. It was on them, and them alone to salvage what was left of their family.

Us two is all we need, thought Cee as he embellished on all of the ruthlessness he had inside of him for this special occasion.

Then, suddenly the laughter came to an abrupt halt. Spits took a deep breath as he turned to check on his boy and what he saw spoiled what little confidence he had left. First, a single shot falling on Ceelow's right shoulder-blade spun him around 360 degrees, and left him with only one arm to continue the massive gunfight. As his body was twirled around from the force of the slug, Spits seemed to be witnessing this all in slow motion. When he'd come around completely, they'd caught each other's eyes one last time. Now was the time. They could say farewell to each other for the last time, the way that they were always meant to. Then, another shot falling directly on his chest made it impossible for him to carry his weapon. He was left with no more resources to be used for defense. He was completely vulnerable.

Spits realized then that Cee didn't have to commit himself the way he'd done. He could have simply seen what was going on and kept it moving. Instead, he'd laid it all out on the line for what he'd always done, and always would be considered his brother. Spits knew with the outcome of this event that Ceelow couldn't have done all the things that were suspected of him. Just earlier that morning, he was kicking himself for not taking care of Cee when the chance was presented. It's funny how much things can change in only a few hours, huh?

When Ceelow finally vanished, so did all of the composure that Spits had left. There was no more sanity left inside of him to hold him back, but he felt helpless without any help. He felt small. He felt like a kid again. He wasn't the big man that he'd grown to be in such a short period of time. There was nothing left of that man. All that was left was a small defenseless boy.

He started shooting wild from behind the car. He couldn't even bring himself to take aim on his enemies anymore. He quickly reloaded once more while still crouched down low to the ground, and continued firing blindly. He continued like this while screaming, "I ain't never goin' to no jail, mu'fuckas! You gonna have to kill me first!"

When the police fire didn't let up, he started yelling, "Take this!" as he shot. "Take this! Take this!" he cried. "Take this!" All he saw were the smoking shells hitting the ground beside him after being discharged from his pistol. Until he heard loud disturbing screams coming from over his shoulder, he had completely lost it. But with this unusual sound coming from out of the air, he didn't know what to do. He peeked over the hood of the car and saw the only thing that could've broken his heart at this point.

He never would have imagined in a million years that in his wild gun-firing, could a little innocent girl be caught in the crossfire. When Spits saw her laid out in her mother's arms, dressed all in white, Spits knelt there on the ground with no more purpose. As her pure white dress was slowly soaked in the dark red blood leaking from her chest, Spits simply lost all of his breath. He felt like he was choking. The more screams her mother let out, the more Spits was unable to breathe. He sat down on the ground with his back up against the car and the gunshots finally stopped. He held his chest tightly and he attempted to get his breath back, but he couldn't.

After a few seconds of choking, a frightening breeze came through and Spits could all of a sudden breathe again. That's when the little girl would no longer give response to her mother's numerous cries to fight. She was gone now and Spits could feel that reality deep in his stomach. He breathed deeply at first, and then slower and slower as the police moved in closer to him. All that went through his head was Pop, Vision, Trigger, Cee…he didn't even blink once as he put his gun in his mouth with one slug left in the chamber.

"NO!" the officers all screamed at once as they lowered their weapons, and then…*BOOM!*

✪✪✪

As one of the worst mornings of Ginger's life was nearing its end, the clouds that had rested over her were getting darker and thicker by the minute. She sat by the window facing her aunt's back porch and stared out of the window helplessly. As the raindrops slid down the window in front of her, so did the tears that came trickling down her face. All of the attempts that Ginger had made to find out what had been happening from back home had fallen short of her satisfaction. No one knew what to tell her regarding Spits' whereabouts. If they were still on the street, they had no clue about everyone that wasn't. There was nothing but complete and utter confusion spread all over the streets of the Bronx on this New Year's Day.

When Tone was awakened from a peaceful nap now well into the afternoon, all he could hear was weeping coming from the other end of the telephone. He rubbed his eyes as he rose and asked, "Hello? Who is this?" After a few more seconds of helpless crying continued, the voice on the other end finally answered.

"It's me," Ginger said. "Did I wake you? I'm sorry."

"Yeah," Tone answered. "It ain't nothin'. I was supposed to be up already anyway, so you did me a favor. What's wrong though, Ma? Why you cryin'?"

"Have you heard anything from Spits, Anthony?" Ginger asked feebly. "I've been trying to get in contact with him now for hours, and no one back home knows where he is."

"Back home?" Tone asked, finally realizing that the number on his cell phone didn't have a New York area code. "Where you at?"

"I came to spend New Year's with my family out here in Orlando," she said. "But something is goin' on back home and no one knows where he is. I need to get in contact with him as soon as possible. It's really important."

"Wait, slow down," Tone said. "What's goin' on up North?"

"I don't know exactly; that's what I need to find out," Ginger stated powerlessly.

"Well, what can I do?"

"I don't know. What can you do?"

Silence fell on Tone and Ginger's conversation and neither one of them seemed to have grasped a possible solution to the problem at hand. They were both left with nothing to add to the quiet hiss of the connecting phone lines. This quiet was only ended when Tone took it upon himself to use a little sarcasm to lighten the mood.

"Well, I could always just fly you to New York," he said with a chuckle. He had no clue that this idea would be taken so seriously when he'd said it, but at this point, anything sounded good to Ginger's hopeless ears.

"Okay," she simply said. "Can you come and get me?"

"I guess," Tone said before he even realized what he was committing himself to. "But–"

"I really need to see my baby, Anthony," Ginger said, sounding even more pitiful. "I don't know what I would do if anything happened to my baby."

After another long uncomfortable silence, Tone reluctantly agreed. He couldn't possibly say no to her, given the state she was in. He agreed to pick her up at her aunt's house, and in no more than two or three hours, they'd be in New York where they could find out everything that had been going on in the hood. Of course, Ginger's mother could know nothing about this. As difficult as it was for her to mislead her daughter just to get her out of New York, she wouldn't be too thrilled to find that Gin was planning on going right back into the belly of the beast headfirst.

Just as planned, Tone called Ginger from fifteen minutes away. They'd planned on meeting at the mall, which was a fifteen-minute walk from Ginger's aunt's house. Before any of her family members knew it, she was gone with only the clothes she was wearing and a small bag that contained some personal things. As she made her way through the storm, its brutality and persistence delayed her arrival at the mall, but she still made it in time to see Tone pulling up in his jet-black Lincoln Navigator. She jumped in and they were off.

The ride to the airport was spent discussing what had supposedly happened in New York earlier that day. Ginger told Tone what her mother had told her and he could not believe it. It wasn't that the story was that far-fetched, but Tone was just the type of person that had to see the shit right in front of his face to believe it. none of the information Ginger provided sunk in to his head at all. He was content with being oblivious until they touched down in New York. He would soon find that Ginger's story was not only one hundred percent correct, but that it was only the half of it.

Only another thirty-five minutes would pass before they were pulling into the parking lot of the Orlando International Airport. After the details of the whole story came pouring out of Ginger as they drove to the airport, it only took for Tone to be informed that two out of the three personal aircraft that were used exclusively for Time Bomb business had been seized by the feds. This is when he finally started to believe what was going on. It seemed as though they'd overlooked one of the smallest details, and that's the only reason they didn't seize all three planes, but that was all Tone and Ginger needed. After filing the proper paperwork in the airport, they were ready to take-off. In fact, everything had been moving so quickly that Gin never once considered her fear of flying. She also hadn't once even realized that this would be her first time flying without Spits by her side. Of course, she would be faced with these concerns sooner than later.

"Yeah, you can just put your shit in the back and ride up front with me," Tone said. "You probably don't want to be alone right now."

"You're absolutely right," Ginger replied. "I've never ridden up front before. I just hope I can handle it. You know, I used to be terrified of flying? The only reason I can get on this plane right now is because of my baby, Spits."

"Oh, word?" he asked. "Well, I'm gonna try and see if we can find a route around this storm. Maybe, just maybe, you'll still feel as comfortable about flying when we land."

They both gave a quick chuckle at Tone's statement, and felt a little bit more relaxed with the trip they had ahead of them. Besides the fact that the weather didn't seem to be letting up any time soon, and despite the numerous warnings they'd received from several employees at the airport, they'd gone out anyway.

As Tone had predicted, once they climbed to the appropriate altitude, things began moving smoother than expected. He figured that they could fly above the storm as opposed to flying directly through it, and he was right. It was only 12:50 p.m., and Tone estimated their arrival in New York at approximately 3:30 p.m.

Everything was going according to schedule, and then the deafening roar of thunder and the blinding shimmer of lightning brought all of Ginger's fears rushing back to her. she tried her best to conceal it, but her limbs began slowly trembling as her eyes grew larger and larger. She started biting her lip as her nerves began to collapse. It was almost like she felt something was about to happen that she couldn't control. *Only if Spits were here*, she thought. In fact, he would only need to hold her hand and tell her, "It's going to be okay," for her to be fine. That's all she would need, but it was too much to ask at that point. She would just have to cope.

As the storm got worse, Tone's plan to fly above it became more and more useless. Their little insignificant jet was now being consumed by Mother Nature and there was little they could do at this point. The downpour that had formed around them was like nothing they'd ever experienced in their entire lives.

"Look," Tone said as he began having second thoughts about their journey. "I know how important it is for you to find out what happened to Spits, but this shit don't make no sense. Now, I think the best thing would be for us to just turn around and wait this shit out."

"Don't you understand?" Ginger asked. "We don't have enough time to just wait this out. I don't know what it is, but something inside of me is telling me that I need to be with him. I can't just ignore those feelings, Anthony. I have to do whatever I can to get back to New York. We've already come this far. Why turn back now?"

For a second, Tone was left completely speechless, then he said, "'Cause I don't wanna fuckin' die out here, that's why." Ginger began crying hysterically from Tone's response, but he was determined to stay focused. "I'm sorry, but I don't think we can make it all the way to New York. We're going to have to turn back."

Just as the words were out of his mouth, they heard an earsplitting boom come from the right side of the aircraft. Suddenly, Ginger became extremely numb all over as caution lights began blinking, needles started twirling around uncontrollably, and warning noises came shooting from everywhere.

"What's the matter?" she asked.

"I don't know!" Tone cried. "I think the lightning hit us!" He took a moment to try and gather himself and figure out their next move, but then he looked out the window. What he saw could only bring one word to his mind, "Fuck!" As Ginger looked to see what had captivated Tone's attention, she too became mesmerized by the sight. There was smoke spewing from their left wing and Ginger could do nothing but stare as well. She was unable to move her body at all.

"Where the hell you goin'?" Tone asked as Ginger got up out of her seat to make her way to the back. "Sit down and put your fuckin' seatbelt back on!"

Tone's cries would fall short of Ginger's ears. She couldn't even begin to consider anything else at this point as she didn't determine the outcome of this situation. With everything that was happening, she only had one thing on her mind. She nervously searched through the bag that she had packed until she found the small velour purse she had tucked deep inside. She pulled the drawstring on the purse and turned it upside-down and dropped the small box that was inside in her hand, and then took a deep breath. She held the box close to her heart, and closed her eyes. She tried her best to imagine Spits there with her. She imagined him sitting there in front of her with a huge inviting smile on his face. She threw out her arms to give him a big hug. When in fact she was only squeezing her own torso, for a minute, she felt like he was really there with her. This was the only way that she could do what she was about to do. After all of the time that passed, she never went a day without thinking about the day she would finally open this box. She imagined over and over again what she would feel and where she would be when she opened it, but never in a million years could she have imagined that it would be like this. She didn't know how long it would take before she was ready, but it had taken the argument that she'd had with her mother earlier in the day to realize.

At last, it was time to open the gift that Spits had given her on the day of their five-year anniversary. She kept her eyes firmly shut to keep the picture of Spits fresh in her mind until the box was completely opened. She breathed in through her nose deeply, and then she blew out of her mouth slowly. When she opened the box, she held it in front of her and imagined Spits down on one knee. She opened her eyes at a snail's pace and completely fell in love with the sight of the ring that was revealed. It was a 3.5-carat, emerald-cut, diamond with baguettes in a platinum setting. She absolutely loved it. Suddenly, a waterfall of tears came down her face, and she wanted nothing more but to be with him. Without even thinking twice about it, she was dialing his number on her cell phone. She didn't once consider the many attempts that she'd made all throughout the day, and she just knew that it would have to go through this time. Then, indescribable excitement flushed through her body as she heard his voice.

"Daddy?!" she yelled with anticipation. "Please tell me that it's you."

With all of the energy that was going through her body, all she could do was cry more when she realized that it was only his voicemail message that she was hearing. She was upset at first, but this was actually the closest she'd gotten to speaking to him all day. At least now she could tell him how she felt.

"Leave a message after the beep, and I'll get back at you when I get back to you. One," said Spits' outgoing message right before a small beep.

"Daddy?" Ginger began as she let out a small sniffle. "I'm sorry...I'm sorry for not being there with you right now, but I didn't know. I couldn't have known. I just found out what was going on back home and all I could think about was being with my baby. I swear if I would've found out earlier, I would probably already be there with you right now. At the least we could be together though all of this. That's all that I ever wanted, was for us to be together forever. I know that now..."

"Ginger," Tone cried from the cockpit. "Get the hell back in here and put your fuckin' seatbelt on! I don't know how long we have before we go down! I'm startin' to lose control!"

"...I had to find that out from the most awkward of places, but it's clear to me now," Gin continued. "I wanted you to know that I love you with all of my heart and I'll never stop loving you. That's why I had to do what I did. I hope you're not mad at me, but I wanted to tell you that I was finally ready to open your gift. It's beautiful, baby, and it's a perfect fit. I want to marry you, honey...now more than ever."

Just as the words were out of her mouth, she was brought back to her reality as a tremendous wind burst sent the plane twirling downward. The sudden jerk threw her from her feet and she flew forward, hitting her back on the cockpit door. A little dizzy, she regained her strength and got back on her feet. Still holding her cell phone in her hand, she made her way back to the cockpit where Tone was. What she saw was absolutely devastating.

The force of the sudden jolt sent Tone from his seat as well. His head got badly bruised as his body flew forward into the window, and he'd lost consciousness. He was bleeding from his head and his mouth, and the plane was falling lifelessly toward the ground.

"I love you, Daddy," Ginger said as she cried, while the plane plunged toward the earth uncontrollably. "I love you."

THE END

AUTHOR BIO

Michael Baptiste, born April 23, 1980, was raised, and still resides, in the borough of the Bronx. As a young'n, he wasn't always focused on his studies, and this led to him dropping out of Evander Childs High in 1996. At sixteen, he passed the test for an equivalency diploma without ever studying. His time following was spent mostly being a knucklehead, but it was not in vain. He soon realized the value of education and decided to pursue a career in computers. It wasn't an easy task, but Michael worked hard enough to graduate from college with honors. Although his experience was in technology, his passion remained in the arts. Along with writing, he produces and records music, and he is also a freehand artist.

It has been a long road traveled for the now published writer, Michael D. Baptiste. He did not always aspire to be a writer; in fact, he still juggles numerous different interests that he shares the same love for. As shown above, Michael also has a love for producing and recording Rap music. As well as his music interests, Michael has always loved sketching, which is now transforming into an urban clothing line that he would like to see take form some time in the near future. Hopefully, triumph in one of these areas will provide the proper platform for success in the others. For now he will be more than happy to accept, with great pride and dignity, to be referred to under the title of "Author."

With much help and influence from his "Wifie," persistence and commitment, plus a little bit of luck, Michael was fortunate enough to have his manuscript grace the eyes of the one and only Zane of Strebor Books International. With this introduction, Michael's future had finally begun to take form. The rest is, as they say, "*history*"...but the future is now. When *Cracked Dreams* is released in October of this year, we will all find out just how far Michael will be allowed to expand on his accomplishments.

All inquiries can be forwarded to info@onlymike.com, and thoughts and suggestions can be sent directly to mbaptiste@onlymike.com. To learn more about Michael Baptiste, please visit www.onlymike.com.

Printed in the United States
By Bookmasters